The Big 5-OH!

**Center Point
Large Print**

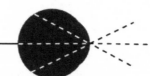

**This Large Print Book carries the
Seal of Approval of N.A.V.H.**

The Big 5-OH!

Sandra D. Bricker

CENTER POINT LARGE PRINT
THORNDIKE, MAINE

Published by arrangement with
Riggins International Rights Services, Inc.

The text of this Large Print edition is unabridged.
In other aspects, this book may vary
from the original edition.
Printed in the United States of America.
Set in 16-point Times New Roman type.

ISBN: 978-1-60285-787-2

Library of Congress Cataloging-in-Publication Data

Bricker, Sandra D., 1958–
  The big 5-oh! / Sandra D. Bricker.
     p. cm.
  ISBN 978-1-60285-787-2 (library binding : alk. paper)
  1. Middle-aged women—Fiction. 2. Large type books. I. Title. II. Title: Big five-OH.
  PS3602.R53B54 2010b
  813′.6—dc22
2010007563

*A big and special "thank you!"
to Tamela Hancock Murray
for opening this lovely door.*

*An enthusiastic "high five" to my
new editor, Barbara Scott.
I'm sure you have no idea what a
unique and special person you are.*

*And a group hug for my girls:
Marian, Jemelle, Debby, and Loree.
You make it such a great adventure!*

*For D: I like you deeply.
Not too much. Just enough.*

1

Prudence leaned over the edge of the pond and gazed at her reflection.

"What's happened to me?" she exclaimed. "I looked like a perfectly normal young donkey when I left home this morning."

"The journey has taken its toll," Horatio HootOwl replied. "But just one dip in the Enchanted Pond, and you'll surely be revived."

Prudence lifted her head and closed her eyes.

"Braaaaaaaay," she whimpered. "Oh, me, oh, my. Braaaaaay."

"No, no," Horatio said, rubbing his feathered wing over the fold of Prudence's smooth ear. "One dunk in the water, and then a nap in the sun, and you'll be good as new. You'll be a new Prudence."

She chuckled at that. "Do you promise?"

"I promise," said her friend. "You'll be a brand new Pru."

❧

Liv dug the shovel into three inches of snow and pushed as hard as she could, then tossed it to

the side of the driveway. Three more reps followed before the muscle down the back of her
arm throbbed in response. It used to take much
longer for her old body to react to physical labor
in this way.

*Time marches on, she thought. Whether we
like it or not.*

"Hey, neighbor!"

Liv looked across the white meadow between
them and waved at her friend Hallie, who stood
at the edge of her garage next door.

Three kids filed past Hallie, all of them bundled
up in coats and boots, hats, scarves, and gloves.
At thirteen, Jason was the oldest. He had reached
the bottom of the driveway by the time Scotty,
the ten-year-old, hurried past his mother. Katie,
age six, scampered behind her brothers, then she
turned and waved at Hallie.

"Later, Mommy."

"Later, sweetie."

"Hey, wait up, you guys," the little girl called.

"Boys, wait for your sister and walk with her
all the way to the bus stop, please."

Jason didn't so much as slow down, but Scotty
came to a full stop until Katie reached him. The
two of them skated along the patches of ice on
the sidewalk.

Liv's heart pinched a little as she watched
them. She'd had more than her share of obstacles
over the years that had kept her and Robert

from having children of their own. Hallie was blessed to have a houseful, and Liv envied her that.

"Coffee?" Hallie called out to Liv.

"Half an hour?"

"I'll bring cake."

The thought of cake cheered Liv right up, and she returned to the chore of shoveling a channel up the driveway so that Hallie could bring it safely to her.

A few minutes later, the snow started to fall again, and Liv leaned on the shovel, breathless, and watched the path she'd just created disappear under a layer of white.

"Ah, crud."

Looking around at the colorless landscape of her suburban Ohio neighborhood, Liv realized there was a time when she had considered her hometown to be one of her greatest loves. Nestled into rolling green hills and bellied up right next to the Ohio River, it was such a beautiful and thriving town. Summers in Cincinnati were blue skies and picnics, and winters were powdered sugar-covered treetops and ice skating on Winton Lake. But all that had changed.

Five years had passed since Robert had died, but passing months on the calendar had a curious way of fogging up the glass through which she peered to try and find the time when she still had him with her. It made her head ache to work so hard at looking back for him, struggling to break through the wall of cancer that stood between present day and her beloved past.

Stage 3 Ovarian Cancer. The English language didn't hold four more terrifying words, and, on the chilly morning of Olivia Wallace's forty-eighth birthday, those words were hurled at her like a dagger with four sharp blades. She remembered it like it was yesterday; this particular glass was as clean and clear to look into as a freshly hung window pane.

Two surgeries, six weeks of chemotherapy, and exactly twenty-seven radiation treatments —all of it as translucent and visible as a neon sign on a spring morning. And now, on the other side of the monster, nothing looked the same anymore. In fact, the first snow of winter had fallen overnight, and it seemed just as dreary and dull as everything else within Liv's recent frame of reference.

As she pulled Robert's old canvas fishing hat from her head and shook off the snow, Liv glanced at the mirror hanging over the cherry buffet in the dining room. It didn't escape her notice that her tedious life and gloomy surroundings weren't the only uninspiring things in the room. Her own reflection looked rather bleak as well.

In the six months since making its original escape, her red hair had finally begun to grow back. Lackluster though it was, and despite those silver streaks all through it, at least she had hair again. Her cheeks were drawn, her green eyes seemed slightly sunken and hazeled, and her fair, freckled skin had gone somewhat ashen. Although her energy levels had finally peaked again, she still looked just as tired and drained as she had felt throughout her recent past.

Liv pressed the button to open the garage, and then quickly latched the door before the outside wind had a chance to make its way through. As she counted out scoops of ground coffee, the *thump-thump-thump* of Hallie's boots on the garage floor signaled her friend's arrival.

"*Buenos días,*" Hallie called as she came through the door into the kitchen. Hallie was always learning something new. Spanish lessons on CD were the project of the moment.

"Morning," Liv returned, setting two oversized cups and saucers on the kitchen table.

"I brought coffee cake."

"What kind?" Liv hoped it didn't have anything healthy attached to it, like fresh fruit. At the moment, she just wanted a pure confection of sugar and sweet.

"Cinnamon swirl."

"Good girl."

"Still warm."

"Even better."

Liv slid across the padded leather bench and

settled into the corner of her kitchen booth as Hallie grabbed plates and flatware before she took the outside chair. Liv watched her as she tangled her fingers into her blonde hair and shook off the flakes of fresh snow and then poured two cups of coffee.

"The first snow of the season," Hallie announced. "Isn't it beautiful?"

Liv tilted into half a shrug, leaned onto both elbows, and propped her face up with her hands.

"Or not," Hallie said, raising an eyebrow at her friend. "Feeling a little blue?"

"Blue and blah."

"Oh, I'm sorry. Anything I can do?"

The funny thing was Liv knew Hallie meant it. If she thought it would raise Liv's spirits to do a little barefoot jig across the linoleum floor of her kitchen, Halleluiah Parish-Dupont would certainly oblige. Her friend was a true-blue cheerleader that way. And at forty-seven years old, it seemed almost wrong that all she needed were the pom-poms to actually look the part.

Liv gave her a smile and shook her head.

"Well. There's cake," Hallie said with hope.

"There is that."

Liv took a large bite and her eyes opened wide at Hallie, and then she smiled.

"This is *sheeriously delishush*," she said through a full mouth. "Did you make *thish?*"

"No. Bender's Bakery on Compton."

After swallowing a couple of times, Liv let her fork clank to the plate. "It's kind of sad that this is the best thing that's happened to me in days, don't you think?"

"This isn't like you," Hallie observed.

"It's not, I know."

"Can't you tell me what's going on?"

Liv cringed and shook her head.

Suddenly, Hallie gasped and slid a hand over her mouth. "Oh, I get it," she said deliberately, nodding her head. "It's the birthday thing, isn't it? Next month is your birthday."

"Afraid so."

"Liv, you've got to give up the idea that your birthdays are cursed. You know that's not how our God works."

Our God. Sometimes Liv wondered if she still knew Him. But Hallie sure did, and that was a comfort somehow.

"I know it up here," she said, tapping her temple with her index finger. "But it doesn't quite make it down here." She smacked herself dead center in the chest several times.

"So what's the plan then? Just mope around and wait for a piano to drop on your head next month?"

Liv shrugged again, and then plopped forward into her folded arms. "Jimmy DiPlantis dumped me on my sixteenth."

"You dated someone named Jimmy Durante?"

Liv raised her head and grimaced. "Not Jimmy Durante. Jimmy DiPlantis. He made out with Rachel Wagner at my Sweet 16 party."

"Well, it's good to know you're not still holding a grudge."

"And on my twenty-first birthday, I slipped on the ice and fell down a flight of stairs. I had a cast on my leg *and* my arm for eight weeks."

"That's awful," Hallie said. "Really. That's *terrible.*"

"On my thirtieth birthday, I had pneumonia, and a fever so high that I lost several days and didn't even realize I'd passed the thirty mark until my birthday the next year. When I finally discovered I was actually turning thirty-one instead of thirty, I was devastated."

"Oh!" Hallie exclaimed and covered her grin with both hands. "Honey. That's . . . horrible."

"I know. And then there was the big blizzard on my thirty-eighth—"

"Oh, no."

"—thirty-ninth and fortieth."

"All three years?"

"All three."

"Oh, my."

"And you were there for my forty-eighth."

"Yes."

"Ovarian Cancer. Stage 3. The worst day of my life."

"But you're healthy now."

"Yep, I am. And here comes my fiftieth, Hallie. Like a locomotive chugging straight at me." Liv leaned back down into her folded arms again, and the dishes on the table rattled when her head dropped. "I'm just too young to be this old."

"You've got to do something drastic, Liv," Hallie told her. "You've got to bust out of this prison you're in. Gloomy weather, birthday blues, expectations of doom. It's just not healthy. You're acting like Prudence, the lop-eared donkey from my mother's books."

Liv raised her head and looked at Hallie curiously.

"She writes children's books, remember?"

"Yes, I remember."

"Prudence only sees the dark clouds."

"You're comparing me to a donkey?"

"Prudence is more than a donkey, Liv."

"Do tell."

"That's not my point. I think you need a vacation."

"So what are you suggesting? A trip to Club Med?"

"No. Not Club Med. But you do need a break."

"No Club Med? That's disappointing."

"But what better place to take a vacation than . . . Florida?"

"Huh?"

Hallie curled her hands into the sleeves of her

blue cable-knit sweater and grinned from ear to ear. "Did I mention to you that my mom has been talking about coming to visit?"

Liv didn't respond. She just stared at her friend with narrowed eyes and a furrowed brow, trying to catch up.

"She hasn't seen the kids in a while, so Jim and I thought she should come for a couple of weeks."

"That's nice. I guess. Since she hasn't been here in a while."

"Do you remember where my mom lives?"

"Florida."

"Yep. *Flor-i-da.*"

"Okay. What are you *get-ting at, Hal-lie?*" she mimicked.

"While my mom comes to Cincinnati, her house on Sanibel Island will be completely empty."

"Uh huh." She still wasn't getting it.

Hallie groaned, and then she leaned in toward Liv for emphasis.

"You could go there, Liv, and lie in the sun, get away from Ohio in winter, and celebrate your birthday at the beach."

"Oh."

"It's brilliant."

"I don't think so."

"Liv."

"Hal."

"You have to do this."

"No. I really don't."

"Wait. You're right," Hallie exclaimed. "You shouldn't go lay by the pool and work on your tan and try to get back some of the strength and joy that all those months of cancer robbed from you. Instead, you should just go back to work in the O.R. Spend your time shoveling snow and getting your birthday sick on. Maybe try some pneumonia again. It's been a couple of decades."

Liv's stomach stood up and fell down again at the mere thought of going back to work. She'd always loved her job. The operating room at Providence Hospital was a well-oiled machine, and she'd always been excited to be a part of it. But now, post cancer surgeries and medical reports of doom that she'd barely overcome, it just didn't seem to be the right place for her anymore.

Becky from Human Resources had contacted her twice in the last week, her messages ripe with friendly enthusiasm. But the thought of returning to work, or even just returning Becky's calls, brought such an ominous feeling to Liv's heart that she hadn't been able to bring herself to dial the phone.

Just that morning, she had lain in bed, her eyes clamped shut and the blanket pulled tight against her chin, and she'd done something she hadn't done in a very long time. She prayed that God would guide her in what to do.

"I don't want to go back to my old life," she'd whispered. "But I can't seem to muster up the desire to move forward either."

Hallie reached across the table and squeezed Liv's hand, yanking her back to the moment. "This is the answer for you," her friend stated, as if she'd been in on every moment's thought. "You haven't had a vacation since the trip to Galveston with Robert six years back, Liv."

The memory pinched her. "I can't, Hallie."

"Yes. You can."

❧

Liv propped the phone on her shoulder with her chin and sighed. She'd forgotten where Hallie had gotten her cheerleaderness. Josie Parish was Hallie's mother. She was Hallie times two.

"Oh, of course, you can, Pumpkin. The house will just be sitting here with nothing to do but provide you a little nesting place."

"Ms. Parish, honestly, I appreciate the offer. I really do."

"Didn't we establish when I was there visiting the last time that you were not going to call me that anymore?"

"Sorry. Josie."

"Okay then. We're on a first-name basis. As close as you are to my Halleluiah, my goodness, we're nearly family. The least you can do is come and babysit my home for a couple of weeks. Oh, do you like dogs, Pumpkin?"

Liv shook her head briskly to make the leap with her.

"Dogs? Umm, yes. I like dogs."

"Oh, that's so good, because my little baby has recently had surgery. She had a bit of a bad jump across the sofa. She's won't be able to travel, that's for certain. You wouldn't mind looking out for her while you're here, would you, Pumpkin? It would really help me out."

"Josie, really, I just can't see my way clear to take a trip right now."

"Of course, you can. In fact, from what my daughter tells me about everything you've suffered through in the last year or so, I'd say you really have no choice. Now, I'm going to make my flight arrangements, and I'll tell Missy Boofer that you'll be here the same day to look after her—"

Missy Boofer?

"—and I'm thinking of arriving on Wednesday. Would that work out all right for you?"

"Well, I—"

"Oh, good. Now I'm off to call Halleluiah and give her the good news. I'll leave you all the information you'll need on the dining room table, and the key to the house will be under the neon pink palm tree in the garden."

Neon pink palm tree?

"Josie."

"Olivia, I want you to know that I do appreciate

this very much. If you weren't going to be here to take care of Missy Boofer, there's no way I could come to see Halleluiah and her family before I get tied up with my next book deadline. You're a little angel is what you are, and I know Jesus will take good care of you here on the island. I have a good feeling about it. I do. My insides tell me your whole outlook is going to change down here, Olivia. The Florida sun has a way of baking up fresh possibilities, you know. And that's all you really need, isn't it? Some new possibilities?"

Liv tossed up her hands and dropped her chin to her chest.

"Okay. Why not?" she said in surrender. "Thanks, Josie. I'll be there next Wednesday."

"Oh, that's wonderful, Pumpkin. Boofer will see you then."

2

Prudence saw the rickety bridge stretched out before her.

She didn't know if she had the courage to make the trek across. The ravine below was jagged and steep. She didn't really want to get to what was on the other side anyway. And certainly not enough to go about it this way!

"I wish I'd just stayed in my meadow this morning," she brayed. "Why, oh, why, did I leave the grasses of home to set out on this terrible journey?"

"You know why," Horatio hooted from his perch at the other end of the bridge. "Now come along and put one hoof in front of the other. Before you know it, you'll have put the hardest part behind you."

❧

Have you left your bags unattended at any time?"

"Umm, no."

"Did you pack your luggage yourself, or did another party pack them for you?"

"I packed them."

"Are you carrying anything sharp in your bags, such as tweezers, scissors, or other cutting instruments?"

"No."

"All right, Ms. Wallace. Here's your boarding pass and your gate assignment. Have a pleasant flight."

As she headed for the gate, Liv remembered the toenail clippers in her pedicure kit, and she wondered if she should have declared them.

"Please remove your shoes and place them in the bin with your purse and carry-on."

Remove my shoes?

It had been a long time since Liv had flown, and she'd heard the stories, but this was far more elaborate than she had imagined. She slowly made her way through the security tower, setting off the buzzer as she did.

"Please step back and come through again."

Groans from the line behind her set her pulse to pounding, but she did as she was told, and the buzzer sounded again.

"Step forward, please, ma'am. Stand here and raise your arms."

The plump uniformed man smelled like tuna and onions. Liv tilted her head away from him and held her breath as she lifted her arms and focused on the business traveler in the line to the left unpacking his laptop from its case.

A louder alarm went off as the security wand floated near her hip, and Liv gasped.

"Oh! I'm sorry," she said, and then she reached into her pocket and produced a jangling key ring. "I forgot I had them in my pocket."

The guard took the keys from her and tossed them into one of her shoes.

"Please step over to the holding area, ma'am."

Woman arrested at airport for carrying too many keys. Detained for two full weeks, entirely missing her Florida vacation. Film at 11.

But a few minutes later, Liv was on her way to the gate, with plenty of time to spare before departure. As she sat down in one of the rows of awkward leather chairs at the gate, she locked eyes with the man seated across from her.

His salt and pepper hair, deep-set brown eyes, and smooth, suntanned skin gave him a Richard Gere quality that made Liv's heartbeat flutter. His smile was as pearly-white as she'd ever seen outside of a commercial, and he gave her a friendly nod that she tried to return, but she was pretty sure it looked more like an odd little twitch. Before she could rectify it and try again, he'd glanced away, crossed one leg over the other, his pleated charcoal trousers draping perfectly as he did. He placed a pair of wire-rimmed glasses on his nose, and then he opened *The Enquirer* to the sports page.

Oh, great. He probably thinks I'm a special

23

needs traveler. How wonderful that she's able to be so independent, the poor thing. I wonder what's with that strange twitch.

☙⚥☙

Jared struggled to focus on the newspaper before he surrendered to the magnetic draw of the woman seated across from him and peered over the top of the paper. He took the opportunity to watch her fuss with something inside her large leather bag.

Green eyes and fire-red hair were a killer combination, and Jared had found himself attracted to her since the moment he'd seen her being frisked at the security gate. She obviously didn't fly often because the whole process appeared to be one surprise after another to her.

Jared was fifty-five years old, and the only hints that the woman was anywhere near his age were the few random streaks of silver glistening in her hair and a remote shadow of . . . what? . . . *weariness?* . . . that he'd noticed in that one iso-lated moment when their eyes had met. He'd seen that shadow before in the eyes of some of his older patients, but Red seemed far too young to have reached that place of tired resolution.

Her loose, S-shaped curls and fringe of long bangs vibrantly framed her oval porcelain face, and a spattering of dark copper freckles dotted her small, upturned nose and pinkish cheeks.

She's just as cute as she can be.

He realized then that any woman over the age of thirty would more than likely object to being categorized as cute.

"Delta flight 1896 will now begin the general boarding process. If you're seated in row fifteen or higher, please step up to the gate with your boarding pass and I.D. in hand."

Jared took his time folding the newspaper, and then he tried not to be rude as he sidestepped an elderly couple so he could take his place in line behind the green-eyed beauty. As she dug through the contents of the satchel that was much too large for her to handle, he noticed a sweet citrus fragrance that he attributed to her shampoo.

"I'm sorry," she said to the gate attendant. "I can't seem to find my boarding pass."

Jared debated for only a moment, and then reached forward and pulled the pass from the outside pocket of her bag and handed it to her.

"Oh." She seemed to glare at him before her face melted into a pretty smile. She thanked him on a bouncing, nervous chuckle and then quickly turned away to walk down the ramp.

After boarding, he paused to help a twenty-something get her bag into the overhead compartment, and then found his place just a few rows behind and across the aisle from Red's seat by the window. The center and window seats of his own row were filled, and the woman next to him reeked of a too-sweet, flowery perfume. As the endless line of people filed in, he hoped no one would take the empty seat on the aisle next to Red.

A buff guy with a duffle headed toward them.

Don't do it, buddy. Don't sit next to her. No, no, no, no, no.

Jared smiled as Muscle Man stepped into the row ahead of hers.

Two more stragglers stumbled toward them, separating before they reached Red. The attendant made her walk down the aisle, checking tray tables and seatbelts, making sure each overhead compartment was clamped shut. Jared tried not to hold his breath until the jet finally left the gate and taxied down the runway.

The engines roared as they left the ground. The couple beside him chattered about seeing their grandchild for the first time in just a couple of hours, but Jared couldn't seem to take his eyes off the lighted seatbelt sign. The instant it went dark, he flipped open the latch on his seatbelt and stood up.

"There's an open seat up the aisle," he told the elderly couple beside him. "I'm going to take it and give you two some room."

"How kind of you."

Jared leaned into Red's row. When she looked up at him and their eyes met again, his breath momentarily caught in his throat.

"Would you mind if I sit here?" he asked her.

"We were pretty jammed in back in my row."

"Y-yes," she said.

"You mind?"

"Yes. I m-mean, no. I-I don't mind," she stammered. And then she took a deep breath and grinned. "I mean, it's fine. Sit here. Please."

"Great," he replied, and he slipped into the aisle seat and loosely buckled his seatbelt. After a moment, he extended his hand toward her and said, "Jared Hunt."

He was stunned by the strength of the handshake she returned, and her wide, toothy smile just about blew him back to his original row.

"Olivia Wallace."

Olivia. Beautiful woman, beautiful name.

"Do you live in the Fort Myers area, Olivia?" he asked her.

"Oh, no. And you can call me Liv. I'm headed down to Florida for a vacation. Sort of. You?"

"Central Florida is home for me. And I'm looking forward to getting back before my son has to return to London. He teaches there and has been visiting for the Easter break. So you're on a *sort of* vacation?"

"Well, it's more like forced R&R." A fraction of a giggle followed, and Jared was enchanted. "My best friend decided I needed it to get over my birthday curse."

"You're cursed?" he asked her. "Maybe I didn't want to sit next to you on an airplane after all."

27

They shared a laugh, and Liv's deep green eyes sparkled like the Gulf of Mexico. Jared found his heart pounding a little harder than it should, realizing once again how electric the attraction was to this virtual stranger. He was no believer in love at first sight but, if he were, he might have taken this for what it would feel like.

"It seems like my birthday is always a conduit for disaster," she told him. "And I have a pretty significant one creeping up on me. Aside from that, I've just managed to defy the odds with cancer, so I'm feeling a little anxious about what's around the next bend."

"Cancer. I'm sorry to hear that."

"Thank you. It was a long road that is, thankfully, finished." She paused, and then tilted slightly toward him so that he got another whiff of that citrus shampoo. "Of course, with cancer, you never really know for absolute certain that it's fully behind you."

"That's the sad truth," Jared told her. "I lost my wife to breast cancer after several battles with it."

The warmth in her eyes nearly burned a hole right through him. "I'm so sorry, Jared."

"Thank you. It was a long time ago. But you never do forget it, do you?"

"I don't think so. But I live in hope."

Oh, Lord. This woman's eyes cut straight through me. What's going on here?

Out of nowhere, the plane jolted, and Liv's hand jerked toward him, and she grabbed his arm and dug in.

"Sorry, folks," the pilot announced. "We're running into some bad weather as we cross the border into Tennessee. I'm turning on the seatbelt sign and would like everyone to remain in their seats with their seatbelts securely fastened until we cross down into Georgia and find some blue skies."

Jared placed his hand over hers and squeezed it. He didn't know how many years it had been since he'd seen a woman over thirty blush, but Liv's cheeks were stained a light crimson.

"I'm sorry," she said, as she pulled her hand away.

"For what? I appreciated having someone to hold on to."

She laughed and, again, it was lyrical. Jared felt his insides twist.

You're not a teenager anymore, man. Get hold of yourself.

"You know," he said, working hard to summon up the verbiage to complete the thought, "I was wondering if you'd like to—"

The jet dropped and bounced, and Liv let out a scream and slapped her hands over her mouth. Closing her eyes, she pulled the seatbelt as snug as it would go, and then clamped down on the arms of her seat.

Even after the pilot let them know that they'd reached clearer skies, Liv remained glued to the armrests, her eyes closed, and her head tilted back. Her lightly frosted lips twitched slightly, and he thought she might be praying. Jared didn't have the heart to intrude, so he put his suggestion that they have dinner on hold until they landed and headed in the direction of baggage claim. He knew she might be flying into Fort Myers and vacationing an hour or more up or down the coast, but he didn't really care how far he would have to drive. He had the unsettling inclination that the possibility of one meal with this woman might have been worth riding a camel across the desert to reach her tent.

After they disembarked Jared stuck close to her as the current of people moved them along, but they were immediately separated by an electric cart and a stream of wayward passengers trying to get out of its way. A flight had just arrived at the gate across from theirs, and the influx of people only made it more difficult to keep his eyes on Liv as the tide dragged her farther away from him.

Jared pushed his way toward baggage claim and scanned the crowd. Not a hint of red hair in sight. The couple from his original row waved at him from the other side, and he tapped the rail in irritation as he waited for the luggage to arrive. His heart pounded out a mantra as he scanned the faces at the carousel.

Where is she? Where is she? Where IS she?

Boxes and suitcases began sliding down the metal ramp and making the rounds in front of the crowd. He moved into a clear spot and grabbed his garment bag as it passed by at knee level. Then he helped the woman next to him as she struggled with an overstuffed canvas duffle and a damaged Samsonite case held together with twine.

"I was afraid that might happen," she told him. "Thanks for your help."

"Any time."

Jared stood back and inspected the throng of people still gathering their belongings. She'd said she was on vacation; certainly, she would have luggage to pick up. But where was she?

He glanced through the windows and noticed a blue Super Shuttle van slowing at the curb. A cop in an airport vest waved the van on after a moment, and the driver slapped the steering wheel before taking off. Jared looked back one more time in hopes of a glimpse of red hair, but she was nowhere in sight.

He slowly made his way to the automatic door, and then stood there blocking the flow of pedestrian traffic as he scanned each and every face within eyeshot. When the blue van came around again and hugged the curb, Jared sighed and reluctantly jogged toward it.

"Jared Hunt," he told the driver as he boarded. "I thought you were lost."

"Not me," he told him, tossing his bag into the rack. "Somebody else."

3

Prudence screeched to a stop and then stood there, planted.

Her eyes stung, and they ached from opening up so round and wide. Once again, she found herself wishing she'd never ventured away from home. She'd never seen a creature like this one in all her days in the valley.

It growled at her and snorted, and there seemed to be fire burning in its bright golden eyes. She tried to run away, she really did, but her legs just wouldn't move from that spot. Surely this beast would tear her to pieces and have her as a midday snack!

"Oh, me, oh, my," Prudence brayed. "What a horrible way to go."

❧

Liv looped the airport three times before finding her way to the parkway. She tossed Hallie's handwritten directions to Josie's home up on the dash of her rental and settled back into the leather seat.

For the twentieth time since leaving the airport, she thought of Jared Hunt and wished she hadn't stopped in the ladies' room. Not that she could have helped it, of course. Nearly three hours on a plane without braving the turbulence to use the facilities, and she would have taken off for the ladies' room at a full run if not for the possibility that he was watching.

The line was long, but she'd hurried through it, only to discover that the beautiful passenger with the toothpaste commercial smile was already gone and out the double doors into the greater Fort Myers area, never to be seen or heard from again. It was a shame, really. Liv had never met a man who could make her heart flutter and her palms sweat; not even Robert had elicited such a reaction. Frankly, she'd long suspected she had passed the age where palpitations and perspiration were still a possibility. It was kind of nice to know she still had it in her. Perhaps she wasn't lost on a downward spiral to an old-age home after all. At least not quite yet.

Liv opened the window and let the balmy breeze caress her face as she followed a Lincoln Continental with a penchant for braking for no apparent reason. The sun was warm and the skies a vibrant blue, hardly a cloud anywhere in sight. Several strange white birds that looked like storks pecked at the ground at the side of the road.

"What in the world?"

As she drove by them, Liv let out a laugh.

"We're not in Kansas anymore," she said. "Or Ohio either."

Josie's house was larger than she'd expected, an L-shaped stucco ranch with palm trees and flowering pink shrubs in the front yard. Several orange-pink and green plastic palms were placed in the rock garden near the front door, and she groaned as she leaned over and picked them up, one at a time, in search of the house key until she found it.

A large glazed Mexican tile was cemented into the stucco over the front door. Enter and be blessed, it read.

"Gladly," Liv muttered.

No sooner had she turned over the deadbolt than the sound of scampering paws and snarling growls drew closer. A matted, hairy thing that resembled a dog, wearing a large lampshade around its neck, barreled toward her, and Liv instinctively backed out the door again and yanked it shut.

The illustrious Missy Boofer, no doubt, she thought, her hand still on the knob.

As the animal threw itself at the front door several times, snorting and barking, she released her hold completely, stepped back even farther, and placed her hand on her hip as she groaned. "Now what?"

Deciding on a different plan of attack, Liv went back to the car and unloaded her luggage to the front porch. When silence indicated that the dog had taken a break, she quickly opened the door, tossed the larger bag inside, and slammed the door again just as Boofer started another tirade.

"Okay," Liv said in as friendly a voice as she could muster, "I understand."

Two more stabs at entering initiated a fury of snarls and barks. When the dog finally settled down, Liv sent a quick wish upward, opened the door, and stepped inside.

Boofer was a four-legged contradiction. Baring her teeth as she growled at Liv, the ball of coarse fur was wrapped in a pink doggie T-shirt with *Princess in Training* written across the back in glittering rhinestones. She ran toward Liv, her big old lampshade rocking from side to side, and she seemed to be spitting as she protested Liv's presence. Missy curled her upper lip at Liv.

Liv took a deep breath, extended her index finger, and, in the loudest voice she could muster, shouted, "Look!"

The dog stopped in its tracks, sliding the rest of the way toward her on its behind.

"I am not a robber. I'm a friend. I come in peace. Your crazy owner has asked me to come here and take care of you, and that's what I'm going to do. You are not going to bite me or growl at me anymore. Is that understood?"

Apparently not, because the dog snarled at her, but only once.

"Okay. Now I'm going to just walk through here, and you can either come with me or not. It's up to you. But you're going to let me pass."

When the dog did let her pass, Liv whispered, "Thank you, Jesus."

Beautiful terrazzo tiles created a subtle pattern on the floor throughout the house, and thick, colorful area rugs gave the place a foundational personality that greeted her from room to room. The kitchen was a Tuscan paradise, with a center island and a magnificent hooded gas stove and grill. Beyond the sliding glass doors at one end of the sunroom was a sparkling blue pool encircled with terrazzo tiles and a free-standing hot tub, barbecue grill, and cushioned bamboo lounge chairs, all caged inside a large, screened lanai. A grassy, landscaped yard extended beyond the lanai, and a tall slatted fence allowed privacy from the view of those occupying the house on the other side.

Boofer remained right on her heels as Liv wandered down the hallway. The walls were dotted with framed photographs of Hallie, Jim, and the kids. She passed a bathroom and two small guest rooms before reaching a master suite that just about took her breath away. Moss green walls surrounded a wood-framed queen bed with striking barley-twisted posters, a headboard of framed panels, and a rosewood inlay with a carved rope molding that arched the design. A thick paisley comforter in greens, golds, and wines extended from a pile of enormous pillows, and the deep emerald green rug covering the tile floor was plush and inviting.

"Well, Boofer, I'd say you've got quite a little setup here in Florida." Boofer flopped to a sitting position beside her. "What do you say you carry in my luggage while I take a nap, huh? Is that a deal?"

The dog just whined and scratched the lampshade with her back paw in an attempt to knock it off. When she wasn't able to break free, she looked up at Liv and growled.

"Hey. What did I say about growling at me?"

Boofer seemed to consider the question, then just dropped to her side and rolled onto the lampshade with a whine.

"That's more like it."

❧

A purple sticky note stuck to the television screen in the living room invited Liv to "turn it on and press play," which she did. She hadn't seen Josie Parish in a couple of years, but the sweet, silver-haired comedienne looked just the same.

"Hi, there, Olivia," she said in her high-pitched Mrs. Butterworth voice as she wrinkled her nose from inside the television. "And welcome to sunny Florida. Isn't it just beautiful? It's not always this pretty, like when we move into hurricane season a couple of times a year, but I predict it will be just lovely while you're here. Oh, other than some afternoon showers that sometimes last about an hour or so, and then they go away and the sun comes out again."

At the sound of Josie's voice, Boofer came running. She made an attempt at jumping on the sofa but missed and tumbled to the floor with a thud.

"Oh, dear!" Liv exclaimed, picking the dog up and placing her carefully on the cushion beside her. "Don't do that again. I can help you if you need to get somewhere."

Boofer laid her lampshade on Liv's knee and looked up at her gratefully.

"I've checked Granny Doogan's Almanac," Josie continued, "and it looks like the weather will be in the low eighties for most of the time that you'll be here on the island. If you want to make the pool water warmer, there's a thermostat on the wall above the barbecue grill. And if you want to make the air conditioning cooler, there's a keypad in the hall next to the guest bathroom."

Liv ran a hand over Boofer's back and smoothed her thick fur, and the dog made a tiny popping noise.

"Oooh, what was that, huh?"

Pop-pop-poppety-pop.

39

"Oh. Boofer. Are you . . . are you all right?"

"Missy Boofer gets one can of special dog food each morning, and then two scoops of dry in the evening," Josie said, drawing Liv's attention back to the screen. "She can have a couple of cookies as a snack each day, and I'll leave it up to the two of you to decide when. She has a section of her own in the pantry off the kitchen. Oh, and the big plastic collar can come off on Monday. If you need it, her veterinarian's information is on the front of the refrigerator."

Pop-pop-poppop.

Liv grimaced and looked down at the dog, who appeared completely unfazed.

"Be very careful with her, Pumpkin. My little puppy dog is a runner. If she sprints by you, just prop open the screen door by the pool, and she'll come back on her own eventually."

Liv cast Boofer a quick glance. "Don't run away, okay?"

The dog made no promises.

"I guess you can figure out by her name," Josie explained, and then she cupped her mouth with one hand and broke into a whisper. "Missy Boofer has a bit of a flatulence problem."

"Your name?" Liv asked the dog. "Is that what that means? Boofing means to—"

Pop-pop-phlooop.

"Oh!" she cried, pressing pause on the television and hopping to her feet.

Boofer stood up on the sofa and looked at her curiously just as the odor reached Liv's nose.

"Ohhh!" she cried, covering her mouth and nose with both hands. "Oh, come on! Are you kidding me with this?"

Pop-pop.

"Stop that! Am I being punked?"

Liv raced toward the sliding glass door to the lanai and yanked it open, waving her arms to coax the sudden stench out the door.

"I see you've met Boofer."

She wheeled around and let out a scream as she came face to face with a tall, muscular young man wearing floral Bermuda shorts, rubber flip-flops, and an open denim shirt. He stood pool-side and held a bottle of juice. Boofer let out one bark and then tottered across the floor and raced excitedly toward the stranger.

"I'm sorry," he said, crouching down to scratch the dog inside the lampshade. "I didn't mean to startle you. Josie mentioned you'd be arriving sometime today, and I just wanted to stop by and see if you needed anything."

"And you are . . . ?"

"Rand," he replied, and he stood up and offered his hand. She shook it tentatively, and then he pointed over his shoulder toward the pool. "The other side of the fence. Your neighbor."

"Oh, I see."

He was young, probably not much more than

twenty-five, and he reminded her of a TV actor on one of the daytime soaps. Liv tried not to stare, but she hadn't seen a rippled chest like his up close in a lot of years, or maybe not ever, at least in person.

"Well, I'm just on the other side," he told her, "if you find you need anything."

"Thank you."

He turned and started toward the screen door at the other end of the lanai, and then he paused and glanced back at her. "Oh, and about Boofer. I dogsat over the summer a couple of times. If you hold back on the special canned stuff and just feed her dry food, you'll be much more comfortable in the long run, if you get my meaning."

Liv chuckled and nodded her head, and then shot Rand a grin. "I appreciate the tip."

"It's really bad, isn't it?"

"Unique. Yes."

"By the way, we're having a barbecue tonight around seven, just some neighbors and a few friends. If you'd like to come over and meet some people, you're more than welcome."

He raked his wavy hair with one hand and took a swig from the bottle of neon liquid, then wiped his mouth with the back of his hand.

"I appreciate the offer," she told him. "But it's my first night here. I think I'll just get settled in."

"Are you sure?" he asked, and something about the way he swaggered, and then smiled at her, gave new meaning to the invitation. "I'd love a chance to get to know you better."

"Thanks, Rand. But I don't think so."

Run along now before I have to call your babysitter.

"All right. If you change your mind, just come on over."

"I'll do that. But don't plan for me."

She stood in the doorway and watched him until he was out the door and had disappeared on the other side of the gate after latching it. She started to close the sliding door behind her as she stepped back inside, but one whiff of what she'd run from a few minutes earlier inspired her to push it open wide instead.

Josie's video welcome lasted another twenty minutes, with tips on the good restaurants, where to go to church on Sunday, and when to expect the pool service. Just about the time that Liv considered turning it off before she was through, Josie told her she could find some other useful information on the dining room table, she wished her a happy holiday on Sanibel Island, and she was gone.

"At last."

Liv dragged her luggage into the bedroom and spent some time hanging things in the closet. She set her suitcase up on the chair in the corner to hold her folded items and lined up her shoes on the floor in front of the window.

Boofer moseyed in, sat down in the doorway, and looked at Liv curiously.

"Well, that killed half an hour," Liv said to the dog as she passed her and headed down the hall. "Now what?"

Boofer scampered behind her, and Liv talked to the dog all the way into the kitchen. "I'll tell you a little secret, Boofer. I'm not too great at the whole concept of vacationing. The truth is I don't really like to have too much free time to think. I'd rather keep busy. Know what I mean?"

Boofer cocked her head, and Liv couldn't help but laugh at the sight.

"Why don't we have a little snack?" Liv suggested. "I'll grab a couple of cookies for you, and maybe one of those apples on the counter for me, and we can go out and sit by the pool. What do you think of that?"

Boofer didn't seem to object, so Liv set about following the plan. She pulled down a serving tray from the shelf in the pantry and grabbed a few dog biscuits from Boofer's private stock. She dipped a spoon into a jar of peanut butter and set the spoon on the tray next to an apple and a knife, and then she grabbed a bottle of water from the door of the refrigerator.

"Let's go," she said, and Boofer followed her straight out the door.

Liv stretched out on one of the lounge chairs and sliced the apple into wedges atop the tray in her lap. Male voices in the distance drew her attention toward the fence, and she recognized one of them as Rand. The other seemed oddly familiar to her as well, which she knew was pretty unlikely, but she strained to listen more carefully anyway.

"Okay if I dump the ice into the cooler and get the sodas and stuff in there?"

"Sounds like a plan. I'll fire up the grill."

They were gearing up for the barbecue that Rand had mentioned. She wondered who the other voice belonged to as she tossed Boofer a meaty bone-shaped treat.

"Hey, Dad, any chance you could make some of that salsa of yours?"

Oh, it's his father, Liv thought, and she couldn't help but wonder what the father of a soap star would look like.

Curiosity outweighed courtesy. It couldn't hurt to have a peek over the top of the fence. Liv set the tray on the edge of the lounge chair and approached the fence. Stepping up on the ledge of the brick planter, she popped her head over the top of the fence.

Rand looked handsome dressed in knee-length khaki shorts and a dark green knit shirt, but where was his father?

At just that moment, a second person emerged

from the house and walked out onto the patio by the pool. Salt and pepper hair, suntanned skin, and a toothpaste commercial smile.

Jared Hunt!

Suddenly, Liv lost her balance and began twirling her arms in circles, desperately trying to stop the inevitable. Then, with a little squeal, she fell backwards off the brick planter and rolled across the terrazzo tile, straight into the deep end of the pool.

4

Prudence could hardly believe her wide donkey eyes!

All sizes and shapes of creatures and beasts milled about in the clearing. There were sheep and cows and tigers and frogs. She even spotted a chicken! And they all shared the path surrounding the pond, conversing like friends while munching on grass and leaves and hopping bugs.

"I haven't seen you here before. Do you live in the meadow?"

Pru craned her neck to look into the gold eyes of the gleaming black stallion that stood before her. He was beautiful, and he took her donkey breath away.

"N-no," she stammered. "I-I'm just passing through."

"Not too quickly through, I hope," the stallion replied with a rich, resonant whinny that rocked her to the core.

❧

Liv hadn't shaved her armpits in two weeks. Frankly, there simply hadn't been the need. In theory, her underarms had become a bit like a sewing kit to her; no one ever thinks about a needle and thread until they split their pants or pop a button. But now she grazed over them carefully with a disposable razor, and then hit each leg twice in the shower to rid herself of what Hallie liked to call "the winter coat." She wasn't facing late March in Ohio any more, and she certainly wasn't going to wear a dress and sandals anywhere without some very keen attention to detail.

Jared Hunt.

She'd repeated his name in her head about a dozen times since spotting him on the other side of the fence. What were the odds? Really, what were they? The handsome guy that she'd lost track of somewhere in the airport terminal— turning up on the other side of Josie Parish's wooden fence!

Liv changed outfits three times before deciding on the brown and pink tie-dyed Ombre dress with ruching across the bodice and spaghetti straps. She was still tying the brown satin ribbon around her waist as she slipped into jeweled pink sandals and wiggled her freshly painted *Cinnamon Toast* toes.

She clasped the palm tree necklace Hallie had given her, one of several Florida-themed early birthday presents, and then stood in front of the full-length beveled mirror and took a long gander at the woman looking back at her. Despite the silver threads running through her hair, and the very, very white complexion that betrayed a long winter season in Cincinnati, Liv took note that she looked a bit revived. She could hardly attribute it to Florida since she'd been here less than twenty-four hours, or to Jared Hunt since they'd only met so briefly.

"I think it must be you, Boof," she said to the Lhasa Apso lying prostrate at her feet. "You make me feel like a new woman."

Boofer's tail thumped several times against the thick green carpet, and Liv tickled the dog's chin with her index finger.

"Okay, now. You be a good girl. I won't be gone long."

By the time she walked through the screen door on the far side of the pool and through the one just like it at the house next door, Liv's heart hammered against her throat.

"Welcome, neighbor!" Rand exclaimed when he saw her, and he greeted Liv with an unexpected embrace. "I'm so glad you changed your mind. Come on in. Let's get you something cold to drink, and then I'll introduce you around."

She struggled against looking too obvious as she scanned the crowd gathered around the pool. Unfamiliar face after unfamiliar face ticked by, all of them slightly aglow from lighted strings of red chili peppers hanging around the whole pool area.

And then she saw him.

With the same mysterious magnet he'd carried with him at their first meeting, some strange centrifugal force drew her straight to Jared the moment their gazes crossed. His eyebrows arched and his chin rose as they headed for one another, and his beautiful toothpaste commercial smile broadened with every step he took.

"Olivia, isn't it?"

"Jared."

"What in the world are you doing here?"

"There you are," Rand said as he stepped up beside her and placed an arm loosely around her shoulder. "This is my father, Dr. Jared Hunt. Dad, this is Olivia Wallace. She's staying at Josie's place for a few weeks."

"What are the chances?" Jared said without dragging his eyes from her.

"I was asking myself that very thing," she replied.

"I'm sorry. Do you two know each other?" Rand asked.

"We were on the same flight from Cincinnati," Jared explained. "I looked for you down at baggage claim."

"I made a stop in the ladies' room on the way," she said, trying to remain casual. "By the time I got to the glass doors, I seemed to be the only one left from our flight."

Jared reached out and took her hand for just a

split second. "It's really good to see you again, Liv."

"You too."

"Well, would you like to meet some people?" Rand asked her. "You don't mind, do you, Dad?"

"Not as long as you bring her back around afterward."

Liv smiled at Jared and then allowed Rand to guide her away, despite the overwhelming desire to stay planted right next to him like one of those deep-rooted sycamore trees back home.

There were neighbors and friends, all of them with names Liv knew she wouldn't remember. And then there was someone named Georgia, impossible to forget.

"Olivia, meet Georgia," Rand said, and the woman with the platinum hair and movie star eyelashes presented her hand as if she expected Liv to kiss her ring.

"Sweet Georgia Brown," she said in a drawl so Southern that Liv could almost smell the mint julep on the woman's breath. "Like the song."

"Liv Wallace," she replied, shaking Georgia's hand awkwardly. "No songs named after me. I did meet a woman named Liv on a train once though."

Laughter erupted out of Rand, but it didn't last long. Sweet Georgia wasn't laughing, and Liv noticed that she didn't look all that sweet at the moment either.

"Is this one of your girlfriends, Randall?" she asked, sizing Liv up in a way that made her wish the fabric of her dress was a little bulkier.

What a question, she thought. *Girlfriend indeed. I'm old enough to be his—*

"Not yet," Rand answered. "But the evening's young, Georgia."

Locking Liv's hand into the crook of his arm, he led her away to the next group congregated along their circular poolside path. She could feel the sharp forks of Georgia's scrutiny poking her in the back as they walked away.

"Bill and Martha, this is Olivia Wallace. She's visiting from Ohio and staying over at Josie's."

Several more introductions followed before Rand finally led Liv to a cushioned rattan chair at a small round table.

"Have a seat," he said, holding the back of the chair for her. "I'll get you a plate and something cold to drink. You've got to taste my dad's salsa."

Liv sighed as Rand made his way across the natural stone pavers toward the buffet set up on a long folding table draped with a colorful sarape blanket.

"I just can't get over you showing up here tonight."

Liv tensed as Jared touched her bare shoulders with two warm hands, and then she managed a grin as he rounded her chair and sat down in the one beside her.

"It's crazy, isn't it?" she asked him.

"Here I was thinking I'd never see you again. And I have my son to thank."

She folded her hands in her lap in an attempt to keep them from shaking. *This isn't high school, Liv. Get hold of yourself.*

"So tell me, how long are you planning to stay?"

"A couple of weeks," she replied. Was it her imagination that he looked disappointed?

"I hope you'll let me show you around."

"I'd like that."

"If I can pry you away from my son, that is."

They both turned toward the buffet table where Rand stood with two full plates in hand, struggling to pull himself away from Georgia and back toward Liv.

"It would appear he's quite taken with you," Jared told her.

Liv chuckled and then shook her head.

Just my luck.

After years of believing the laws of attraction had all been overturned, she had finally met someone who made her heart race again. But it was his son who was rushing her way like a bull charging through a china shop door.

"I got you a little sampling of everything," Rand said, setting the plates down on the table. "What would you like to drink?"

"Diet soda?"

"I'll be right back," he declared. Then, after just a couple of steps, he turned back toward his father and pointed at the second plate. "That isn't for you."

With a twinkle in his eye, Jared plucked an unidentifiable appetizer that looked like a miniature turnover from the assortment of snacks before him and popped it into his mouth.

"You're impossible," Rand groaned.

"What kind of pie is that?" she asked Jared once Rand was out of earshot.

"You've never had an empanada?"

Liv shook her head. Not only had she never tasted one, she'd never even heard of one.

"Try it."

She lifted a pie from the plate in front of her, examined it carefully, and then took a bite.

It had taken such a long time after cancer treatment to get her appetite back that bold tastes were now always a wonderful surprise.

"What's inside?"

"Chorizo."

"Now in English?" she suggested on a chuckle.

"Chorizo," he repeated. "A type of pork sausage, spiced with paprika and garlic and red pepper. It's a traditional Spanish or Latino meat that they fry into this pastry dough to make an empanada."

Liv's mouth was burning, and Rand arrived with beverages just in the knick of time. She grabbed the cup out of his hand and gulped down the soda.

"I was expecting an apple pie filling or something," she told them, and both Jared and Rand laughed. "But this is really, really good!"

"Sometimes you'll see them filled with fruit or pumpkin," Jared explained. "But these are traditional *tapas*. Appetizers."

"Wait till you try the salsa," Rand added.

It seemed like several days had passed, but Liv realized it was just that morning when she'd driven in from the Fort Myers airport. She recalled spotting an odd, long-necked bird along the side of the road and thinking what a strange and different place she was in. Now, as her lips burned and her eyes watered from the compelling new cuisine, and her pulse raced from the crackling nearness of Jared Hunt, she wondered if Delta had actually flown her out of Ohio, over the Grand Canyon, and into some parallel universe where birthday curses were unknown and the locals ate delicacies like salsa and little spicy pies.

Hey, what if I wake up younger in Florida Land? With smaller feet and no wrinkles. Oh, and what if there's chocolate with zero calories on this planet!

Why not? In a world where it seemed like everything was new and different, and where anything was suddenly possible, it couldn't hurt to waste a wish or two.

And if Sanibel Island, Florida, was light-years away from Cincinnati, Ohio, the most obvious alien in this new world was heading straight for her.

"So, Olivia Wallace," Georgia Brown sang in her thick Southern drawl as she plopped down in the chair next to her and crossed her legs into a twisted pretzel, "I just heard you're a temporary visitor to our sleepy little town. Tell me, how long are you staying? And just what are your intentions with our young Randall while you're here?"

❧

There was a special meter not widely known in the region, and Jared had long been the keeper of it. He liked to call it the *Georgia Brown Richter Scale,* and it measured the levels of embarrassment caused in others by his nurse. The meter gave Jared a little electrical shock every time Georgia's seismic activity was on the rise. And this was a doozy.

"Liv, why don't I walk you home?"

She didn't even respond. Olivia just popped up out of her chair and took his lead.

"Very nice meeting all of you," she tossed back at them, already in full retreat mode. "Rand, thank you so much for inviting me. It was really lovely."

Once they'd stepped outside the patio door and the screen had tapped shut behind them,

Jared and Liv turned toward one another. Her green eyes sparkled, and a full-on grin spread across her face. "Thank you," she said in a whisper. "She's a pill."

"She is."

"What is she, someone's crazy aunt or something?"

Jared felt a rush of heat as he replied. "Sort of. She's my nurse."

"Are you ill?"

"No, no," he laughed, and then he realized she was only joking. "I'm a doctor, remember? She works for me."

"Ohhh," Liv sniggered.

"Although I'm not feeling all that great right now."

"Shall I call a nurse?"

"No. Please."

Jared instinctively reached toward her face and smoothed back a wayward curl that had fallen across her cheek. As she looked up at him and smiled, it took everything honorable in him not to lean in for a kiss. He reminded himself that he was not a teenager, he was a gentleman, and this was a true lady. They'd only just met for the first time that morning on an airplane that felt to him as if it had crossed some great divide.

"Would you like to go for a walk?" he asked and was relieved when she nodded.

Jared's hand hovered on the small of Liv's back

as he guided her toward the concrete sidewalk leading to the corner illuminated in dim yellow light from the street lamp.

"So how long have you lived here?" she asked, tucking her hands deep into the pockets of her dress as they strolled along.

"About fifteen years. Rand was just a kid when we left Chicago and bought this house, and his mother was still alive."

"I've been in Cincinnati for my whole life," she told him. "Born and bred." She tilted her head slightly and grinned at the taut canvas sky. "There's about a foot of snow on the ground there right now, and I'm walking under a full moon, wearing a sleeveless dress."

"I know."

"You do?"

"I left a foot of snow behind in Cincinnati when you did this morning."

"Oh, that's right," she commented, and then she stopped walking and turned toward him. "Isn't that strange? It feels like such a long time ago."

"I was thinking that myself tonight."

Jared offered her his arm, bent at the elbow, and she took it. They meandered down the street, arm in arm, and Jared found himself wondering if the sweet scent tickling his nose emanated from the neighbor's garden or Liv's smooth, fair skin.

"What are your plans while you're here?" he

asked her when they reached the corner and turned to the left.

"I'm not sure," she replied. "Read a couple of books. Get some sun. Sleep until ten o'clock every morning! I'm on a mission to escape."

"From?"

She paused for a long moment before answering. "Me, I guess."

"You'll have to explain that to me."

"Well, I told you this morning that I've just been through the war."

"Ah, cancer. Yes. And I recall mention of a birthday curse as well."

"Right. It's a pretty big one headed my way next week."

He took a minute to try and guess which one was looming. Forty? Forty-five?

"My birthdays have traditionally been ripe with disasters," she continued. "Seriously, it's like some sort of annual dark cloud that comes back around every year about this time."

Jared looked up at the full silver moon and then grinned. "Good news. Not a cloud in sight."

Liv pinched his arm playfully and then patted it several times. "Well, keep a close watch, Dr. Hunt," she told him. "There's probably a typhoon on the way."

"That's the spirit," he replied, squeezing her hand. "Positive thinking is so important."

5

Prudence didn't like surprises.

She didn't like the way her blood pumped harder, or the way her eyes popped open so round that she could hardly blink. And she especially didn't like the way her whole donkey body froze with solid, rusted fear.

But when her steady friend Horatio was taken by surprise right before her, well, Prudence found out that was the scariest thing of all.

❧

At the back of her groggy mind, Liv recalled the vow she'd made when crawling into bed the previous night. After so many years of rising early for work in the O.R., and then months of 6:45 a.m. wake-up calls to make it to the center in time for her daily eight o'clock radiation treatments, Olivia was bound and determined to sleep until nine or ten o'clock on this vacation of hers.

So why was the alarm screaming at her?

She peeled open one eye and blinked several times.

7:12 a.m.

She reached over and smacked the snooze button on the top of the alarm clock, but nothing happened. The racket just continued.

Opening the other eye took considerably more effort, but she managed, and then propped up on one elbow and groaned. It wasn't the alarm clock going off, it was the *Lhasa Apso*.

Boofer was on a tirade in the other room, going off like a storm siren. As she tossed her legs over the side of the bed, Liv wondered if the aforementioned typhoon had found her and this was Boofer's way of warning her to run for safety.

"Boofer!" she exclaimed as she hurried down the hall, tugging at the belt of her robe. "Quiet! Boofer!"

If Liv spoke dog, she was quite certain that the indecipherable diatribe would add up to something with quite a few expletives. When she reached the dining room, the ball of multi-colored fur stood on her back legs, her front ones pressed against the slider, her little Princess T-shirt cocked sideways, and her lampshade collar scraping against the glass as she growled and snarled at something on the other side of the window.

"Boo-fer! Please!"

When the dog turned back toward her, the collar caught her off balance, and she toppled over to the floor with a whimper. The long brown-on-black-on-white fur around the dog's face was blown back in a way that made her look as if she'd been riding with her head poked out the window of a fast-moving car. Her bright pink tongue hung off to one side, and her brown eyes were as wide and round as disks.

"What is wrong with you?" Liv asked as she placed Boofer back on her feet again.

Movement beyond the window drew Liv's attention, and she squinted as she watched something large and white skim the surface of the water across the length of the pool. She made sure her robe was securely shut as she threw open the slider. Before she could even take a step out onto the patio, Boofer barreled past her, barking at a pitch that Liv thought might just succeed in shattering glass.

Her front paws were planted so close to the edge that Liv worried the dog might fall in, and she lifted Boofer into her arms and took the dog's place at the edge.

"Hey!" she called out to the elderly man as he reached the far end of the pool. "Excuse me? Hello!"

He was eighty if he was a day, with pasty white skin and yellow-silver hair. He raised the small blue goggles to his forehead and squinted at her.

"Josie?" he said in a raspy Grandpa McCoy voice. "That you?"

"No, it's not," Liv replied. "Josie is—"

"Hah?" he snapped. "Whadja say? Hearing aids are out. Speak up, woman."

Liv saw the realization stain his face as she walked along the edge of the pool toward him.

"Who are you?" he demanded.

"I'm Josie's houseguest," she returned. "Who are you?"

"Houseguest. Where's Josie?"

Liv groaned and turned her head away as the old man climbed out of the pool, his lime green and yellow swim trunks dipping low as he did. She hurried to grab the towel thrown across the patio table and tossed it toward him, but she was a little disappointed when he merely tied it around his waist, facing her with a sagging bare chest. Boofer growled at the man, and Liv inwardly acknowledged that she shared the dog's point of view.

"Who are you?" she repeated.

"Clayton Clydesdale," he answered as he poked his index finger into his ear and plunged it like a stopped-up drain. "Like the horses."

"And what are you doing here, Mr. Clydesdale?"

"I'm swimming. What's it look like? Josie lets me swim laps in her pool a couple times a week. Now who are *you,* and what are *you* doing here?"

"Olivia Wallace. Josie's daughter Hallie is my best friend."

"Hallie with you?"

"No. Josie's gone to visit her in Ohio, and she invited me to stay here while she was gone."

"What happened to that fool dog? Got the mange?"

Liv didn't like all the questions, especially before eight in the morning. She eyed Clayton with caution as he fetched his hearing aids from a nearby table and twisted them into his ears.

"Mr. Clydesdale, I'm going to be here for the next two weeks, and I'd appreciate it if you didn't just let yourself into the pool while I'm here."

"Gotta do my laps," the old man grunted as he adjusted one of the aids in his ear. "Don't know how to do that without letting myself into the pool."

"Maybe you could use the community pool," she suggested. "I saw that there's a very nice one just a block over. Only while I'm here, if you wouldn't mind."

"Maybe."

"Well, I'd appreciate it if—"

"Maybe not."

Without another word, the old guy slipped into rainbow-colored rubber flip-flops, tightened the towel around his waist, and headed straight for the screen door.

"What's your name again?" he called from the open doorway.

"Olivia. Wallace."

"See you later, Olivia Wallace."

"Not if I can help it," Liv muttered, scampering toward the screen door and locking it behind him once he was gone.

She padded back to the house and once inside set Boofer down on the floor, and then flicked the lock on that door too.

"How about some breakfast?" she asked the dog. Boofer trotted happily behind her into the kitchen. "None of that special wet dog food for you, either, my friend. There's lots of doggie nutrition in the dry stuff, without the whole digestive . . . situation."

She filled the pink bowl with kibbles and set it on the floor. Boofer sniffed at it, and then looked up at Liv and barked once.

"I know. This isn't what you're used to. But you know what? You won't starve. And I won't have to deal with finding a store where Floridians buy their gas masks."

Boofer slumped with disappointment and ignored the kibbles.

"I don't think you understand, Boofer. That special dog food of yours is lethal." Boofer tilted her head. "Well, I know. Not to you. But certainly to me. And you don't want that, do you?"

The dog apparently had to think that one over before delivering her final conclusion.

After breakfast, Liv pulled on a pair of denim

capris and the short-sleeved white T-shirt with a glitter palm tree on the front that Hallie had given her with the necklace.

"To put you in the mood for a Florida vacation," she'd said.

She strolled into what appeared to be Josie's home office and stood before the floor-to-ceiling bookshelves that occupied one entire side of the room. There were at least a dozen different Bibles on the top shelf. The others were dotted with the names of the classics, mingled with contemporary thrillers, whodunits, and flowery romances. Liv pulled a cozy mystery off the shelf and read the back cover while Boofer made herself at home resting against Liv's leg.

"Who would have guessed Josie had such eclectic tastes," she said out loud, casting Boofer a smile as she replaced the book and selected a romance novel from the next shelf down.

She hadn't even finished skimming the three short paragraphs on the back cover before Jared Hunt bounced into her thoughts, transporting her back to a moonlight stroll and warm brown eyes that seemed to lay into her like some sort of branding iron.

"Maybe not a romance today," she said, placing the novel back into its spot.

She continued to scan the bookshelves, landing on a colorful section of books, all with different titles but the same recognizable font style. The first one was *A Brand New Pru* by Josephine Parish, and Liv tugged it out and looked at the cover. She'd been hearing from Hallie for years about the series of *Prudence* books Josie had written, but she'd never seen one before, and she recalled Hallie comparing her to the downtrodden donkey in the stories.

Liv stepped out of her sandals, curled into the corner of the settee, folded her legs beneath her, and started to read. Only a few pages later, a *thud-thud-thud!* at the front door sent Boofer into a barking frenzy, and Liv set down the book and hurried out to answer it.

"Good morning, beautiful!"

"Rand. How are you?"

He passed right by her, tapped Boofer on the top of the head, and stepped into the foyer. With his sun-kissed hair and skin and gleaming white teeth, he looked a lot like someone who might pose for the cover of a Florida travel magazine.

"You have your father's smile," she told him.

"I also have his twenty-eight-foot Sun Runner."

"Which, in English, means what exactly?"

"It's a boat," he announced. "What do you say we pack a picnic lunch and motor around the island for some sun and surf? Maybe go snorkeling."

Liv folded her arms and smiled. "Rand, how old are you?"

"Twenty-six."

"Do you know how old I am?"

"I don't know. Forty?"

"No," she replied, and then stopped herself. "Thank you, by the way. But no. I am not forty. I'm not even forty-five."

"Really?"

"Really."

"So do you want to go?"

"Are you asking me on a date, Rand?"

"I'm inviting you out for some lunch," he corrected. "If we happen to fall in love while we're eating, then so be it."

Liv grinned in spite of herself. "You are a very charming young man, Rand."

"If you think this is charming, you haven't seen anything yet."

"But I am not going to date you."

He regarded her strangely, and then took a step back. "You're not?"

"I'm not."

"Are you hung up on the age thing?"

"Extremely."

"And if I were forty?"

"I'd be grabbing my shoes and running toward the marina with you."

"That's so wrong, Liv."

"I think so too. But it's just how wrong I'm going to be. And you need to respect it."

Rand shrugged and pulled the door open. Turning back to her, he smiled. "So it's definitely no."

"It's no."

His hand flew to his chest and he sank back against the door jamb as if he'd been wounded. "You're harshing my mellow, Liv."

"Am I?"

He shrugged again and stepped outside. Just as he turned back toward her for one last objection, Liv grinned at him.

"Good-bye, Rand."

And she closed the door.

~⁂~

"Good morning, Mrs. Hennessy. How are you doing today?"

Doris Hennessy was one of Jared's longest standing patients. Meaning she was ninety-three years old, and she was *still standing*.

"My bursitis is acting up, Jared, and my grand-kids are coming to visit."

"Mary Kate or Mary Grace?"

"Mary Grace. She's just had her third baby, you know."

"I didn't know," he told her, lifting her arm with caution until she winced. "Congratulations. That makes you a great-grandmother. Quite an accomplishment."

"Well, I'd like to be able to hold the baby. But my arms are aching so badly."

"Have you been taking your anti-inflammatories?"

"Yes."

"And have you iced your shoulder?"

"No."

"Why not?"

She pushed her wire-rimmed glasses up on her nose and thought about it. "It didn't help last time, Jared."

"All right. Then let's try some heat therapy. Okay with you?"

"Sure."

"Can I have a listen?" he asked her, holding up the stethoscope draped around his neck. She nodded, and he pressed it to her back. "Big deep breath now. Good, you sound nice and clear. I think you're going to live longer than anyone on this island."

"Good. I considered the alternative, and I decided against it."

Jared laughed at that. "I'll have Georgia set you up with a prescription for therapy over at the clinic. I want you to go in every weekday through the end of next week. Can you do that for me?"

"I think so."

"Do you have someone to take you, Doris?"

"Yes."

"I don't want to see you driving that car anymore, do you hear me?"

"I won't."

Mrs. Hennessy had been visiting a friend over on Captiva a few months prior, and she'd backed her car right into Harry Stafford's golf cart.

"You call me if you can't get someone to drive you, all right?"

"I will, Jared."

"Now let's go see Georgia, and she'll fix you right up."

Mrs. Hennessy linked her arm through Jared's, and it reminded him of someone else. Liv had held his arm that way when they'd gone for a walk around the neighborhood the previous night.

"Hey, Mrs. H, how have you been?"

Rand stood at the counter chatting with Georgia and Audrey as Liv and Jared came around the corner.

"Dr. Hunt, your son gets more handsome every time I see him," Doris told him.

"Oh, and he's well aware of that, I'm sorry to report."

Rand smacked his father's arm and let out a laugh.

"To what do I owe this visit?" Jared asked him, after walking Doris to the door.

"I thought you might want to grab some lunch," Rand replied. "They've opened a new Chinese place down on Pine."

"Oh, you don't want to go there," Georgia interrupted. "It's all grease and MSG."

"I happen to enjoy a little grease with my food now and then," Rand teased.

71

"Well, I was thinking more about your father's constitution, Randall."

"Whoa! O-kay now!" Jared exclaimed. "That's the last time I want to hear any office conversation that revolves around my constitution, thank you very much."

"So what do you say, Dad? Lunch?"

"I told the Gordons I'd stop out and see them this afternoon. I think I have enough time to grab a bite beforehand, but how about something a little less risky than Chinese?"

"Whatever. You're paying. You name the place."

"Oh, I see. The salad bar it is then."

"C'mon, Dad. Have a heart."

They reached a compromise on the way to the Lazy Flamingo for fried grouper sandwiches.

"So what are you up to today?" Jared asked as he stirred sugar into his tea.

"Well, I thought I was going to take the boat for a spin, but my date bailed."

"Sorry to hear that. Losing some of that mojo of yours?"

"Absolutely not," Rand declared, wiping his mouth. "Just the opposite. I'm too young and virile for Liv to handle."

"Liv," Jared stated.

"Yeah, I asked her out, and she turned me down flat."

Jared tried not to smile, disguising it with a

knitted brow and serious expression. "Did she now."

"Said she wasn't going to date me, no way, no how."

"Harsh."

"That's what I told her. Harshing my mellow, big time."

"Harshing your mellow," Jared repeated.

"Yeah. Stomping my mind. Blowing my zen."

"Ah."

Jared wished he'd been a fly on the wall for that conversation. Not that he found any joy in his son's mellow being stomped, but he figured it wasn't any great betrayal as a father that he was relieved Olivia Wallace wasn't suddenly dating his son.

"Maybe you should give her a run."

Jared jerked back to the moment and stared down his son. "I beg your pardon?"

"If I'm too young and intense, maybe she'd give an old guy like you a run for his money."

"I don't know what to respond to first."

"Okay, sorry. You're not an old guy exactly. But next to me, come on, Dad. Let's face it."

The waitress set the check down in front of Jared and, without missing a beat, he slid it across the table toward Rand.

"Thanks for lunch," he said in his best grandpa voice. "Now this old geezer needs to be on his way."

Rand laughed and pushed the check back at Jared. "I must have left my wallet in my other pants."

"Whippersnapper."

"Relic."

"When do you go back to school again?"

6

Prudence looked around and realized how far away her meadow home was now. She gazed at the sparkling pond and the rocky hills that surrounded it, and she wondered if she would ever again make it home to her meadow.

"Everything is so different here," she told Horatio in a soft, thoughtful bray.

"Different can be good," her wise friend replied. "Sometimes different builds a bridge between what you are and what you can be."

❧

O h, Clay is harmless," Hallie said with a chuckle as Liv stood at the glass door, the phone tucked between her ear and shoulder.

"He is so annoying," Liv replied as Clayton touched the flagstone at the far end and then flipped backward for another lap across the swimming pool. This time, it was the backstroke. "He's out there right now after I expressly asked him not to let himself into the pool area while I'm here."

"He didn't ring the doorbell, did he?"

"No. He slit the screen and unlocked the patio door."

"Oh, boy. And that woke you up?"

"Yes. Well, no. Boofer's reaction to a stranger on the property woke me up."

"Oh," Hallie sighed. "How is Boofer?"

Liv glanced around. Missy Boofer's little doggie T-shirt was bunched up above her mid-section, and the lampshade collar was squished sideways as she lay sound asleep on one of the throw pillows on the sofa.

"I expect her to start snoring any minute."

"I guess she got over that whole 'stranger danger' thing then."

"She did," Liv replied, turning her attention back toward the pool just in time to catch a glimpse of Clayton adjusting his low-riding swim trunks and tying a neon tie-dyed towel around his waist. "I'm not sure I ever will, though."

Hallie laughed. "I'm sorry, Liv. I'd forgotten all about the cast of characters down there."

"Impressive. How did you manage it?"

"Motherhood. It takes up too many brain cells. I'm on spring break overload. Have you met anyone else in the neighborhood?"

"I met Jared Hunt on the plane down here, and then discovered he lives right behind Josie."

"Ooh, Jared. Isn't he yummy?"

Liv decided not to reply. "And I met his son, Rand."

"Rand is there?"

"On holiday while school is out. I guess he's a teacher."

"He teaches American Lit at an all-girls school in England."

"Can you imagine that?" Liv asked, and then she chuckled at the thought of an audience of teenage girls pretending to listen to monologues about Keats and Faulkner but thinking only of the bronze, godlike instructor at the front of the class. "Anyway, they had a barbecue my first night here, and I went over and met some of the locals. Had some great Mexican food. Carne asada on the grill. Some *cherry riso* sausage. Oh, and these little pies called *empinojos*."

"Empanadas?" Hallie giggled.

"Whatever. They were delicious."

"It sounds like you're having a good time then. Admit it."

"If I could get the chance to sleep past dawn, I'd be golden."

"So have you made any plans for your birth-day?"

Liv sighed. "Not yet."

Outside, Clayton shook his head in swift, side-to-side gestures, as if he had long locks of hair to drip dry.

"We were talking about it last night, Liv, and here's what I think you should do—"

"Listen, I'm going to take another shot at reasoning with Michael Phelps' great-grandfather before he leaves. Can I talk to you later?"

"Sure. Give my love to Jared and Rand, will you?"

"Will do."

Liv pulled open the slider and stepped out to the patio just as Clayton reached the screen door at the other side.

"Mr. Clydesdale?" she called, but he didn't flinch. "Mr. Clydesdale?" she shouted louder, but to the same reception.

Liv noticed Clayton's two small hearing aids still strewn on the table, and she hurried to fetch them, cringing as she placed them in the palm of her hand. Then she jogged across the lawn after him.

"Mr. Clydesdale!" she exclaimed, as she touched him lightly on the shoulder. He jumped and turned to face her with both fists raised, causing Liv to step back in defense.

"You forgot your hearing aids," she said, mouthing the words with animation.

"Hah?"

"Your hearing aids. You left them."

She opened her hand and showed him, feeling a little wave of queasiness as she did. Having some old guy's waxy ear buds in her hand made her want to rush back into the house and scrub all the way up to her elbows.

"Ah. Thanks." He snatched them from her without ceremony and twisted them into his ears like knobs on a bedroom door.

"Mr. Clydesdale, do you remember that we spoke about your not using the pool until Josie comes back?"

"Josie?" he said, and then he softened for just an instant. "When's she coming back?"

"Not for two weeks," she explained.

His gruff scowl back in place, he declared, "Can't go two weeks without doing my laps."

"Okay," Liv replied, searching for another tack. "And you don't feel like you could use the community pool for two weeks?"

"Too far," he said, adjusting one of the hearing aids. "I'd have to crank up the car for that. It's better to just walk across the street."

"O-kay. Well. How about you do your laps a little later then?"

"Early riser," he snapped.

"I believe you. But I would like to *NOT* be an early riser. And the dog barks every morning when you let yourself in, and it wakes me up."

"Mangy dog."

"Mr. Clydesdale, please. I'm on vacation. I'd like to sleep in past sunrise each morning."

"Yeah. Okay."

"Then you won't come earlier than nine?"

"No earlier than nine. Got it."

"Thank you."

"Yeah," he grunted. "You want to swim with me some morning?"

Liv cocked her head like a dog who heard a whistle two blocks over. "I'm sorry. What?"

"Swim with me," he snapped. "Maybe get some lunch."

The old guy wiggled his eyebrows at her, and Liv took an instinctive step backward. Was he *flirting with her?!*

"Um, no. Thank you. But . . . no."

Turning on his heel and stomping away from her, he shot one curt wave into the air and back at her from above his head.

Liv started to comb back her hair with both hands, then froze, staring at them in midair. With a second thought, she dropped her arms to her sides and headed into the house to give those hands a good scrub.

❧

Liv wondered when it was in history that bathing suits went from the knee-length shorts and tank-top versions to a couple of patches of fabric held together by a few strings. Stretching her very white leg across the length of the lounge chair, she looked down at the one-piece alternative she'd hardly been able to find in the sea of midriff-bearing options in Hallie's summer closet.

"I am not wearing a bikini," she had told her friend in no uncertain terms.

"I don't even own a bikini," Hallie had retorted. "These are just two-piece bathing suits. They cover more skin than your bra and panties."

"But I would not go out in public in my underwear."

"Where are you planning to swim? Silver Key?"

"What's that?"

"The nude beach. But you're not going there, Liv. You'll be completely alone, just you, the water, and the sun in my mother's very private backyard!"

Very private, she laughed to herself now as she recalled her conversation with Hallie. *Nothing private about this particular backyard!*

But with that false promise of privacy in mind, Liv had borrowed a bright red one-piece with ruching across the top and large gold buckles holding the straps in place.

She said a silent prayer that Clayton, or worse yet . . . *Jared!* . . . didn't stop by, as she took a long draw from the glass of lemonade on the table beside her. Boofer had found a little circle of space to curl into beside her on the chair, and Liv ruffled the only patch of the dog's fur in sight.

"We really need to get you out of that ridiculous T-shirt," she remarked, and Boofer lifted her head hopefully. "Would you like that?"

In response, the dog rose to her feet and seemed to smile.

"*Princess-in-training*," she read with disdain before trying to pull the pink T-shirt over the lampshade. "Well, that's not going to work, is it?"

Liv unfastened the collar and laid it to rest on the tile floor beside her chair.

"Don't get too excited. You're only paroled from this thing long enough to get this ridiculous shirt off of you."

But the moment the Princess-in-Training turned back into a dog again, Boofer made a break for it. She flew through the air and toward the slider, then whimpered when she discovered she'd been closed off from the inside of the house.

"Come on, girl. Come back here."

Liv approached the dog slowly, lampshade in hand but tucked strategically behind her back, and then she lunged toward her. Boofer took off running around the rim of the pool.

"I understand, I really do," Liv empathized on her second lap of pursuit. "But it's for your own good. You just need to wear this collar for another week or so, and then you're free."

Liv soon realized they could circle the swimming pool for days, and she doubled back in hope of catching the dog on the other side. Boofer, however, was not to be outsmarted, and she just turned and ran back in the opposite direction too.

"Oh, come on."

"Need some help?"

She stopped so quickly in her tracks that she stubbed her toe, and she winced as Jared came through the screen door.

"I've got a runner," she told him, nodding toward Boofer in her doggie standoff at the other side of the pool.

"You take the east road," Jared teased. "I'll take the west."

They each followed the rim of the pool, closing in on Boofer, who still looked as determined as ever to make her escape. She wiggled a bit when Jared picked her up, but then she eased into his soothing voice and the warmth of his gentle hand petting her fur.

"Thank you," Liv said as she clamped the collar back into place. "You've saved me from the stigma of being outsmarted by a dog."

"I'm sure you would have prevailed," he commented, setting Boofer down on the tile to scamper off toward the house, "just by virtue of having thumbs and all."

"Well, I don't know," Liv replied with a laugh. "My thumbs weren't doing much for me."

"Were you going for a swim?"

Time probably didn't really stop, but it felt to Liv as if it had. Clenching her jaw, she glanced down at herself and then clamped her eyes shut. "Would you . . . mind . . . turning around?"

Jared chuckled. "What?"

Liv's head popped up and, with her hands firmly planted on Jared's shoulders, she turned him. "Please. Turn around?"

"All right, all right," he said in surrender, raising his hands in the air like a man taken prisoner.

"Thank you," she said, backing away from him. "Thank you. Just stay that way for—" Liv scampered on tiptoe around the pool toward the sarong folded across the back of the chair. "—just one more minute." Even tied into place, one of those long, pasty legs of hers poked out, and she felt only a little less naked.

"Can I turn around now?" Jared asked, and the amusement in his voice was unmistakable, even before he chuckled.

"Laugh it up," she told him as she re-tied the sarong. A little lower on the hip might cover more leg. "You have no idea what a favor I'm doing for you. The glare alone from my lack of tan could easily blind you."

"Olivia. I'm turning around now."

She yanked at the hem of the sarong as he did, and found herself feeling very much like she'd gone to that Silver Key beach after all.

"Liv," Jared said as he approached her, and then he took her hand into both of his and planted a soft kiss on the knuckle of her middle finger. "You're stunning."

"And white," she added.

"Lovely."

In a downcast whisper, she added, "Completely devoid of muscle tone."

"Liv."

"Sorry."

The reality of her own self-deprecating insecurity began to settle in on her, and Liv was sinking into the mortifying tide.

"I'm not usually this . . . this . . ." She paused and then couldn't help but smile. "Well. Not this bad, anyway."

"Look," Jared said, "I'm sorry I intruded. I didn't mean to embarrass you, or catch you at a moment when you didn't want to be caught. I really just stopped by to invite you out for dinner."

"And instead you got a heaping serving of my neuroses."

He laughed. "Would you like to have dinner?"

"Y-yes," she managed. "I would."

"Great. I'll pick you up at the front door at six-thirty. Is that all right?"

"Perfect."

"I'll be going now."

"And I'll just be hiding here in this big hole I've dug for myself."

"I'll leave you to that then."

Liv didn't move a muscle as she watched Jared stride across the patio. He turned back and gave her a smile before heading out the door, and then he was gone.

She waited until she heard the clank of his screen door on the other side of the wall, and then she sank to the chair and buried her head in her hands.

"What, are you in the eighth grade?" she whispered to herself. "You're forty-nine years old, not twelve. And he didn't just ask you to the prom!"

Still, Liv was on the phone with Hallie in nothing flat, asking about the best place to find a new dress for dinner, and what to do about her pasty white legs.

"Liv!" Hallie gasped. "What if you two fall in love? Will you move there?"

"Goodness, no," she laughed. "Can you see me living down here?"

"Kinda."

"Well, you're insane. I'm not moving to Florida, and I'm certainly not falling in love."

"All evidence to the contrary," Hallie said.

"I'm just exercising some new muscles, that's all. I haven't been asked out on a date in forever." *Unless you count Jared's twenty-six-year-old son, of course.* "It's just so nice that someone, somewhere actually notices that I'm still a woman."

"Where's he taking you?"

Liv bit her lip. "I forgot to ask."

"Well, that's okay. Everything in Florida is

pretty laid back and casual. You don't want to overdress. What about that sundress you packed?"

"Nope. I wore that to the barbecue."

"Well, look for something casual and pretty like that."

"Where do I go?"

"I'll talk to my mom and call you back in ten."

"Thanks."

Ten minutes turned to twenty, but Liv made the best of the gap by touching up the polish on her fingernails and toes. By the time Hallie called back with the names of two local boutiques and a department store exclusive to Florida, Liv had changed clothes and was ready to go shopping.

She wasn't even out of her car yet when she spotted the dress she knew she was going to wear. A sleeveless black crepe shift with subtle beading detail on the high neckline, and it would go perfectly with the black open-toe pumps that she hadn't worn once in the two years since she'd bought them.

It took five minutes to grab the dress in her size and try it on. Ignoring the price tag took a little longer, but not much. While standing in line behind another customer at the register, Liv grabbed a bottle of wave-enhancing liquid that promised to make her spiral curls glossy and fresh. A bottle of bronzer for her colorless Ohio legs made it to the counter just in time as a last-second impulse purchase.

She was back home again in under an hour. Unlike every other woman on the planet, Liv had never been a big fashionista, or much of a fan of the whole shopping experience. But this was a record even for her.

With just three hours between her and Jared, Liv decided a long soak in the tub might soothe her frazzled nerves. This would be her first date since Robert had died more than five years prior, and she couldn't help asking herself why she was taking this turn. While she and Rob hadn't had some great love affair for the ages, they'd been happy and content and in sync. When she lost him, Liv grieved his passing for a long time, and she told herself that she'd had love in her life. Now she would enter a new phase and find out what it was like to strike out on her own. She went back to nursing, and she took some art classes, and she even battled cancer and won. Coupling again was the farthest thing from Liv's mind—until she boarded the plane to Florida and met Jared Hunt.

Just the thought of him made her feel a little like the heat had been turned up beneath her bathwater. The mirror and windows were all steamed up . . . and so was Liv.

"What's going on with me?" she said aloud, and Boofer opened her eyes and looked up from the nap she was taking on the fluffy bathroom rug.

She wondered for a moment if she'd made a bad decision by accepting his dinner invitation. After dinner, then what? Where could they realistically go from there? Jared was settled in Sanibel, and Liv's life was anchored to Cincinnati.

"Olivia," she sighed, dipping down low in the water until her shoulders were completely covered with bubbles. "What are you doing?"

7

The stallion swaggered toward Prudence and shook his magnificent mane.

"Have you trotted around the pond yet?" he asked her. "It's beautiful scenery."

But Prudence didn't answer. She just put one hoof behind the other and backed away from him slowly.

"Where are you going?" the beautiful black horse inquired. "There's so much to see in this valley."

Prudence picked up backward speed and, in doing so, she got her back hoof tangled in her tail and fell down flat with a thump. Embarrassment crept over her like honey from a tree on a hot summer day, and she pulled herself up and took off at a full gallop.

"Where's she going?" the stallion asked Horatio.

"To lick her wounds," Horatio replied with a crooked owl smile.

"Did I wound her?"

"No. Prudence does that all on her own."

Liv crossed one leg over the other and leaned back in the supple leather seat. Beside her, Jared rested a hand over the slope of the wheel while he accelerated with the other. Gliding across crayon-green water in the twenty-eight-foot boat Rand had hoped to borrow from his father for their lunch date, Liv couldn't help but wonder what Rand would think of her dating his dad instead.

"Are those shells on the beach up there?" she asked. "There must be thousands of them."

"Sanibel Island runs east to west," Jared explained. "But Gulf tides run north to south, pushing and pulling at the beaches. As a result, a ton of small feeder fish and seashells are forced up to the shore. This is one of the most popular areas of the whole state for shell collectors."

Liv sipped from the plastic cup of sweet tea Jared had poured for her just before they set out on their cruise.

"Look over here," Jared said, and she leaned over the side just in time to catch a glimpse of two dolphins arching alongside the tip of the boat.

"Oh, look at that!" she exclaimed. "They're so beautiful."

Liv pressed against the edge for several minutes, watching them dance in and out of the foaming waves in the path of the boat. In the distance, passengers on another craft waved at them from beneath a brilliant gold and orange sail that looked to Liv to be a hundred feet tall.

When she sat down in the leather seat across from Jared, he smiled at her. She couldn't help herself, and she beamed back at him.

"What are you thinking?" he asked, and she gulped around the lump in her throat.

"The truth?"

"Of course."

"I was thinking that you always look like some-one in a toothpaste commercial when you smile."

Jared's laughter bellowed against the back-drop. "I think that's probably a compliment."

"It is," she reassured him.

"Do you want to know what I think of when you smile?" he asked.

"I . . . think so."

"Every time you smile at me, from the first time in the terminal at the airport in Ohio, all the way to right now," he said, "I'm reminded of that one moment each morning when the sun comes up for the first time."

Liv swallowed again and just stared at him. She couldn't even blink.

"Too much?" he asked, and as she gulped for a third time, he confirmed his own suspicions. "It is. I'm sorry. I didn't mean to embarrass you."

"You didn't embarrass me," she told him

once she found her voice. "You stunned me." No one had ever said such a lovely thing to her before. Not even Robert in all the years that they were married. Her smile had just been compared to a sunrise.

Is this guy for real?

In Liv's experience, which was admittedly somewhat limited when it came to men with pearly white smiles and glistening brown eyes, or really just men in general, those who said such romantic and wonderful things were certainly after one of two things: Sex, a lofty pursuit which would end in the ultimate thud of disappointment; or money, which would turn out to be about as fruitless as her bank account. Liv wasn't poverty-stricken or anything, but cancer had robbed her better than any gold-digging man ever could.

"I'm not a drinker," Jared told her when they were seated at the restaurant. "But if you'd like some wine—"

"Oh, no, thank you. I'm not a drinker either." She hoped he wouldn't laugh, but . . . "You know what I'd really love, though?"

"Your wish is their command."

"A big, cold root beer."

"You know what?" he said with a glint of amusement. "That sounds really good." Glancing up at the waiter, Jared inquired, "Do you serve root beer?"

"Yes, sir."

"Excellent. Two frosty mugs of it, my good man. And keep 'em coming."

The waiter hardly cracked a smile, which made Jared and Liv both laugh right out loud, punctuating his exit.

Jared was such a lot of fun to be around, and once again Liv found herself wondering when the other shoe might drop.

If something seems too good to be true, she thought, *it usually is.*

Perhaps this would be Liv's greatest birthday disappointment of them all. Finding out that Jared Hunt was flawed and deceptive beyond the façade of a dazzling smile and general perfection would leave pneumonia and broken bones and various birthday calamities strewn in the dust.

But she didn't have to find out just then, did she? She could at least enjoy one early evening cruise and a seafood dinner with him before the shoe broke through the clouds and hurled out of the sky toward her.

"I've never been to a restaurant where you could arrive in a boat instead of a car," she told him.

"I never had either before moving to Florida. The lifestyle takes some getting used to, but now I can hardly remember the bitter-cold winters of Chicago."

"Cincinnati's not as cold as Chicago," she admitted, "but winter is engrained in me. Of course, I was just shoveling out of two feet of snow a couple of weeks ago."

"Give it time. The Florida sun will melt the memory away in no time at all."

The waiter set down two mugs of foamy root beer on the table between them, and Liv opted for a straw.

Lifting his drink into the air, Jared toasted. "Here's to warm hearts and melted snow."

"And forgotten frozen tundra," she added with a grin.

"Ohhhh-ho-ho," Jared hooted at first taste. "I haven't had a root beer in ten years."

"Ten years!" she exclaimed. "You poor, deprived soda drinker. I myself am a bit of a connoisseur. In fact, I can tell you that this particular brand of root beer was brewed on a northern slope . . . probably on a Tuesday . . ." She paused seriously and took a long draw from the straw, swishing the creamy liquid around in her mouth before swallowing for dramatic effect. "Barq's is my guess. 2009. It was a very good year."

Jared snorted and then transitioned into a rich and resonant laughter that Liv thought almost took the form of music.

The waiter stepped up to the edge of the table, ready to take their dinner orders. Instead, Jared cast Liv a playful expression before asking, "Just out of curiosity, what brand of root beer is this?"

"Barq's, I think," the fellow replied, and the two of them shared a laugh that excluded their waiter. "Is there something wrong with your drinks?"

"No, absolutely not," Jared replied. "They're delicious. Obviously a very good year."

The poor guy didn't quite seem to know how to respond, so he raised his pad and set his pen to it. "What can I get you?"

Liv let herself sink back into the leather booth as Jared ordered salads and a platter of peel-and-eat shrimp. She hadn't had shrimp in such a long time and, as she glanced out the window at the emerald-green Gulf waters just beyond the dock, she realized this would be about as fresh as a seafood meal could get.

"Tell me about your life back in Ohio," Jared invited her. "What do you do there? Aside from shovel snow, that is."

"Well, I live next door to my best friend and her family. And I like to paint and sculpt," she told him, absently pushing the straw in circles around the inside of her glass. "I work full-time in the operating room of a busy hospital."

"A nurse?"

"Yes. Well, I was."

"It's a little early for retirement, isn't it?"

"Thanks for noticing," she replied with a grin. "I think I mentioned the other night that I'd been diagnosed with cancer."

"That's right. Was it breast cancer?"

"Ovarian."

"Ovarian, and you're all clear now?" he asked.

"I am."

"That's quite a blessing. Ovarian is one of the rough ones."

"It is indeed," she agreed. "But . . . they're all rough."

"True enough," he said thoughtfully, and then he narrowed his eyes at her and smiled. "I seem to recall something else you've mentioned, more than once. Something about a curse and a fairly significant birthday sneaking up on you."

"Ah, yes. The birthday curse," she replied just as the waiter set two beautiful green salads before them, and then dropped a heaping platter of cold shrimp on the table between them.

"Will there be anything else?"

"Not right now," Jared answered. "Thank you."

While they polished off every one of the little critters, filling an empty plate to overflowing with discarded shells, Liv proceeded to entertain Jared with the dark comedic tale of the string of annual disasters that had plagued her for most of her life.

Jared could hardly believe it when he glanced at his watch and realized they'd been in the restaurant for more than two hours. After the shrimp came a shared slice of key lime cheesecake and countless cups of decaf. And truth be told, when they made their way down the dock and boarded his Sun Runner, he wasn't ready for the evening to end.

"I haven't had such a good time with someone in a long time," he told her, the boat skipping across the bay.

"Thank you," she replied, and then she lowered her eyes, preventing him from searching them for a trace of reciprocation. "The meal was lovely," she finally added.

Jared flicked on the stereo. The Michael Bublé CD was still loaded; he'd had it playing while he cleaned the downstairs cabin the previous afternoon, and it made a nice soundtrack against the low-setting sun and vibrant purple sky.

He glanced at Liv and found her swaying to the music, her full, red lips mouthing the words of the song as she stared out over the darkened water. The sun was a ball of fire on the horizon that set her short red hair ablaze in its reflection. She pulled her shawl around her shoulders and arms, and he noticed the creamy porcelain skin of her hands as she folded them in her lap.

Jared's gaze began moving beyond her to the ocean view when he did a double take. Beneath the knee-length hem of her black dress, his attention was drawn to shapely legs, crossed at the ankle.

What in the world? he thought as he took a closer look.

He wished he'd have darted his eyes away just a second faster, but Liv caught him gawking, and she followed suit. As she looked down at her own legs, she gasped, covering her mouth with both hands.

"What is that?" she cried, popping to her feet and running a hand over one bright orange, striped leg. "Jared, what is it?"

It looked for all the world as if she'd been spray-painted.

"I don't know," he said, grabbing a towel from the bench behind him and handing it to her. "Try this."

She did, and nothing changed, and then sudden realization seemed to overwhelm her. Jared watched as she heaved a belabored sigh and dropped back down to the seat.

"I can't believe this."

"What is it?" he asked. "An allergy, maybe?"

"No."

"What then?"

Liv looked up at him with dewy eyes and a crooked attempt at a smile. "It's bronzer."

"Bronzer?"

"I bought it this afternoon," she admitted. "My legs were pasty Ohio white, and I didn't want to be embarrassed. I thought a little bronzer might . . ." She trailed off without finishing, and dropped her face into her hands.

Jared tried to keep his grin in check, but he couldn't help himself, so he just lowered his head and angled his face away from her. Once composed, he rested his hand on her shoulder and patted it gently.

"I look like I was left out for a couple of months after a rain. I'm rusted!" she exclaimed. "This is so embarrassing."

"This is not embarrassing," he reassured her. "It's just another beauty product gone mad. It happens all the time. My nurse, Georgia, came in one Monday morning with hair as green as seaweed."

Liv separated her fingers and looked at him hopefully from between them.

"I kid you not. She is a peroxide-bleached blonde, she got hold of some new product, and her hair went completely green. They couldn't dye it back for a week, so she had to just wear that green hair. It wouldn't have been so bad if she were Irish instead of Southern Belle."

Liv snorted, then buried her face in her hand again as she giggled.

"Or if it had been March instead of July. She could have blamed it on St. Patrick."

After a moment, Jared reached over and pried Liv's hands away from her face, and then pulled one toward him and planted a kiss on one knuckle.

"Besides, as long as it's not a jumpsuit you're wearing by the side of the road," he told her, "you look very nice in orange."

Liv punched at him and chuckled.

"I've heard sometimes chlorine water causes the fake-bake stuff to fade," he suggested. "Why don't you come over for a coffee and soak your legs in my pool?"

"No. Thank you, but—"

"C'mon."

It hadn't taken much convincing, and Jared was thankful for a reason to remain in Liv's company a little longer. There was something about this woman, something he couldn't quite label or explain to himself. She gave off a ray of light that warmed him to the core. He hadn't even known he'd been cold.

The pool lights cast a pale ice-blue sheen on the water, and movement sent wavy lines of light across the surface. Jared strode toward her, tray in hand, as Liv perched on the edge of the pool, legs extended out over the concrete steps, rubbing them vigorously with both hands.

"Do you like cappuccino?" he asked.

"I do, but I can't have caffeine this late or I'll be up all night."

"It's decaf," he told her. "I have the same problem in my old age."

"Hey. Did you just label me *old?*" she teased.

"No. I labeled me that way."

"Oh, okay. That's all right then."

"Hey."

Jared rolled the hems of his trousers up to just below the knee, and then sat down beside Liv on the flagstone, the tray of coffee between them, both sets of legs dangling over the edge of the pool steps. The underwater light magnified the difference in their skin pigments; his suntanned legs looked as white as a starched sheet in the reflection, and hers were orange, like the top layer of color on a piece of candy corn.

"I've had a really good time tonight, Jared," she said, and her voice was as soft and sweet as a lone flute playing in the distance. "Thank you for inviting me."

"Thank you for coming along," he replied. "I'm glad to know you enjoyed yourself."

"Aside from the whole orange leg thing," she told him with an arched brow, "it's been perfect."

"I told you. I think you look beautiful in orange."

"It is my color," she acknowledged, and they shared a smile as the now-familiar sweet citrus scent of her shampoo wafted by him.

Jared knew it was too soon, but he didn't allow himself a moment to think it through. Throwing caution to the wind, he reached toward her and skimmed the line of her jaw with his finger, and then he drew her face toward his into a kiss. It was consciously soft at first, nothing pressing or too intrusive, just the momentary meeting of their lips. They parted for an instant, and then came together again. He wasn't sure if it was his doing or hers, but they both leaned into one another, a nonverbal agreement from both sides of a magnificent and tender kiss.

"Whoa! Go, Dad!"

A moment like that is never interrupted without a screeching, shattering jolt, and Jared felt it all the way to his waterlogged toes. Liv flushed with embarrassment, and Jared glared at Rand and his companion where they stood facing them from the other end of the pool.

"I didn't know you had it in you, old man," Rand teased, and the young woman with him jabbed him in the ribs with her elbow.

"Is there something I can do for you, son?"

"No, I didn't know you were home," Rand said, leading his friend by the hand around the curve of the pool. "This is Shelby. We met at a singles mixer at church last week, and then we ran into each other again last night at the movie. Shelby, this is my dad, Jared Hunt. And our friend, Olivia Wallace."

"Nice to meet you," the petite blonde offered.

"We were thinking of hanging poolside," Rand

told them. "But I think we'll leave you to the pool and we'll go inside. Challenge you to a game of Scrabble, Shelby?"

"I love Scrabble!" she exclaimed.

"Me too. Let's go. Good to see you again, Liv. G'night, Dad."

Just before the sliding door slipped shut behind them, Jared heard Rand speak ever so softly.

"What do you know! My dad kissed a girl."

Jared glanced toward Liv and she grinned.

"I guess his old man surprised him," he remarked.

"He called me a 'girl'!" Liv added with excitement.

8

"Why are you so sad?" Horatio asked Prudence as they counted the ripples in the water from the edge of the pond.

"Because," she replied. "Everything's going so well here in the valley."

"You're sad because you're so happy?" her friend asked.

"Well, yes. I'm sad because I know the happy is sure to end soon."

"That makes no sense at all. Aren't you, after all, already a brand new Pru, just like I promised you would be?"

"This kind of happy never lasts," Prudence explained. "We can't stay here forever. One day soon, we'll have to set out again for home and go back to the meadow, leaving the valley far behind us."

"And that will be a sad day?"

"A very sad day," Prudence admitted. "I think it will be the saddest day of all."

❧

The evening ended on a high note, but dawn brought with it an old and familiar frustration:

old being the operative word in this particular instance.

Liv checked the clock. 5:52 a.m. This was outrageous, even for Clayton Clydesdale!

Liv's teeth were clenched so hard that her jaw ached. She pulled on sweatpants beneath the long sleepshirt she'd worn to bed and stalked toward the back door amidst a peal of barks and growls and snarls.

"Boofer! Quiet!"

With all of the unexpected strength that anger affords, she flipped on the patio lights and threw back the sliding glass door. Stomping out to the patio, she searched the water for any sign of Clayton or bright neon chartreuse swim trunks, or some equally shocking apparel.

Shocked is what Liv got, times ten. But not because of the color of any ensemble Clayton was wearing. In fact, Clayton was nowhere to be found.

Instead, moving steadily across the patio from the open screen door was an alligator. Destination: swimming pool.

Liv shrieked, and the five-foot reptile paused, turning its head full of teeth toward her. She tried to gasp, but her lungs were completely devoid of anything resembling air, and the world began to spin. She was locked in a cyclone of teeth, scales, and black eyes.

The ringing in her ears evolved into high-pitched barks, and she realized that Boofer had passed her by and was heading straight for the creature at the other end of the patio.

"N-nooooo," she cried, finding her feet just in time to rush forward and pull the dog from the ground by the rim of her lampshade collar.

"Eeeeeeeeyy-yyyeeeeeee," she screamed, running on sharp tiptoe straight into the house.

Liv slammed shut the door and locked it before ever looking back. But when she did, the gator had transported itself completely across the patio and was no more than five feet away. She shot a quick and generic prayer of thanks upward for the wall of glass that separated them as she fumbled with the phone.

"Y-yes, hello? I n-need some h-help, please. There's an in-intruder."

Liv could hear her heartbeat pounding in her own ears, but the 911 operator was calm as she asked for Liv's name and location and the whereabouts of the trespasser.

"Well, he was on the patio," she said, wide-eyed, as she peered out through the glass. "But now he-he's in the pool."

"I'm sorry, ma'am. Did you say the intruder has gone for a swim?"

"Y-yes. I just saw his tail disappear into the water!"

"His . . . I'm sorry. Did you say *his tail?*"

"Dad, you better get up."

"Hmm? Why? What time is it? It's Sunday."

"Well, it's only seven, but you're going to want to see this."

Jared stretched and then opened his eyes with reluctance. "Rand, what are you talking about?"

"Something happened next door. To Olivia."

An inner spring he didn't know he had launched Jared straight out of bed and to his feet.

"Don't panic. She's all right. But there are rescue workers and news crews jammed around her house. It seems there's a gator in Josie's pool."

"A what?"

Jared didn't wait for further explanation. He hurried into the bathroom and was dressed and out the back door in under five minutes.

Rand wasn't joking about the hordes of people, and Jared pushed his way through onlookers and reporters and cameramen until he reached the sidewalk. Rounding the house, he headed toward the front door but was stopped by a gathered crowd there as well.

"I didn't know what to think, really," Liv said, bright lights illuminating her, and several microphones placed in front of her. With her hair disheveled the way it was and wearing sweats, Liv looked just about as cute as Jared could stand. "I mean, the dog was going crazy, and the sun wasn't even up yet. At first, I thought it was the elderly neighbor who uses the pool to do laps a couple of times a week. But then I found myself face to face with something much more frightening than Clayton Clydesdale!"

The reporters laughed as Jared caught Liv's eye.

"Jared!" she called, and then she thanked the news crews and excused herself.

Peeling herself away from them, she headed straight for him, deliberate and full speed ahead. She almost jumped into him, encircled his neck with her arms, and cried, "You won't believe what's been going on here!"

"I heard. Are you all right?"

"I think so. I'm still shaking in my boots." Jared looked down at her bare feet, and she wiggled her painted toes and added, "So to speak."

"The dog?"

"Boofer is a moron. Ran straight for the big old thing like there was something she could actually do. But I grabbed her and ran inside and then called 911. One of the reporters told me that alligators shy away from humans, but this one ran right after us, Jared. I think Boofer looked a little too much like breakfast."

Jared's heart squeezed. His brain knew that the woman before him was an intelligent, captivating, adult woman. But something about her just then, in her "Sleep Is Good" T-shirt and her pinkish toenails and orange-tinted feet, with her chin-length spiral curls waving in all directions, made him almost believe she was just a teenager home from a weekend sleepover and telling the tales of her many adventures.

He placed an arm around her shoulder and directed her toward the house. "Let's go inside."

She allowed him to lead her past the swarm, chattering all the way about the gator's black eyes and scaly skin and massive pointed tail.

"Thanks, guys," Jared said with a wave before closing the door on the reporters and neighbors gathered outside.

"Let's see if they got him," she cried, scampering through the length of the house and stopping next to Boofer at the patio door. "Oooh, Jared, look!"

He stepped up beside her and watched as two workers in dark olive uniforms used a contraption with two large wooden pegs connected by a thick, looped nylon rope to restrain the creature.

"I should be taking pictures," Liv said through the fingers clamped over her mouth. "Josie and Hallie will never believe this."

"With all those reporters out there, I don't think you'll have any trouble getting your hands on a visual or two for them."

"This is so surreal," she said and looked up at

him with wide, curious eyes. "I've never seen anything like this before. One time, a deer got locked in someone's screened-in porch up in Ohio, but all they had to do was open the door and let it out."

Jared chuckled. "You'll want to make sure you keep that screen door shut, going forward."

"I was sure it was shut," Liv replied. "Clayton tore the screen to unlock it the other morning. Maybe the latch needs to be fixed."

Jared turned serious and pressed her around to face him. "What do you mean?"

"Oh, Josie lets the old guy across the street use her pool to do laps a couple of times a week. I asked him not to come while I was here because he was setting Boofer off and it would wake me up. So I locked the screen door, but he just tore a little piece of the screen so he could unlock it and let himself in."

"Are you joking?"

"I wish."

Jared put his arm around Liv's shoulder, turning their attention back to the gator and its captors out on the patio.

"I'll speak to Clayton."

"Yeah? Good luck with that."

❧

She hadn't really meant to accept Jared's invitation to attend church with him, but there she was anyway, sitting beside him in the fourth pew on the right side of the crowded little chapel.

The last time Liv had set foot inside a church was the day of Robert's funeral. All of the events and sensations of that day were still so intermingled, in fact, that even now she could almost taste the permeating scent of the roses cascading over the top of his casket.

She hadn't realized when she left the church that morning that she was leaving more behind than her life with Robert, or that she was embarking on such a lonely and isolated journey as she staggered through the large mahogany doors. She'd left her faith behind her on that pew along with the hymnal and the folded bulletin with Rob's picture on the front. She'd meandered outside into a crisp November morning, leaving behind her unwavering belief in God's good intentions toward her. Her trust in Him evolved that day into just an unnoticed, stagnant entity hanging heavy in the air with the fragrance of those flowers on Robert's casket. From that very day to this one, she still avoided both God and roses.

Eluding thoughts of God was no easy task either, especially during eighteen solid months of battling cancer. She'd closed her eyes before each of her surgeries, and opened them again afterward, with the Lord's name perched right on the tip of her tongue. His song could almost be heard behind the clanking metal of the MRIs and the *click-click-click* of the radiation therapy equipment. And yet it was a song never quite sung, a Name never uttered, a healing presence never acknowledged. Liv knew she would be ashamed of herself if she had good sense or the ability to overlook her own pride, but she had neither.

So there she sat, Jared beside her, looking so handsome in a crisp charcoal suit with tone-on-tone navy shirt and tie, smiling Sanibel Islanders all around them, and the middle-aged Pastor Phillips standing at the pulpit, assuring them that there was no offense their Lord could not forgive.

No, Olivia. Keep it together.

Despite Liv's best efforts, a spout of emotion welled up inside of her, and tears sprang to her eyes. In her attempt to blink them back, they got the better of her and plunked out, cascading down both cheeks in fat droplets.

Oh, come on. Not now.

But if there was any one thing that Olivia Wallace remembered about the God she used to serve, it was that His timing was all His own. And He had apparently chosen this particular moment, as she sat next to Jared Hunt in his tiny island church, to draw her heart back toward Him.

"In the gospel of Luke, chapter fifteen," the pastor explained, "the Lord shows us a picture-type of His love as the prodigal son returns home. 'But when he was still a great way off, his father saw him and had compassion, and ran and fell on his neck and kissed him. And the son said to him, Father, I have sinned against heaven and in your sight, and am no longer worthy to be called your son. But the father said to his servants, Bring out the best robe and put it on him, and put a ring on his hand and sandals on his feet. And bring the fatted calf here and kill it, and let us eat and be merry; for this my son was dead and is alive again; he was lost and is found.' "

Oh, good grief. Not now!

That was all Liv needed. She lowered her head as the tears began to flow in uncontrollable waves. After a moment, she felt Jared's arm around her shoulder, and he offered her a white cotton handkerchief. She didn't even know men still carried them.

"Are you all right?" he asked in a whisper.

"Fine," she managed, taking the handkerchief and wiping her face.

Jared's arm remained around her until the service concluded, and he placed his hand on the small of her back as he led her out of the church afterward.

"It was lovely," she told Pastor Phillips as she filed past him.

"Thank you. Come see us again any time," he returned. "Morning, Jared."

"Morning, Ed."

Liv slid into the passenger seat and flipped down the mirror to wipe her eyes before Jared joined her.

"Want to tell me?" he asked once he'd yanked the door shut behind him.

"Oh, I don't know," she said, keeping her head angled away from him and concentrating on the line of traffic leaving the small parking lot.

"No worries," Jared commented, and he turned over the key in the ignition. "I was thinking we could go home and change, and then maybe pick up a picnic lunch at the marina and head out on the water for a couple of hours. What do you think?"

"That sounds so great."

An hour later, after changing into black, knee-length cotton shorts and a bright-white tank top, Liv used a sponge and some foundation to patch the orange streaks still showing on her legs. Piling her curls into some semblance of an upward sweep, she fastened them into place with a tortoise-shell clip and headed out the door.

She waved at Clayton Clydesdale when she reached the bottom of the driveway, but he simply grunted and darted his attention to the fat, bright orange cat hiding in the underbrush of a shrub in need of pruning.

"Come on now, Morey," she heard him snap. "Get out of there right now and c'mon home."

Finally, the cat dashed past him and over the

stairs in one giant leap, straight through the open door and into Clayton's house. Without casting a look back in her direction, the owner of the enormous cat followed suit, slamming the door behind him.

"I take it you spoke to Clayton," Liv said when Jared joined her at the bottom of the drive.

"No, not yet. Why?"

"Oh," she replied on a sigh. "I guess he's just rude today for good measure."

"Have you met Clayton?" Jared asked with a laugh. "He's rude every day of the week and twice on Tuesdays. The only creature on the planet who's seen his softer side is that cat of his."

"Morey." Liv nodded.

"The thing weighs about two hundred pounds, has lived as long as Clayton, and has his owner wrapped right around his giant orange paw."

Liv laughed and touched Jared on the arm. "It's good to know he actually *has* a softer side."

"Who? Clayton? Or the cat?"

Half an hour later, Liv and Jared headed out into the open Gulf off the shores of Sanibel Island.

"I thought we'd head toward Captiva," he told her as they left the marina.

"O-kay!" she called, producing a pair of sunglasses from her purse and setting them into place.

"Are you wearing sunscreen?"

"Aye-aye, Captain," she replied. "You?"

"Yes, ma'am."

"We're all set then."

Liv bit her lip. She would need the courage to talk to him about what happened in church, and she didn't know where to start.

She looked out over the Gulf and watched the dark green ripples on the surface of the water dance beneath foamy caps. Sunlight reflections ricocheted, leaving golden glitter in their path. Dolphins rolled like smooth hoops along the boat's course, and Liv extended her hand over the side into the soft spray of water. After a few minutes she took a deep breath and swallowed hard before turning back and curling sideways in the leather seat, her legs folded beneath her as she faced Jared.

"You know," she began, and he glanced over at her. "Before today, I hadn't been inside a church for a very long time."

"No? Why not?" he asked with casual curiosity.

"I'm not sure I can explain it, really. After my husband died, I went into a bit of a funk or something. I know it sounds crazy since he didn't just pack up and move out, but I felt rather abandoned."

"I can understand that."

"You can?" She was hopeful.

"Of course. You plan your life with this one

other person, and then, without warning, all of your plans fall to the ground."

"That's exactly how it felt," she told him. "And I suppose it seemed a bit like God had abandoned me too."

Jared nodded.

"Anyway, I was really touched by what the pastor preached about this morning. How the prodigal son's return was received by his father, how all was forgiven."

"I'm guessing you needed to hear that."

"I suppose I did."

"Were you a believer?" he asked. "I mean, before your husband passed away."

"Yes."

Time ticked by in perfect cadence with the thump of the boat coasting over wave after wave after wave. It felt as if several minutes had passed since she'd confessed her former Christian faith, but Jared punctuated it by reaching across the seat and squeezing Liv's hand.

"Welcome back," he said.

Liv's eyes filled up once again, and she smiled at Jared through salty emotion. Then, once he'd returned his attention to the open sea ahead, she closed her eyes and laid back her head.

I'm so sorry, she prayed in silence. *I didn't even know I was turning away until I was already gone. Thank You for forgiving me . . . and for welcoming me home.*

When she opened her eyes again, Jared smiled at her. He extended one arm toward her, and she scooted across the seat and leaned into his embrace.

"I'm really happy you're here," he told her, and she nuzzled her head against his shoulder.

Liv couldn't remember the last time she'd felt so content and happy, and she determined that she would call Hallie as soon as she got home and thank her for insisting she make this trip. Perhaps she had succeeded in breaking the long line of birthday-cursed years by coming to Florida and getting a new perspective.

She smiled as she pictured them, all the mangled and battered birthdays, flying and bumping into the surf behind her.

9

"Pru! Pru! Calm down!" Horatio implored, but Prudence continued to wail.

"Oh, braaaaay. Braaaaaaaay."

"What is it? What's wrong with her?" the stallion asked Horatio in a cautious whisper.

"Prudence has a very low threshold for change," the owl replied.

❧

Hurricane season doesn't start until June, Gayle. But the way those winds kicked up this morning, I could have easily forgotten that. These pictures are live from the Fort Myers airport. This storm cell came right out of nowhere with winds at 20 miles per hour and golf ball-sized hail."

"Welcome to Central Florida, ladies and gentlemen."

Liv tucked her feet beneath her and turned up the volume. Boofer, freshly liberated for the first day from her lampshade-shaped ball and chain, snuggled up against Liv's knee as she watched local newscasters belabor the details of the storm that had summoned her from bed at six-thirty that morning.

Liv wondered if she was going to have even one morning while on vacation in Florida where she would keep that promise to herself and sleep until ten. At this point, an eight o'clock wake-up call seemed like an extravagance.

"It's 7:18 a.m., and this storm warning will remain in effect until 9:30—unfortunately, right through drive time, so be careful out there."

Well, if she wasn't going to have the opportunity to sleep in, at least she didn't have to suffer through a morning commute. That was something, anyway.

She sipped from her coffee cup and hadn't had time to set it down on the table beside her when—

Snap—crackle—POP! The entire house went dark and silent.

Boofer's head darted up, questions burning in her big brown eyes.

"Don't worry," Liv reassured her, fluffing the fur at the back of her neck with soft, easy strokes. "It's just a power outage from the storm."

The eager whistle of the high winds filled the silence and, out of the corner of her eye, Liv noticed something large fly past the sliders. She jumped up from the sofa and hurried to the glass doors as one of the large wicker chairs rolled across the length of the patio like a tumbleweed.

Slipping into the rubber sandals she'd left by the door, Liv pulled open the glass sliders and scurried outside. The large wooden table next to the hot tub seemed like a good bet, so she scuffed the lightweight rattan chairs toward it and tucked them between the table and the stucco wall. As she looked around to see what else might need to be weighted down, Boofer scuttled past her and pushed open the unlatched screen door, making her escape before Liv could even turn around.

"Boofer! Come back here!" she called, holding the door handle with tight frustration. "Boooooofer!"

She'd taken only one solid step past the doorway before she was stopped right in her tracks by the instant illumination of a lightning bolt that cracked straight through the trunk of a small palm tree less than ten yards in front of her, splitting it down the center like a sharp knife through a loaf of bread.

A raspy scream broke out of her throat, and Liv stood there trembling, her eyes wide, rain pouring over her from the turbulent, greenish sky as she stared at the smoking carcass of the palm tree. It looked like a sliced pineapple on a barbecue, with one side of it toppled over on the lawn. A clap of thunder made her jump backward, and she stepped back into the patio. Remembering Josie's warning about the dog being "a runner," she propped open the screen door and hurried back into the house for a safer pair of shoes and an umbrella.

As she sprinted down the hall and into the bedroom, Liv couldn't help but wonder if this was her birthday-cursed fate. While rushing out into a thunderstorm to retrieve Boofer, would she be struck by lightning and split down the middle like that palm tree?

She was taken from us too young, the reverend would surely say at her underpopulated funeral. *After miraculously surviving the ravages of cancer, she was taken just a few days before her 50th birthday by a lightning bolt with the perfect, improved aim of a God intent on catching His prey at last.*

The moment she set foot outside the front door and popped open the flower-trimmed umbrella, a gust of wind assailed her, whipping away just as fast, and turned the umbrella inside out.

"Well, of course," she groaned, tossing the skeleton toward the door. Still, she persisted in her search for the dog in the pelting rain that stung as it pinged against the bare skin of her face.

"Boofer!" she screamed into the wind as she made her way down the driveway. And then in a low rumble, she added, "You annoying little ball of matted fur. Get your gaseous little fanny back here!"

Just about the time that she realized how fruitless it would be to continue searching the inclement neighborhood, Liv heard two quick telltale bark-growls from behind her, and she took off running toward the house.

"Boofer!" she called again, and Liv caught a glimpse of Boofer's hind quarters as the dog disappeared through the flapping screen door.

Liv followed Boofer and then latched the door behind them. But as she jogged across the patio, she noticed that the dog was dragging something along with her.

"Boofer, what is that?" she asked, approaching with caution.

At first, it looked like a stuffed toy that had been dragged through the mud. But as Liv caught sight of a patch of bright orange fur, her heart dropped with a grievous thud.

"What have you done?" she cried, slipping open the slider and shooing the dog inside.

She slammed the glass door behind Boofer, and crouched over the muddy heap on the tiled patio floor. Emotion crept over her, and tears sprung to life as the realization inched its way from her heart to her head.

Morey.

Clayton Clydesdale's beloved, ancient cat lolled before her in a mound of mud and fur, lifeless.

Boofer sat in silence on the other side of the glass, watching.

"What did you do? Why did you kill Morey?" Liv cried, and the dog slinked away. "Oh, Lord, what do I do now?"

She recalled Jared's account of Clayton's love for the cat, and she cringed, dropping her drenched face into her hands, sobbing. A conglomerate of fragmented thoughts and ideas skipped across her mind. She should go across the street and knock on Clayton's door, repentant and sorrowful, and confess to him that Boofer had taken the life of his best friend.

Oh, God, no. Please. I can't do that. I can't bear to do that.

Perhaps she could just wrap the cat in something soft and bury it in Josie's yard and never speak of it again. But then she pictured Clayton, for months on end, walking the neighborhood and calling the cat's name. He'd never find closure.

And then an idea tiptoed across her mind: part compassion, part cluck-cluck-chicken.

She would sneak across the street and lay the furry little thing on Clayton's screened porch where he could find it, but without a total confession of the horrible dog across the street and the overzealous capture of Clayton's longtime friend. But as she looked at the muddy thing at her feet, Liv knew there was more that needed to be done. With all the care and caution she could muster, Liv picked up the limp cat corpse and set it to rest across her arm, and then carried it into the house.

In the kitchen sink, she used warm water and gentle blue dishwashing liquid to cleanse the mud from the cat's fur. Then she cradled its massive body, wrapped in a terrycloth towel, and transported it to the bathroom counter, where she used her own comb and blow dryer to finish off the deed.

Knowing full well how ridiculous the whole scene was, Liv chose to choke back the objections, offenses, and off-color zingers that raced across her mind in deference to the higher road. It would be so much easier for Clayton to find Morey in this condition than to find the muddy heap of dead cat that Boofer had brought home.

The rain hadn't stopped, but it had at least let up. The sky was murky gray and green, and Liv hoped that the dark gloom of the morning would camouflage her movements. Clutching the clumped-up towel, she set out down the driveway.

Please don't look out the window. Don't look out the window. Please don't look out the window.

Her frantic wishes pounded against her brain in perfect rhythm with her steps as she tromped across the street, over the sloshing lawn, and up the three front steps. She took a deep, shaky breath and creaked open the porch door, and then unfolded the towel and carefully rolled Morey's corpse to the floor in front of a wooden rocker with a Tampa Bay Buccaneers pillow angled into the seat.

She used both hands to mold the cat into a circle, and she rubbed one finger along the length of his nose.

"I'm so sorry," she whispered and then folded the towel over her arm and took the first step toward her hasty retreat.

But before her escape could materialize, the thing Liv feared most happened. The front door flew open, and Clayton whooshed through the doorway toward her and whacked her hard on the arm with the back of his hand.

"What'd ya do?" he shouted, and his narrowed eyes burned a hole right into her. "First, you tell Doc Hunt you don't want me swimmin' in Josie's pool, and now this? What'd ya do, ya dern fool?"

"I'm sorry," she said. "Clayton, I'm so sorry."

The old man pushed past her and seized Morey's lifeless body from the floor and cupped the cat with both hands.

"Get outta here 'fore I call the cops and have you arrested!"

"Clayton, I'm—"

"Out!"

Liv rushed through the door, barely clearing it before Clayton yanked it shut with a bang.

"Don't you ever come back here again!" he yelled.

Liv just stood there on the lawn, looking back at the house, her pulse thudding in her veins, tears standing in her eyes, and rain pouring down over her. A clap of thunder punctuated the slam of Clayton's front door, and she turned around and started across the street.

It was only then that she noticed Jared making his way toward her, a jacket draped over his head.

"What was that all about?" he asked her. "Are you all right?"

She couldn't answer him. She just let him shelter her beneath the jacket as they hurried up the drive. A clap of thunder crashed, and Liv took off running, leaving Jared far behind her as she ran into the house.

"Olivia?" he asked once they were both inside.

Liv turned toward him and opened her mouth to speak, but she burst into sobs instead.

"What? What is it?" he inquired, letting her fall against his chest before circling her with his arms. "What did Clayton do?"

"Do?" she sniffed. "He didn't do anything. I did it."

"What did you do?" he asked with tenderness as he looked down into her eyes.

"It's too horrible. I can't tell you."

"Okay," he said at last. "Why don't you go and get into some dry clothes? I'll make a pot of coffee."

"Boofer killed him, Jared." The words just detonated out of her, and then Liv covered her mouth with her hand.

"Killed . . . who?"

"Morey."

"What?"

"Clayton's cat. Boofer got outside, and she killed the cat and dragged him back here. He was all muddy and dead, and I didn't know what to do, so I washed him up and I took him over, and I was going to leave him there on the porch so Clayton wouldn't know it was my fault. It was a horrible thing to do, I know it. I'm a horrible person, Jared."

His laughter caught her off guard, and Liv scorched him with an angry glare.

"I'm sorry," he said, and he collected the chuckles as they rolled out toward her. "I'm sorry. But Boofer didn't kill Morey, sweetheart."

"Yes, she did."

"No. She didn't. Morey died last night, and I helped Clayton bury him under the shrubs in the front yard."

"Wh-what?"

"Liv, Boofer didn't kill the cat. But I'm guessing she dug him up."

The power was back on in the neighborhood so, as Liv dried her hair and changed into fresh clothes, Jared took over the kitchen. While a fresh pot of coffee brewed, he lowered English muffins into the toaster and sliced a few mushrooms and an onion into a skillet. Once sautéed, he added half a dozen eggs and pushed it all around into a scramble.

"That smells so good," Liv said as she hopped up to the stool on the other side of the counter.

Her cheeks were pink, and her red curls framed her face like a halo. Jared felt a flutter overtop his ribs when their eyes met and a smile spread across her porcelain face like warm butter on hot toast.

"Coffee?"

"Please."

He poured her a cup and slid it toward her, then watched as she doctored it precisely with milk and sugar.

"Feeling better?"

"I am," she told him. "But I'm going to have to go over and talk to Clayton to explain."

"I'd wait a day or two on that," he suggested, vowing to make it over before she had the chance and try to pave the way.

"I feel horrible, Jared. The poor old guy buries his beloved cat, and this dog digs the thing up, drags it home, and I wash and fluff its fur."

Boofer slipped under the counter and laid her chin atop her paws with a whimper.

"Bad dog," Liv snapped.

"But not as bad as you thought, right?"

"True."

Jared coaxed the eggs out of the pan onto a couple of plates, and then transferred the English muffins.

"Hey," he said as he rounded the counter and sat down on the stool beside her. "Which day is your birthday, by the way?"

"Never mind," Liv replied with a chuckle, and then took a bite of eggs. "Mmmm. Very good."

"Thanks. Now the birthday question?"

"I think I answered you."

"That wasn't an answer."

"It just wasn't an answer you liked. But it was an answer."

"C'mon. When is it?"

Liv slid off the barstool and padded into the kitchen. "I want jam. Do you want some?" And then she shot him a wicked grin that felt like a hot branding iron.

"None for me," he commented, a forkful of eggs poised in front of him. "It's okay. You don't have to tell me. I'll just call Hallie and ask her."

The comment had the desired effect. Panic rose in her green eyes faster than he could swallow his eggs.

"Friday," she said. "Happy?"

"Thrilled. How about I host a little party for you?"

"A party!" she exclaimed, and then she laughed at him. "Who would come?"

"Clayton, maybe?" he teased.

She pretended to take a playful stab at him with the butter knife in her hand, and then she shook her head.

"I'd really rather just let my birthday float on by, if you don't mind."

"If we whisper, it won't know we're here?"

"Something like that."

"I happen to think your life is worth celebrating," he told her, and he hoped she didn't gauge the high level of sincerity behind the words. "We could have a barbecue or maybe a little gathering at a restaurant on the beach."

"Jared. Let it float," she said, waving her hand past him like a helium balloon caught on a breeze.

They sat beside one another eating their breakfast in silence, until Liv reached over and squeezed Jared's hand.

"My birthdays are a disaster," she said, turning toward him and leaning in. "Every year. And I came down here to try and escape it—change the tide a little."

"A celebration dinner with total strangers isn't different enough for you?"

Their eyes met, and Liv choked back her coffee before they shared a laugh.

"Fine," he continued. "No party. How about we cruise over toward the lighthouse and go snorkeling at Edison Reef? Just the two of us. Then I'll grill up some steaks down in the galley, and we'll watch your birthday float by."

"Deal," she replied.

"Deal."

10

The water rippled across the Enchanted Pond, and Prudence kept a watchful eye on its surface.

"Are you looking for something?" the stallion asked her.

"Yes," she told him without so much as blinking. "Something unexpected."

"You're expecting the unexpected?" he inquired, and then he shook his dark mane vigorously. "I don't understand."

"Something's going to happen," Prudence declared. "And I want to be ready when it does."

"Well, that's just absurd," said the beautiful horse. "Expecting the unexpected makes the unexpected expected. So it's not unexpected anymore."

Prudence jiggled her head from side to side as she tried to figure that one out. "Is that a riddle?" she asked.

"I think you're the riddle, my donkey friend."

Once it had cooled, Liv sliced the nine-by-twelve-inch pan of pumpkin cake into squares and transferred them to a large plastic plate she had found on the top shelf in the pantry.

"Low in fat, low in sugar, high in taste." That was the way Hallie had always described her special pumpkin cake recipe. When Liv looked for something to bake and take over to Clayton's house beneath a waving white flag and a sincere apology, it seemed like the perfect choice. If he slammed the door in her face and the offering made a round trip back home, at least she wouldn't gain too much weight when she ate the whole thing by herself.

This must be what it's like to mosey, she thought, realizing that she was meandering across the street, plate and proverbial hat in hand, at a snail's pace.

"Lord, I know it's been a while since I've prayed, but . . . please don't let him injure me in any way. You know how fragile I am, and I really think the old man could take me."

Climbing the couple of stairs to the front door was like scaling a mountain, and she raised her hand to knock at the door. Before she could lay knuckles to wood though, the door flew open and Clayton stared her down.

"Whadya want?"

"Mr. Clydesdale, I want to apologize."

"What for?"

He wasn't going to make it easy.

"For everything," she replied. "For the misunderstanding about the pool—"

"Misunderstanding," he coughed. "You not wantin' me there is pretty clear, young lady. No misunderstanding there."

"And about the . . . your . . . about Morey."

His face fell so fast at just the mention of his cat's name that it made Liv want to cry.

"I'm so sorry for your loss."

He didn't say anything for what seemed like an hour; he just glared down at his feet as if they'd done him some terrible injustice. "That all?" he asked, finally.

"Well, I made you some pumpkin cake," she told him, holding the plate out before her, feeling as though she needed to prove it to him. "I thought maybe we could have a cup of coffee and share a piece."

The old man glanced up at her, one eyebrow much higher than the other, his mouth pursed far off to one side.

"Can I come in?"

Clayton seemed to be thinking it over, and then suddenly, he yanked open the door and left it hanging there while he wandered off toward the kitchen.

"Don't have any milk. You'll have to drink it black."

Liv stepped inside and closed the door behind her. "That'll be fine," she said as she hurried into the kitchen after him. "Maybe just some sugar?"

"Got no sugar neither."

"Oh. Okay. Well, black is good. Nothing wrong with a nice, strong cup of black coffee."

A few seconds later, Clayton set down two steaming mugs, both of which bore the Tampa Bay Buccaneers logo, and one of which had a chip missing on the rim. Hers, of course.

He plunked two plastic Bucs plates down on the table and helped himself to the cake, leaving Liv to fend for herself.

"I wanted to explain to you about the pool," she said.

"No need. Doc Hunt told me all about it."

"He did?"

"Yeah. I'll be swimmin' laps in his pool until Josie comes home."

"Well. All right."

He softened, but only slightly, his fork in midair as he said, "You're on vacation, and you don't need to be startled first thing in the morning by me."

"Well—"

He crammed the fork into his mouth and shook his head.

"Josie's been gone a long time now."

It hadn't been such a long time. Liv realized that Clayton must really like Josie.

"She'll be home soon."

"Good cake."

"Oh, good. I'm glad you like it. It's Hallie's recipe."

"How is Halleluiah? She ain't been down here in a gap o' time. Guess she's pretty busy with all them kids."

"I don't know how she does it. She's a pro at keeping up with all they have going."

"Nice girl, Hallie. You tell her I like her cake."

"I will."

Liv grinned and took a bite of it herself, and then held her breath as she washed it down with a sip of the thickest, blackest coffee she'd ever tasted. She had visions of it eating through the lining of her stomach upon arrival.

"Also," she began, and then wished for a second that she hadn't, "I wanted to explain about the other day. With Morey."

"No need. Doc Hunt explained that too."

"He did?"

"Yup. Said you wouldn't be havin' a meal with me neither. But here you are with cake."

"A meal?"

"I mighta said I was thinkin' about that. Maybe havin' a lunch or a supper with ya."

"Oh."

"The doc nipped that idea in the bud."

"He did?"

"Says you're not interested in lunchin' or nothin' else with me. Seems like maybe he's the one wantin' to take you to supper."

"Well," Liv began, and then she sighed and gave her temple a swift rub with the back of her hand. "Clayton. I just wanted you to know . . . I just wanted to say to you . . . that I didn't realize Morey had . . . passed away."

"Yup. You figured that mangy dog o' Josie's killed him."

"Well, yes. That's what I thought."

"And you figured I'd get over that as long as you cleaned him up real nice."

The way he was looking at her caused Liv to spontaneously burst with laughter. "It seems kind of strange now that I hear you say it."

Clayton plucked another square of cake from the plastic plate and dropped it to his own.

"Anyway, I'm just so sorry, Clayton. I really am. About everything."

"I believe you," he snapped. "That's enough apologizin'."

"Okay."

"You wanna go out for supper?"

Liv grinned. The old guy was nothing if not persistent.

"No, thank you, Clayton. But I appreciate the thought."

"Whatever. Your loss. I still got moves, you know."

"I can see that."

The silence that followed was broken with the soft clank of fork to plate, the slurping of coffee, and then the thump of Clayton's cup back to the wooden table. Liv searched her mind for something, anything, to stir up some conversation.

"You sure do seem to like the Buccaneers," she said. "That's a football team, right?"

Clayton lifted one eyebrow and then peeled an odd smile across his face. "Tampa Bay Buccaneers, woman. 2003 Super Bowl champions. Raymond James Stadium, the *Crown Jewel of the NFL*. Ring any bells?"

"Sorry."

Clayton groaned as he downed the rest of the coffee from his team's cup.

"I've never been much into sports. Except for figure skating."

"Figure skating!" he exclaimed, and then he clamped his eyes shut and shook his head. "That ain't a sport, girl."

"It is," she insisted.

"Nope, not a sport, with all that twirlin' and leapin'."

"But there's a beauty to the twirling and leaping, Clayton. It's art on ice."

"Hockey. That's art on ice."

Liv chuckled. Clayton smacked the table so hard that she jumped, and then they both laughed.

"Does Tampa have a hockey team too?"

And there went that silver eyebrow again, straight up into an arch over his narrowed gray eye.

"Tampa Bay Lightning?" he clucked.

"Also a jewel of some kind?"

"Not lately, no."

❧

"So what's this I hear about our Randall getting serious with someone?"

Jared looked up from his desk and peered at Georgia over the rim of his glasses.

"He had a date scheduled with Edna Stanton's granddaughter for this weekend, and he called her and canceled, saying that he'd met someone and it was getting serious."

Serious. Now there was a word Jared couldn't quite wrap his brain around when used in association with his son's love life. "Really."

Georgia slipped down into one of the chairs flanking his desk and tapped her pointy pink fingernails. "And Lila and Joe spotted him at the mall in Fort Myers with a young, petite blonde. Do you know the girl?"

"He's been spending some time with a blonde named Shelby," Jared speculated, and then he rolled his pen across the stack of paperwork before him. "But he hasn't mentioned that they're *serious*."

"It's about time for Rand, wouldn't you say?" Georgia inquired with a just-spotted-the-canary grin.

"He's leaving to go back to London in another couple of weeks."

"Maybe Shelby's going with him."

Jared thought that over and then shook his head. "They just met."

"Stranger things have happened, you know."

Liv floated across his mind, and Jared smiled. *Stranger than meeting someone and knowing them for twenty minutes and then calling it serious?* "You're right," he conceded. "You just never know, do you?"

"Well, keep me posted on the love affair, will you?"

Jared's neck jerked a little as he looked up at her. "What?"

"Rand and this Shelby person," she explained. "I'll want to know when to start shopping for a dress for the wedding."

"Oh."

Of course. Rand and Shelby. That love affair. Not the one with Liv.

Not that it was an actual love affair. But Jared wondered, if not, what then? Like Rand, Liv would be packing her bags and leaving Sanibel soon. Would he and Shelby cry in their tea together, lamenting over lost loves and missed opportunities?

Georgia headed out to reception, and Jared leaned back in his chair. Pushing his glasses up to his forehead, he rubbed his burning eyes and speculated about Liv's departure. What would life be like for him after she returned to Ohio? For someone who'd occupied a spot in his world for such a short time, the thought of her going away certainly had sketched out a dismal portrait of the future.

Jared turned over the page on his desk calendar and counted down the days until Liv left on the thirtieth. For a moment, his thoughts stretched about inside his brain, like a beam of white light searching open waters from the top of a lighthouse, pursuing some possible scenario where he and Liv weren't forced to say good-bye. But Jared knew the situation was stacked firmly against them. They didn't know each other well enough to wager something more permanent. Yet their feelings had developed at an unexpected rate.

At least he was fairly certain it was *their feelings* in the mix. He'd hate to think he was the only one with this stirring inside of him.

"Guess who's here," Georgia whispered as she poked her head around the doorway. "Speak of the monkey himself."

Before Jared could respond, Rand rounded

the corner and plopped down in one of the chairs across from him.

"What's up, son?"

"I was thinking it seems like good weather for a sunset cruise."

"I'm guessing you're not inviting me to join you."

"Hah!" Rand spouted. "No. I was hoping you'd let me borrow the boat."

"Will you be cruising alone then?"

"No," he replied. "Don't be ridiculous. I'll be with Shelby."

"The two of you are spending a lot of time together."

"Yeah."

"Anything you want to tell me?"

"Like what?"

"Anything about Shelby?"

"Well, she's cool," Rand replied with a shrug, and then Jared noticed a smile quivering at the corner of his mouth. "What else do you want to know? She can't hold her sugar; she gets a head rush if she eats something sweet. And the girl cannot sing a single note in key."

"But?"

"Yeah," he acknowledged. "But. She's pretty great."

"I'm glad you've met someone who can make you happy, son. But I hope you're taking it easy."

"What do you mean?"

"Let's face it, Rand. You've never been much of a one-woman guy. And if you've met someone who can make you feel like you want to be that guy now, well, that kind of emotion can be fairly heady stuff the first time around." Rand's curious expression convinced Jared that he needed to be a little clearer. "Traditionally, the male of our species isn't entirely lucid during times like these."

"I get it, Dad. I get it. So can I borrow the boat?"

"You may."

"Thank you."

"Any chance you'll be interested to spend five or ten minutes with your old man sometime between now and the time that you pack up and leave to go back to school?"

"I'm sure I can squeeze you in at some point," Rand teased. "Maybe breakfast on Thursday. Say 11 a.m.?"

"Breakfast at 11!" Jared exclaimed. "I hope you won't be expected to teach 8 a.m. classes again next semester. Your students might be forced to start a wake-up-professor service."

"Hey, that's not a bad idea. I could work that into the syllabus as a class project—part of their grade. No, no, really. This is a pretty great idea!"

"Get out of here."

Rand made a fist and extended it, bumping Jared's with a grin.

"Later, Dad."

"Later, son."

The instant the front door thumped shut, Georgia stood in the doorway smiling at Jared.

"Find out anything?"

"Nothing I didn't know before. For instance, my son has a mind of his own, and any sage advice from his ancient father is going to be disregarded in the shadow cast by a pretty blonde and a sunset cruise."

Georgia chuckled. "The more things change, the more they stay the same."

"You said it."

"So," she breathed in that I'm-leading-up-to-something-so-prepare-yourself way he'd come to know so well. "What are your plans for dinner tonight?"

And then the familiar squeeze of discomfort just below his ribs.

"Salmon on the grill, a bike ride, and an early night of it," he stated, trying to sound casual.

"You know what? You could still do all those things if you came to my house for the meal and the swim. I've got a couple of T-bones defrosted."

Jared leaned back in his chair and smiled at Georgia. She ran his professional life like a fine Swiss clock, and she was one of the best nurses he'd ever encountered. But her interest in taking over his private life as well, although flattering, was just not something in their stars.

He'd been as polite as he could possibly be on several occasions, trying to explain how valuable she was to him professionally, believing every time that she understood. And then a few months later, each and every time, she batted those mascara-laden lashes at him, smiled her most cunning smile, and invited him to dinner. Or a movie. Or a museum show in the city.

"Thanks for the invitation," he replied. *Polite but firm.* "But I'm going to head home."

"Are you sure?" she prodded. "Because I—"

"I'm sure," Jared told her, and he looked her in the eye and then smiled. "You have a nice evening."

He felt the thud of her disappointment deep within him. He hated rejecting her time and time again, but he just didn't know how to get through to her. Georgia was a lovely woman, a true Southern belle in every sense of the term. And she kept all the plates of his medical practice clean and spinning. But she just didn't appeal to him on a romantic level. Not like—

The momentary thought of Liv stroked his heart like a velvet glove.

"Good night then," Georgia said, and he nodded as she disappeared into the hallway.

Jared knew there was no future with Liv either, but for different reasons. He'd been searching for a solution to the odds against them almost since the first day they'd met, and there didn't appear to be a ray of hope in sight. But even so, he was determined to enjoy every moment with her until there were no moments left for them. Then he would go back to his practice and his boat and the den that needed painting. Until then, however—

"Liv, it's Jared," he said the second she answered. "Do you feel like a bike ride?"

11

"Why, oh, why, did we ever come to this enchanted place?" Prudence asked Horatio.

"Don't you remember, my donkey friend? You weren't happy in the meadow."

"Of course I was! What are you hooting about? That's crazy. I was happy. I was content."

"Do you think I never saw you? When you'd amble out to the edge of the meadow and stare longingly down the path? I could see the hope for something more in your eyes back then."

"Did I?"

Prudence brayed softly and dropped her head. She did remember. Life had seemed like one gray day after another there in the meadow. But it was home, and she would have to return because that's what donkeys and hoot owls did—they eventually went home. Didn't they?

Now that she'd seen the colors of the rainbow in the sky over the Enchanted Pond, *she wondered how she'd ever go back to living an ordinary green life again.*

❧

I haven't been on a bike in twenty years," Liv said as she hoisted her leg over the bar for a second try. The muscle up the back of her thigh strained as she did.

Uh oh. If my muscles are pulling just from getting on the bike, what are they going to think when I try pedaling more than three times around?

"I'm sorry we don't have the girl version for you," Jared said as he watched her. "Just men here at Casa de Hunt."

"It's okay," she groaned, making the third time the charm. "Go easy on me, okay? I hardly even walk except down the driveway to get the mail. And even at that, the weather has to be ideal or I let it pile up in the box."

"I'm a doctor," Jared teased. "Don't tell me these things."

"Then I won't let on how much red meat I consume either."

"You said you were turning over a new leaf, right?" Jared quipped. "We'll start with exercise and work from there."

"How long did you say this trail is? When you suggested a bike ride, I thought you meant like around the block."

"There are lots of places to stop and rest."

"Oh, good. Is it too soon to stop?"

Jared laughed. "Just follow me."

"Do you have a set of heart paddles with you? In case I need resuscitating?"

"Come on. Follow the leader."

Liv was thankful that Jared's driveway had a slight decline to it, and she coasted down to the street and pedaled up beside him.

"So far, so good," she said when he cast a glance at her. "How much farther?"

Jared laughed again. She loved the sound of his laughter. It was so carefree and melodious, like a song playing from a radio nearby.

The bike paths were wide and asphalt paved, and they created a well-used system all their own on Sanibel Island. Liv dropped back and followed Jared through the neighborhood and across a causeway. The path was smooth and straight for a period, and then it began to curve through overhangs of lush, green shade trees.

Other riders nodded and waved as they passed. A toddler in a safety seat strapped to the back of her father's bicycle, her blonde curls bouncing on the breeze, opened and closed her fist in a clumsy wave.

"Hi, there," Liv sang as she rode by.

A pair of overweight riders huffed and puffed as they approached, and the first one called out a breathless greeting to Jared.

He waved. "Good for you, Desiree. That's what I like to see."

The woman behind Desiree tried a tight smile that melted down into a steel jaw. Liv nodded her head.

"I feel your pain," she said as they glided by one another.

Liv took note of Jared's solid, suntanned calves as he pedaled ahead of her. She imagined that her own, still lightly streaked with orange remnants of bronzer, looked like sausage casings stuffed with tense, balled-up knots. They pulsed with each push of the pedals, and her lower back burned.

She'd never been much of a gym dweller, but cancer had taken what little energy she'd had and tossed it into the basement closet with discarded curtain rods and a box of ceramics from her creative period. Building up her strength again had been a slow process, and there was still a long way to go. Much like making it to the end of this bike trail she was on.

It was such a healthy lifestyle in Florida, particularly in comparison to the long winters she'd endured back in Ohio. The Sunshine State allowed a year-round array of activities, and even the oldest citizens indulged. She thought about Clayton, swimming his laps in his neon swim trunks, and she smiled.

In Cincinnati, people pretty much took to their

houses after Thanksgiving and didn't come out much at all until the spring thaw. She imagined Jared, in jeans and a sweater, pedaling through the winter and into the spring, when he would no doubt change into a pair of Bermuda shorts and press on.

"How are you doing?" Jared called back to her.

"A little out of breath," she returned, trying not to let on that it was more than a little. "But I'm good."

"There's a bridge up ahead. Just beyond it, we can pull over for a rest."

She didn't admit how elated she was to hear it, but the muscles burning in her legs when she finally pumped the brakes confirmed the private sentiment.

She waited until Jared turned his back before she hauled her leg over the bike and limped off of it, stifling the grunt that threatened to accompany the action.

"Lemonade," he said as he headed for a wooden bench beside a tall palm tree.

She made a thudding sound as she collapsed to the bench, and Liv grabbed one of the large sippers in Jared's hands. She didn't even struggle to conceal her frantic desire to get some of the cold liquid into her.

Sip-swallow-sip-swallow-sip-swallow.

"Oh, that's so good. Thank you."

Jared's mouth twitched at one corner as he

asked, "Liv? Are you all right?"

"I guess I can't keep it from you any longer," she admitted through hyperventilation. "I'm one hundred and thirteen years old."

"Ah."

"And I'm guessing you are seventeen."

"Bless you."

A sudden grabbing at the back of her knee caused Liv to impulsively slam her sipper into Jared's chest. Letting out a mournful cry, she grabbed the back of her leg with both hands.

"Liv?"

"My leg. My leg! *MY LEG!!*"

"Okay, flex it. Move it, like this," he said, taking her ankle into his hand and guiding the movement.

"Yowwwww. It hurts. It *HURTS!*"

"It's a cramp."

No. Ya think?

"Make it stop."

Jared failed in stifling a chuckle, but continued to pump her leg out and back several times before the pain began to subside. And as the pain left her, embarrassment moved in at stealth speed to replace it.

"Better?" he asked.

"A little."

"We'll just rest a while longer."

"Like until tomorrow?"

Jared grinned. "I have an idea. You wait here

and rest. I'll be back in a few minutes."

"Where are you going?" she asked as he mounted his bike.

"Just relax. I'll be back soon."

"Jared."

"Relax."

"But—"

"Soon."

She watched him ride away before shaking her head and dropping her face into her hands with a groan.

Woman crippled trying to ride bicycle in days leading up to her fiftieth birthday. Doctors say they've never seen anyone in such terrible shape. Full interview with handsome and horrified cycling companion, with film at eleven.

Liv wondered where Jared had gone. Perhaps to a nearby store for some ice. Or to retrieve a takeout Geritol cocktail, decorated with a little paper umbrella for good measure.

Another wave of debilitating charley horse pain assaulted her, and she began pumping her leg again until it passed. Her borrowed bicycle caught her attention, taunting her with the realization that she was going to have to climb aboard again and manage to pedal herself back to Josie's house. The mere thought of it was almost more than she could bear, but Liv vowed that she was not going to let Jared see her limping home, pushing the bike down the road as she leaned on it for support like a geriatric with a walker. She would somehow manage to lift her leg over the bar one more time, take her place on the miniscule triangular seat, and pedal her way back with a pasted-on smile and her head held high. She could still collapse, she assured herself, behind closed doors, later, after Jared left.

She was still working on putting some resolve behind the plan when a car pulled up right in front of her. She peered into the window and saw Jared's smiling face, and then she heaved a huge sigh of relief as he hopped out, hurled her bicycle into the trunk, and offered her a hand.

"Let's go, Grandma," he said. "Your chariot awaits."

"Oh, thank the Lord."

⌘

Liv sat submerged to her shoulders in the steaming whirlpool of Jared's hot tub while he tended to salmon on the barbecue grill at the other end of the patio. Closing her eyes, she leaned her head back against the rim and flexed her ankles, making circular patterns with both feet.

"Do you want to come and have some dinner?" he called to her.

"Can't I eat in here?"

"Not so great for the digestion," he replied. "But I'll meet you halfway with a plate."

"Deal."

Liv climbed out of the hot tub, careful to do it while Jared's back was turned. The evening had been humiliating enough without him catching a full body shot of her in a swimsuit, for crying out loud. She wrapped her sarong around her waist and tied it into a knot at the hip. Stepping into rubber sandals, she scuffed toward him with a capricious smile.

"Any better?" he asked her.

"Much."

"Good," he replied, setting down two Talavera-style plates bearing salmon, grilled asparagus, and baked potatoes wrapped in aluminum foil. "Everything you'll need is on the table. Sit down and relax."

"You're a very kind man, Dr. Hunt," she said, easing down into the nearest chair with a slight whimper. "And I am eight hundred years old."

"Well, you wear it well," he told her. "You don't look a day over a hundred and thirty-five."

Balling her fist up and shaking it at him, Liv clucked, "Funny. You're such a funny guy."

Jared opened a carton of fat-free sour cream and doctored his potato. "The truth is," he told her, "I should have realized that your body has recently completed a round of cancer treatments." Then, without hesitating, he reached across the table and did the same for Liv's potato as he continued. "You weren't ready to ride a couple of miles. We should have started out by circling the block."

Liv laughed.

"Salt and pepper?" he asked.

"Please. I was trying to impress you," she said, and then cringed at the admission. "How'd I do?"

"You'd be hard pressed to do anything I didn't find impressive, Liv. I don't know if you've noticed, but I'm kind of taken with you."

Liv glanced up from her dinner, and his eyes caught hers. She gave a halfhearted attempt to look away, to no avail.

"The feeling's mutual," she finally told him.

Jared's smile warmed her face, and then the heat moved down her neck to her shoulders and chest.

"That's odd," he commented, and then he took a bite of grilled salmon.

"What is?"

"It feels like the miles between here and Ohio just doubled somehow."

Liv set her fork down on the rim of her plate and softened with a smile. "When I planned this trip, I sure didn't plan on you."

"Any chance you've fallen in love with the place and might have thoughts of making a move?"

Liv sighed. "I couldn't do that even if I wanted to. My job is there. My friends. My doctor."

"There are doctors here," he reminded her. "In

158

fact, I happen to know a few of them."

"My life is in Ohio, Jared." The words, although true, felt suddenly hollow and sharp-edged.

Jared pushed the food around on his plate with the tip of his fork in silence. "I understand," he finally said. "But what about extending your trip? Is that a possibility?"

She couldn't say the thought hadn't crossed her mind a few hundred times already. But her disability leave had already been exhausted, and her savings cushion was just about depleted.

"I don't know," she told him. "It's complicated."

Josie's coming home and will want her house back. I only have five more years before I'm eligible for early retirement at the hospital. My follow-up appointment with the oncologist is scheduled for a week from Friday.

The thoughts buzzed, and her stomach rocked.

Picking up her life and moving to Florida because of a man she'd just met? The idea was absurd! Who did that kind of thing? And yet—

"Hey, Dad. Olivia."

Liv's head popped up as Rand led Shelby across the patio toward them.

"Hi, Rand. How are you?"

"How was the sunset?" Jared asked.

"Magnificent!" the girl piped up.

"Olivia, you remember Shelby Barnes?"

"Of course," Liv said. "Good to see you again."

"You too."

"Can we join you two for a minute?" Rand asked, and Liv took note of his cautious tone.

"Of course," Jared replied. "Sit down."

Rand and Shelby exchanged wary, nervous smiles. Rand scraped his chair closer to hers, and then took Shelby's hand.

"This looks ominous," Jared observed. "Do I need to strap myself in?"

"Maybe," Rand admitted.

"Randall. Did you wreck the Sun Runner?"

"No, Dad. The boat is fine."

Liv noticed that Jared started to ask an additional question and then stopped himself, looking to Rand.

"Well," he began, and then he glanced at Shelby for an encouraging smile and a nod. "Dad. When I head back to London to start the spring session, Shelby's going with me."

"Really."

"I know we haven't known each other for long," Rand began, taking on the somewhat frantic cadence of motivation to get his final shots in before his father's objections. "But we've known each other long enough to know we're in love. And we're getting married."

Liv pursed her lips tight, her eyes darting from Rand to Jared and back again.

"Married."

"And we'd like to do it here. Before we leave."

Liv admired Jared's calm demeanor at the

timbre of this news. Less than two weeks ago, Rand had knocked at her own door, inviting her out on a date. And now here he was, stiff and guarded, announcing his plans to marry Shelby Barnes.

"How old are you, Shelby?" Jared asked.

"Twenty-two."

"Have you spoken to your parents about this?"

"No, sir."

Jared paused and rubbed his temple.

"The thing is, Dad," Rand interjected, "we're not here to ask your permission. We're just here to tell you our news."

Liv winced. *Probably not the wisest plan of attack,* but . . .

"And I was hoping you'd be my best man."

Nice save.

Rand stood up first, and then Shelby popped up in response, slipping her hand into his.

"We're on our way over to speak to Shelby's family. You take some time for this to sink in, give it some thought, and we'll talk again tomorrow."

Jared nodded. Caught in the headlights of his son's departure, he sat motionless and silent until well after the now-engaged couple was gone from sight.

"Are you all right?" Liv whispered as she cupped her hand over his. When he didn't respond, she added, "Jared?"

161

"I'm sorry," he said. "I must have nodded off. I just had the most unbelievable nightmare."

She couldn't help herself, and she released a sudden burst of laughter.

"I'll just clear these dishes," she said, stacking his plate onto hers. "I'll wake you in a little while."

12

Prudence slinked back toward the pond again, and this time she held her breath as she did. With all the caution and care she could muster, and her eyes clamped shut, she stepped right up to the edge of the water.

She eased one eyelid open, and then the other, daring to look at her own reflection for a second time.

"It's always a surprise," she told Horatio as he fluttered to her side.

"What's that?" he asked.

"Seeing yourself from outside yourself, instead of always only seeing the rest of the world."

"Ah," Horatio nodded. "You're right about that. It can be quite jarring."

❧

On the one morning that Liv might have slept in, when there were no neighbors (or reptiles) taking liberties in the swimming pool, and Boofer was uncharacteristically quiet atop her bright pink bed cushion, Liv couldn't sleep.

She brewed a cup of herbal tea at 2 a.m., took a

spin around the dark house at 3:30, and was wide-eyed and alert, flat on her back and staring at the ceiling, as the digital clock blinked 5:41. She couldn't get the picture of Rand and Shelby out of her mind.

More to the point, it was Jared's reaction to their news that was stirring up her anxiety.

There they'd been, talking in loose terms about the future over salmon and asparagus, Liv stumbling around her thoughts, hoping against hope for a way that she wouldn't have to say good-bye to Jared. And then . . .

Rand and Shelby want to get married.

After knowing each other not much longer than Liv and Jared had, they were ready to peel away their inhibitions and dive into the marriage pool. No life preservers, no inflatable orange jackets, just them and the choppy Gulf of Matrimony. It wasn't until she'd seen Jared's reaction to the news—he'd compared it to a "nightmare"—that she realized how truly foolish she had been. Rand and Shelby's announcement acted as a mirror reflection in which Liv was able to see a clear and shining truth. She and Jared were no more ready to make a change in order to be together than Rand and Shelby were. Yet for those few minutes leading up to the awakening, she'd been harebrained enough to swim around in the fantasy.

Boofer didn't make a sound as she hopped up to

the bed, slipped into the curve of Liv's arm, and lay down. The dog gave her new friend an understanding glance and then sighed as she closed her eyes.

Poppety-pop.

Liv chuckled as she stared her down, but Boofer was unfazed.

I knew it was a mistake to bring home a chunk of salmon for this dog! Back to dry food and Milk-Bones.

She clamped her eyes shut and whispered a little prayer that she might come to her senses about Jared.

"Let me just enjoy the time we have together, and then have the strength to walk away from him and go home."

Boofer punctuated the prayer with a sleepy groan.

"And amen," Liv added.

As the clock rolled over to 6 a.m. Liv made the decision to put her feet back to the floor. There was nothing more unproductive than thinking in the dark, and so she made herself a fast cup of coffee and then headed into Josie's office to fire up the computer and set about changing the course of her morning.

With her birthday looming, and subsequent plans for snorkeling with Jared, Liv determined not to head into another activity without being fully prepared. She wasn't going to let the fact that she'd never been snorkeling or scuba diving, or even fishing, in her life become another bike ride in the making! And so she navigated to her favorite search engine and typed into the box.

Snorkeling for dummies

Amazed that there was actually a book by that title, she scrolled through some of the results before trying a different tack.

Sanibel snorkeling preparation

The World Wide Web could be counted on for nothing if not diversity. As she worked on her coffee, Liv learned all about the gear that would be used and the reason for each piece, the surprising world beneath the surface of the sea, and what to expect from a day on the water.

She scribbled down items for a *Seaside Survival Kit.*

- Sunscreen. *Of course.*
- Sunglasses and hat. *To shield the sun.*
- String cheese or peanut butter crackers. *In case of low blood sugar.*
- Hand sanitizer. *For icky ocean things.*
- Insect repellent. *Pesky mosquitoes.*
- Vinegar or rubbing alcohol. *In case of jellyfish sting.*
- Breath mints. *Just in case.*

She hit PRINT on a how-to list that rattled off

while she changed into her swimsuit. Then she grabbed the snorkeling equipment she'd spotted in a net bag hanging on the hook inside Josie's front closet and headed out back to the pool.

Liv sat on the edge of the first step and slipped large green flippers over her feet, then accidentally sloshed the how-to paper with water, smearing some of the fresh ink.

"While standing in shallow water," she read aloud, "practice putting your face below the surface while looking through the mask."

Liv wiggled her flipper-covered feet in a sort of greeting before tilting back her head and lifting the mask like a headband.

"If your mask or snorkel should fill with water," she read, "this can be a frightening experience. Take great care to learn the process of clearing the equipment prior to your day of snorkeling—o-kay! To clear the snorkel, exhale strongly through your mouth, which will send the water up and out of the tube. Some snorkels are fitted with . . . blah blah blah blah."

Liv swished the snorkel around in the pool water, and then pressed it to her mouth. Breathing in hard through her nose first, she then blew out, sending water sprinkling out of the tube.

"This seems easy enough," she declared, and then slipped the mask into place for her first snorkel-swim in just four feet of chlorinated water.

Jared squinted, trying to figure out what was at the center of Josie's pool. At first, it looked to be a large, red plastic plate bobbing at the surface. And then it took an odd curve, and a border of solid white appeared on one side.

He moved closer to the edge of the pool and pushed his sunglasses down to the tip of his nose and peered over them.

It's someone's . . . bottom, he realized, and then his laughter rang like a church bell. *A backside, just floating in the water!*

The round, red bottom submerged just then, followed by two green flippers, kicking and splashing. When she came up again, the sight of Liv—her red curls dark and slicked straight back from a face almost completely obscured by a bright blue mask, with a lemon-yellow snorkel extending over her head like a one-sided antler—doubled him completely over. He snorted, leaning on the back of one of the patio chairs to catch his breath.

"Whad?" she exclaimed, standing in the shallow end of the pool, her foggy mask suctioned to her face and her hand folded against her hip. "Whad're you laughing ad?"

"I wish you had my perspective," he replied with a chuckle.

Liv pushed the mask up over her forehead and

glared at him. "I knew the minute I decided to try this that you would come through that screen door. I just knew it."

"Listen, Jacques Cousteau," he said, shaking his head, "I'm driving out to Naples to check on one of my patients. Are you interested in coming along?"

"Where's Naples?" she asked as she peeled the mask over her head.

"Less than an hour. But it's worth seeing, if you're interested."

"Okay."

She stared at him for a long moment and then planted her hand on her hip again and raised an eyebrow.

"What?"

Liv raised her hand and flicked her fingers at him. "Go," she sang. "Go, go, so I can get out of the pool."

"I've seen you in your swimsuit before, you know," he teased, but her fingers just danced that much faster, pointing the way toward the screen door. "All right. I'm going."

He sauntered toward the door at a snail's pace for effect. When he heard Liv groan, he broke into a full grin.

"I'm telling your patient, you know. What a terrible doctor you are, making them wait like this."

Jared shot her a glance over his shoulder, and

Liv cried out immediately, "Jared Hunt, turn around and get off this property right this minute."

He laughed out loud as he opened the screen door and stepped out onto the lawn.

"One hour," he called.

"O-kay," she sang back to him.

"Okay then."

"Go-o."

"Go-ing."

"Now-ow."

"Go-one."

Jared walked home with that grin plastered across his face the whole way. As he poured himself a cup of coffee, he realized that his face kind of ached. No matter how he tried, however, the smile was going nowhere, and he had Olivia Wallace to blame.

She was just the most adorable creature he'd ever met. Modest and insecure, charming and funny, smart and completely disarming, Liv was what Jared would have created if given the chance to put together the perfect woman.

I'm in real trouble here, he realized as he strode into his home office and plunked down in the leather desk chair.

He gulped from the warm cup and then set it down on the desk and leaned back into the chair.

"I've only known her . . ." he began, and then fell silent.

This is absurd. She's leaving and going back to Ohio next week. What are you going to do, propose?

Jared's gaze floated to the framed picture of Rand on the corner of the desk. His son's huge, engaging smile always pinched at his heart. When he was a little boy, that smile seemed too big for his little face but, as he grew into it, Rand learned how to master it.

If only he'd use it for good instead of evil, Jared joked inwardly.

Rand could get just about anything he wanted in life because of that smile, and now his father wondered if that was a blessing or a curse. In fact, he could almost manage to blame that smile for the fact that a young and innocent twenty-two-year-old blonde had agreed to marry him after knowing him for only a few weeks.

He wondered what Shelby's parents had to say about the announcement, and whether they felt a little panicky when they thought about the reality of their daughter pledging her entire life to some professor with a great smile, who would be dragging her an ocean away from the life she'd only just begun to build.

Youth offered a certain advantage to Shelby and Rand that Jared didn't have. At fifty-five, he certainly couldn't turn his head and ignore the flags and alarm bells going off at the thought of making such an impulsive commitment, or at the thought of asking someone else to make it. Liv had a life of her own in Ohio. She had friends and a job and a home. Hallie was her best friend. She surely wasn't going to leave her behind, uproot her entire life, and move more than eight hundred miles on the off chance that a physical attraction with Jared would turn into something lasting. And yet, even the mere thought of it now summoned a spicy-scented hope inside of him.

Jared groaned. He tilted his head back and clamped his eyes shut and shook his head.

Get a grip, man.

For a moment, he wished he hadn't given in to the temptation to invite Liv to ride along to see Fletcher in Naples. A couple of hours alone in the car might have been helpful just then. But ever since they'd met, Jared had been making the most of every possible interlude, inviting her to dinner and lunch, out on the boat, even stopping by with no solid reason for doing so. There was something about Olivia Wallace, and he felt uncharacteristically helpless in the fight against it.

Case in point: An hour later, when she opened her front door and stood before him in a teal-blue sundress the color of the Gulf, with her fire-red curls piled upward and an eager smile spread across her porcelain face, Jared sent a quick and silent prayer of thanks upward for the next several hours in her captive company.

The ride to Naples flew by on wings of conversation that never once ebbed. From their marriages, their early lives, his in Chicago and hers in Ohio, to their favorite books and music, one topic to another to another. Nothing was off-limits.

"You're kidding. You've been reading Josie's *Pru* books?"

"Go ahead. Mock me. But there's a depth to those characters," she defended. "For years, Hallie has been telling me I reminded her of *Prudence the Donkey*, and I have to tell you that I kind of get the comparison now."

"Do tell."

"*Prudence* resists change of any kind. She's cautious and awkward and somewhat paralyzed by her own circumstances, whatever they may be."

Jared glanced over toward Liv. "That doesn't sound like you."

"Are you kidding? I'm a mess. Pru and I were separated at birth."

"I don't see that," he insisted, shaking his head.

"What, then?" she asked, her voice soft with trepidation. "I wonder what you're seeing that no one else does."

He made a right on Fifth Avenue Parkway and then eased into traffic as he thought that over.

"The Olivia Wallace I've gotten to know is sweet and hopeful," he explained. "Maybe you strike me as a little cautious, but in a vulnerable

173

and charming way. Paralyzed by your circumstances? Not a chance, lady."

Liv laughed, and Jared shot her a smile as he
pulled into a parking place. Even her laughter
tugged at him.

"What is this place?" Liv asked.

"The trolley stops here at 11:48," he told her.
"Fletch will be on it."

"Fletch?"

"Fletcher Banks was a patient of mine over
the summer," he replied. "He had a mild stroke
while visiting his daughter on Sanibel. But she
called my office a couple of days ago and said
that he hadn't been to see his own doctor since
returning to Naples, and she's concerned. I told
her I'd stop by and have a chat with him."

"He lives on the trolley route?"

"Nope. Rides them. He's lived in Naples for
all of his eighty-one years, and he's all about
historical facts and stories. You'll love him."

Jared grabbed his medical bag off the floor of
the back seat and led Liv to the wooden bench at
the stop. They sat down, and he glanced at his
watch just as the trolley pulled up in front of
them.

"11:48," he said. "Right on time."

Jared paid the driver as they climbed aboard,
and he and Liv sat down in the bench seat across
the aisle from Fletcher Banks.

"Fletch. How are you doing?"

The old man grimaced, and then the light of recognition finally flicked on.

"Dr. Hunt? What're you doing out my way?"

"This is Olivia Wallace, Fletch. She's visiting from Ohio."

"Pleasure," Fletcher nodded.

"I thought I'd give her a history lesson on this beautiful city."

"You? What do you know? You're a Yankee."

"Well, maybe you can help me with that."

Fletcher grinned and stared at his feet. "Rose send you?"

"She's worried, Fletch."

The old man groaned as he pulled himself to his feet. "C'mon then."

Jared shot Liv a smile and a nod, and the two of them disembarked and followed Fletcher across the sidewalk to the bench. Jared pressed his finger against Fletcher's wrist to check his pulse, then asked him, "Have you been taking your meds?"

"Yep."

"Have you had any symptoms since you've come home?"

"Nah."

"No shortness of breath, no racing pulse or headaches?"

"None to speak of."

Jared produced his stethoscope and slipped it under Fletcher's T-shirt. "Deep breath." When he'd heard enough, he asked, "What does that mean? 'None to speak of'?"

"A couple of headaches," Fletcher admitted.

"Fatigue?"

"I'm eighty-one, Doc. Of course I'm tired."

Liv chuckled.

"Okay, Fletch. Here's what I recommend," Jared said. "I'd like you to check in with your regular doctor this week. I can call and get you an appointment, but I need you to commit to me that you're going to show up."

Fletcher looked into Jared's eyes for a long moment and then lowered his gaze in surrender. "Yeah, I'll go."

"I have your word on that?"

"You do."

"Because you know I'll turn right back around and drive down here and take you myself, with Rose in the seat next to me."

"All right, all right," the old man twittered. "You tell me when, and I'll go see Doc Jansen."

Jared's gaze met Liv's, and she grinned at him.

"That's what I like to hear," Jared said, tapping Fletcher on the shoulder. "Now where's the best place around here to take you and my friend to lunch?"

13

The moon hung low in the sky, and its reflection off the Enchanted Pond made the meadow look as if the midday sun was shining down. Some of her new friends were playfully batting around a ball of brush, and Horatio HootOwl watched them from a branch overhead.

All seemed right in the clearing that evening . . . until Prudence found herself face-to-face with a scowling billy goat with dark, narrowed eyes, that is.

❧

Goodness me! It seems like you've been here a very long time," Georgia sang on that velvet Southern drawl of hers. "How much longer will you be with us here on the island?"

Liv forced a smile upward, making the conscious choice to avoid answering the latter part of the inquiry as she replied, "It feels just the opposite to me. I feel like I've only just arrived."

"You and Jared are certainly spending a lot of time together," she said, and Liv followed the track of Georgia's long red fingernails as they raked her teased-and-sprayed platinum coif. "Just about every time I see you, he's right there at your side."

"He's been showing me around Sanibel. Making sure I have a good time."

"He's polite that way," Georgia nodded. "But I wouldn't read too much into it if I were you. He's just that nice to everybody."

Liv felt the rumble of a groan move up from the pit of her stomach, but she managed to harness it before it reached her throat.

"Everybody in this part of the state knows Jared," Georgia expounded. "And they just love him."

"I'm sure they do."

Are you listening, Lord? Are you getting a load of this? Where is Jared?

Her question was answered immediately as she spotted him, heading toward her, beaming from one ear to the other, and carrying a large paper plate bearing a concoction that looked a little like a giant mangled donut.

"What on earth?" she asked as he reached her.

"Jared Hunt!" Georgia exclaimed. "You are not going to put that thing into your body."

"I most certainly am," he retorted. "What kind of trip to the fair is complete without an elephant ear?"

"A what?" Liv cried.

"Elephant ear," Jared repeated, and then he

broke off a piece of the thing and held it to her mouth.

"Mmmm," she nodded after tasting it. "What is it?"

"Fat and cholesterol, sprinkled with sugar," Georgia stated.

"It's a sort of twice-fried donut," Jared corrected, and he elbowed Georgia playfully. "With powdered sugar. It's a Florida tradition!"

"Which explains your booming medical practice," Georgia added.

"Look, a table!" Jared exclaimed, and he grabbed Liv's hand and dragged her off toward one that had opened up on the fringe of the concession area. "Georgia, see you in the morning!"

There was no mistaking the disappointment on the woman's made-up face, and Liv almost felt sorry for her. Her feelings for Jared were obvious, and it couldn't be easy for her to see him holding hands and sharing elephant-sized treats with another woman.

"Are you up for the Ferris wheel?" Jared asked her once they were seated.

"Promise you won't laugh?"

"I promise to try not to laugh."

"I've never been on one before."

Jared raised an eyebrow and stared at her.

"I know. But it's true. What can I say? It was a sheltered life."

"This is a night of firsts then," he told her. "Your first elephant's ear, and your first ride on the Ferris wheel."

Liv's stomach did a little flip-flop as she gazed at the ride off in the distance.

"Are you game?" he asked.

"I am."

"Excellent."

Once they had devoured most of the confection, Jared tossed the rest into a nearby trash barrel and took her hand again. They navigated the cresting waves of people along the way, and then stepped into line.

"You know what's funny?" she asked him.

"Do tell."

"It's forty-one degrees in Cincinnati today. I saw it on the weather channel. And here I am, getting ready to ride a Ferris wheel at an outdoor fair in eighty degrees. I love that."

"We should call Hallie and Josie and tell them," he said with a laugh.

"Jared. That would just be mean."

"Yeah. You're right."

Then on second thought, she giggled as she added, "Maybe we'll call them later."

Liv's breath caught in her throat twice, once as she stepped up on the platform, and another when she and Jared sat down on the hard plastic bench seat, and the fair worker lowered the bar over their laps and snapped it into place. She gasped as the wheel began to turn and the ground moved away from them. After several more stops to load passengers, the movement became far more gentle and smooth.

She squeezed Jared's hand as they rolled up-up-upward, and her eyes felt as if they were glued wide open by the time they reached the top and all of Sanibel Island appeared to stretch out like a lighted carpet at their feet.

"Fifty years old, and I've never done this before," she exclaimed.

"You like it then."

"Oh, Jared, I love it."

She gazed into his eyes and saw the reflection of the ride's lights there and something else too —another reflection, something akin to admiration, or possibly joy. She wondered if it belonged to him, or was it her own joy shining back at her?

"Jared, I—"

She stopped herself. What was she thinking? The words that were just about to skip off her tongue in such a carefree and unguarded manner were so uncharacteristic for her.

"What is it?" he asked, and then he brushed a lock of hair away from her face. "What were you going to say?"

"I, uh . . ."

I love you.

She bit back the words until she felt the puncture in her bottom lip.

I love you so much.

The warmth in Jared's eyes stroked her cheeks and, as their gondola moved over the arch at the top of the ride and started its downward slope again, Liv's stomach went with it.

Jared didn't chase her words again. Instead, he placed his hands on either side of Liv's face and guided her toward him. When their lips touched, a crackle of electricity sparked between them, and the breeze pushed her hair around in a way that made Liv think of a growing nest of cotton candy. Suddenly, she was cocooned by the sweetness of their kiss, the citrus taste of her hair dancing on the twilight of a perfect day, the utter bliss of unprofessed love lingering at the tip of her tongue.

I love you.

She couldn't speak the words. It was too ridiculous. She'd known him for about twenty minutes! And yet . . .

Jared tangled his fingers into her spiral curls and tugged gently, elongating her neck and allowing the back of her head to fall against his open hand.

Oh, Lord. What's happening to me?

Jared's lips eased away from hers as the wheel rolled to a stop at the platform, and Liv's eyelids were heavy as she tried to blink her way back to the moment. The fair worker took care of that for her as he snapped up the bar and stepped back.

His voice broke through and sent her plummeting back to earth. "Watch your step."

Jared's hand felt like a hot brand on Liv's back as he led her across the platform and down the stairs.

"What would you like to do now?" he asked her.

"I, uh, think I'd like to visit the ladies' room."

One foot in front of the other, she reminded herself as she marched toward the painted-brick building and followed the metal arrow adorned with a hoop skirt and high heels. Once inside, Liv leaned over the chipped porcelain sink and ran cold water over her hands.

Jared's kiss still tickled her lips, and the warmth of his handprint still glazed her back. Even in all her years with Robert, Liv had never felt this kind of connection with a man, and yet she'd only known him for little more than a week. It made no sense. And Olivia Wallace was nothing if not sensible!

"So we meet again."

She darted her gaze into the mirror, and her eyes met Georgia's in the reflection.

"You look a little 'deer in the headlights,' " the woman pointed out as she painted a clean line around her lips with a hot-pink brush.

"First ride on a Ferris wheel," she commented.

"That's not the flush of an amusement park ride," Georgia said, poking the lip brush into its tube and tucking it into her purse. "That is something else entirely."

Liv lowered her eyes to the floor for a moment and then looked back at Georgia and made a failed attempt at a smile.

"Can I be blunt, Olivia?"

Must you?

"I suppose."

"I've been watching you with Jared ever since you arrived that night of the barbecue. I don't know if you're aware of this, but I don't just work for Jared. I've known him almost since he moved here from Chicago. I've put a lot of time and energy into this man. I think you know what I mean."

"Well, I—"

"Let's call the Queen of Hearts just as she is, shall we, Olivia? I haven't put in all these years with Jared just so you could mosey into town and undo everything in a matter of days. If you think I'm going to let that happen, well, you're just as wrong as Splenda in the sweet tea. Do I make myself clear?"

"I—"

"Good, because surely the time has almost come for you to go back to your life up in Ohio and leave the rest of us to our lives here."

Liv watched Georgia smooth her helmet of hair with both hands, lick her lips, and touch up her lip gloss with the fingernail on her pinkie, and then Georgia's eyes poked a hole in Liv as she regarded Georgia warily.

"It's good advice I'm giving you here, Olivia. Move on and leave Jared where he belongs."

"With you," Liv replied. "Just to be clear, that's where you think he belongs?"

"More to the point, not with you. I think we both know that's true."

"Thanks for the tip."

"Like I said, you're Splenda in the sweet tea, darlin'," Georgia remarked. "It just doesn't belong."

Georgia's spiky little heels *tap-tap-tapped* against the concrete floor as she made her determined exit.

She'd referred to Liv as a deer in the headlights, but the reality was that she felt more like a gazelle caught in the crosshairs of a mountain lion. And this bleached-blonde cat had barely broken a sweat as she'd torn Liv to pieces, leaving her carcass there in front of the bathroom mirror at the fair.

Liv paced in front of the counter, her coffee cup sloshing a little as she moved.

"I don't know why I let her talk to me like that. I mean, I didn't say a word in response. And it's none of her business, is it? If I want to have a little vacation fling, or if I want to fall in love and marry Jared after knowing him only thirty minutes, well, that's my decision. And Jared's. It has nothing to do with whether she's been trying to land him for five years or five decades! The nerve of that woman. Honestly! Can you believe the nerve of that woman?"

Clearly, Boofer could not.

"You're a good listener," Liv told the dog, and then she slid her still-full coffee cup across the granite countertop. "But I was sort of looking for some input, Boof. What do you think?"

Boofer stared at her for a long moment, wide-eyed, and then just rolled over to her side to take a nap.

"Oh, fine."

Liv opened the sliders as wide as they would go, crossed the patio, and sat down in the wicker lounger. There were a dozen other chairs and loungers surrounding the pool, but for some reason this was the one she always chose. Stretching out on it, she tilted back her head and closed her eyes.

Day Ten in Florida. Just a couple more days to go, and then back to the real world.

And in that moment, something dropped on Liv with a thud! She opened her eyes with a slight *boing!* and stared straight ahead.

"It's my birthday."

Liv almost couldn't help herself, and she winced. She scanned the sky on the other side of the screened lanai, searching for whatever disaster was sure to overtake her at some point that day. Perhaps the gator would come back, which, of course, made her think of Georgia Brown.

One potential disaster after another meandered across her horizon, and then those of the past began to play out before her. She was almost relieved when her cell phone jingled from inside the house, and she hurried in to find it. By the time it was in her hands, however, the caller had gone to voice mail, and Liv pressed the button to listen to the message.

"Olivia, this is Becky from Human Resources at Providence. We have a situation here. Irene Stamopolis has had a stroke, and Jennifer Cavanaugh has given her notice, so we're more short-handed than ever. I need to hear from you about coming back to work on Monday, or I'm afraid we're going to have to fill your slot. We just can't hold it indefinitely, Olivia. You know how things are around here. Give me a call, please?"

There it went again. Liv's heart thudded at the pit of her stomach as she flipped shut the phone.

The understanding kindness in Becky's previous messages had left her voice, and now she was all business. Liv knew she shouldn't be surprised. Becky had been calling her since before she left Ohio, but she just couldn't wrap her brain around making plans to go back to her pre-cancer life. Liv loved her job in the operating room, and her team was a tuned machine. But more than eight months had passed since she'd stood beside them, and Liv had begun to doubt that she had the edge of an O.R. nurse anymore.

"It's probably like riding a bike," Hallie had reassured her.

Thinking of her most recent efforts with a bicycle, Liv tossed her head into her hands and laughed out loud, thinking that she sounded a little like a seal.

"What's so funny?"

Her neck snapped slightly as she raised her head to find Jared standing in the open doorway, a small white bakery box in his hands.

"Not much," she replied.

"Just the hysterical laughter of a birthday girl?"

"Something like that. Come on in."

Jared crossed the living room and sat beside her on the sofa. He set the box on the coffee table and lifted the lid. Fragrant espresso and chocolate wafted from inside, and Liv peeked over the side to see a small birthday cake flanked with two tiny palm trees sculpted out of dark chocolate.

"Oh, Jared."

"Happy Birthday," he offered. "I thought we'd put it in your fridge and then have some together tonight."

"That's very thoughtful."

"So are you up for a day of snorkeling?"

Liv didn't look into Jared's eyes as she nodded, and he raised his hand with caution and tipped her face toward him.

"What is it?"

"I have to go home."

"When?"

"Tomorrow."

Jared didn't come close to disguising his disappointment. "I thought you were here until Tuesday."

"That call was about my job," she replied, opening her palm to reveal her cell phone. "I have to be back at work on Monday, or they won't hold my job for me."

It seemed as if several minutes passed before Jared uttered, "Oh."

"Josie won't be back until Tuesday, though. Do you think Rand would take care of Boofer in the meantime?"

"Between the two of us, Boofer will be just fine."

"Thank you."

"You really want to go back?"

"I'm working on wanting to," she said with a grin. "You know, I used to love my job so much. I just feel like such a different person now. It's been a little difficult to start thinking about going back to my old life."

"Which is why you came to Florida."

"Right. To get myself ready."

"And?"

Liv chuckled. "I'm not ready."

"Then I don't think you should," he said. It was disguised as a joke, but there was no mistaking the undertone of hope.

"Oh, Jared," she said with a sigh, and then she leaned into him and let him slide his arm around her shoulder. Liv wondered how ten short days could have cradled a nest of friendship that felt so natural and comforting. "I have to go back. I need my job. All those months of cancer really took a toll on my financial life. And I only have a few more years before I'm completely vested for retirement."

"Hmp." She looked up at him with curiosity. "Then today is our last day together."

Thud! There went her heart again.

"We'll make it a day to remember. We'll go snorkeling, barbecue some steaks, and make some memories out on the water. What do you say?"

Liv nodded with determination.

"Sound like a plan?" he asked her.

"It's a plan," she agreed.

But that was the problem with making a plan, Liv remembered. It was like raising a white flag to everything on earth that could fall in the way.

14

Prudence dropped her head, and one of her ears fell across her eye. "It's a scary thing," she told Horatio. "Change."

"But there are two very different kinds of change," her friend explained. "Change in your circumstances is always a little scary. But change from within . . . that's a blessing to behold."

❧

"All right, Georgia. Tell him I'll meet the ambulance at the hospital."

Liv looked down at herself. Hallie's bright red bathing suit mocked her from beneath the white eyelet peasant-style coverlet and red Capri pants with white pearl buttons at the cuffs.

"We're going to the hospital?" she asked with a wince. "I'm not exactly dressed for anything except a drive to the Gulf."

"I'm sorry," Jared replied, squealing into a U-turn. "It's Clayton. He's having chest pains and shortness of breath. They're taking him to Fort Myers."

"Oh, no."

"I'm sorry to derail our plans, Liv. Hopefully, we'll still get to the marina later this afternoon."

"No," she objected. "Don't worry about that. Please."

Her white flip-flops smacked out a goofy little rhythm as she tried to keep up with Jared, up the sidewalk and down the long linoleum hallway of the hospital. In the elevator, she raked her hair with all ten fingers, and then she scurried out behind Jared.

Georgia's scowling face was the first thing that drew Liv's attention as she and Jared arrived at the desk. Georgia looked as if she'd just bitten into a big, bold, sour lemon and didn't mind letting on how she felt about it.

"He's in Exam Room 3," Georgia explained as she interlocked her arm with Jared's and whipped him around and down the hall. "They're doing an EKG right now. His rhythm is erratic, and his pulse is 122."

"Okay," Jared said, and then he turned around toward Liv as he continued to walk backward. "Have a seat over there. I'll be back as soon as I know something."

Liv nodded, and then he was gone.

Slipping down into one of the leather chairs in the lobby, Liv caught the eyes of a little girl, reclining across her mother's lap while Mom smoothed her dark brown hair in long, gentle strokes. Liv smiled first, and the girl returned the smile with a tired, honey-coated effort.

"I got a fever," the little girl stated, and it took Liv a moment to realize the comment was directed at her.

"You do?" she returned. "I'm sorry to hear that."

The girl's mom grinned at Liv in a knowing way, and then Liv cocked her head and leaned toward the little girl.

"You just rest. They'll see you very soon."

"My name's Sarah," she said. "I'm seven."

"Hi, Sarah. I'm Liv." She decided to skip the age update.

"That's a funny name."

"It's short for Olivia."

"Oh. I don't have a short-for."

"You don't need one. Sarah is a beautiful name."

"I was named after a lady in the Bible. She wanted a baby real bad, but she never could have one. Then when she was really, really old, God said she could have one, and she laughed at Him."

"I remember that story," Liv replied. "I think I might have laughed too."

"Yeah, but God did it anyway. He's like that."

Liv exchanged a glance with the girl's mother, and then she leaned her chin on the palm of her hand and said, "Sarah, you're a very sweet little girl."

"I'm much sweeter when I'm not 102."

"Is that your temperature?"

"Yep. Anything over 101, we have to come to the hospital."

"Do you get fevers a lot?"

"Yeah, I do. My immunes don't work so good."

Sarah's mom leaned down and kissed her daughter's temple. "We normally go to the pediatric clinic, but the wait was so long there this morning that I decided to come here. I'm not sure that was the best move because we've been waiting for over two hours."

"Can I get her something? Maybe some juice?"

"Really? That would be so great. I didn't bring anything."

"Absolutely."

A small cubbyhole around the corner held a limited selection in vending machines, so Liv took the elevator to the second floor and sought out the cafeteria for something more.

Little Sarah's flushed face and deep brown eyes preyed upon her mind as she walked the buffet line and chose boxes of orange, apple, and cranberry juice. She'd been working the operating room for so long that Liv seldom had the opportunity to deal directly with patients, much less children. Something about meeting Sarah made her wonder if a move from the O.R. to the pediatrics clinic in her hospital might be something to think about.

In the elevator Liv leaned back against the

padded tapestry wall and smiled. Suddenly, that one little glimmer of hope about making a change that might bring her life into focus again was starting something within her—a fire. And she could almost feel the warmth from the spark the moment had created. A simple consideration had been stoked into a full-blown revelation in just a few minutes, and Liv felt certain it was the leading of God. It had been such a long time since she'd experienced answered prayer, but she still could recognize it right away.

Leaving Jared behind was going to be such a difficult thing for her, but having a plan—something hopeful to go back to—at least took the sting out of it. For the time being, anyway.

"I didn't know what you'd like," Liv said as she crouched before Sarah. "Orange, cranberry, or apple?"

"Apple, please."

Liv poked the straw through the top of the box and slipped the plastic off the straw. "Sip slowly, okay?"

"All right."

"What do you say?" Sarah's mom asked her daughter.

"Thank you, Liv."

"You're very welcome, Sarah." Liv ran her hand over Sarah's hair, and then she kissed her finger and pressed it against the girl's hot cheek. "You feel better, okay?"

When Liv got to her feet again and turned around, Georgia was leaning against the desk watching her. Liv took a moment to take a deep breath and press her coverlet with the palms of both hands before walking toward her.

"Too bad Jared missed that," Georgia said with a whisper. "I'm assuming that was the plan?"

"You know what they say about *assuming,* don't you, Georgia?" The quip had just crackled out of her, and Liv was both appalled and amused at her uncharacteristic bravado. "Now if you'll excuse me, I have a call to make."

"Well, Clayton has asked for you, if you can spare him the time."

"Where is he?"

"Exam Room 3," she replied, pointing the way down the hall.

Liv made her third or fourth wish about being dressed differently as she *slap-slap-slapped* down the hallway in her flip-flops. But all thoughts of silly clothing and rubber shoes disintegrated when she turned the corner and saw Clayton. His suntanned face was ashen, his eyes clamped shut, and he was tethered to several machines with tubes and sensors.

Jared looked up from beside Clayton's bed, and their gazes locked for a long and lingering few seconds.

"How is he?" she finally asked, and Jared clenched his square jaw.

"Holding his own for the moment."

"Was it a heart attack?"

"Yes. I've called in a specialist, and we're going to prep him for surgery."

"I'm in the room, you know," Clayton said, his eyes still pressed shut.

Liv chuckled and rubbed her hand over his arm.

"How are you feeling, Clayton?"

"How do you think I feel?" he asked, snapping open his eyes. "Then I hear you're here and that you didn't even come to see me."

"They were sort of busy saving your life," Liv replied with a smile. "I thought I'd hold onto my greetings until after that was taken care of."

The corner of Clayton's mouth quivered before he gave in to it and let out a chunky laugh that ended abruptly and turned into a cough.

"Is there anything I can get you?" Liv asked him, and Clayton shook his head.

"Nothing I'd ask ya for in mixed company," he replied, eyeing Jared with a serious glare.

"Well, I'll be right down the hall if you think of anything."

"You gotta go so soon? I thought you might distract me from this surgery talk."

"You just do whatever Jared tells you to do. And I won't go far."

Just as she started to pull away her hand,

Clayton reached out and grabbed it. When she looked into his eyes, he winked at her and squeezed her hand before letting it go.

"Glad you're here," he said in a raspy whisper.

"You feel better, will you?"

"Workin' on that."

Jared gave her a nod before she stepped out into the hallway. "I'll be out in a little while."

Instead of heading for the lobby, Liv turned in the opposite direction while digging in her bag for her cell phone. She took a deep breath as she dialed, and then released it slowly and leaned back against the wall while she waited for an answer.

"Becky. It's Olivia Wallace."

"Olivia! I'd begun to think you'd disappeared from the planet."

"I know, I'm sorry. I've been on a little vacation in Florida. In fact, I'm still here."

"I see. That poses a problem because I was really hoping you would come back to work on Monday. When do you return from Florida?"

"Becky, I've been thinking about it, and I'm going to see if I can change my plane reservation to come back this weekend. I'll be back at work on Monday."

"You will?"

"Yes. I appreciate your patience with me."

"I'll let Valerie know you'll be back, Olivia. I think she'll be very happy."

"Becky, can you tell me something?" Liv began, and then she paused to pull the words together in her head. "You mentioned staffing problems in one of your messages, and I was wondering if you could tell me . . . how wide-spread are the shortages?"

"Oh, we're down an employee or two in virtually every department at the moment, Olivia."

"What about the pediatric clinic? Are you short there too?"

"Let me check," Becky said, and Liv could hear the turning of pages through her cell phone. "Yes, we're down two nurses and one doctor."

"Do you think there would be any chance that I could transfer to the clinic?"

"Well . . . I don't know. I'd have to look into that."

"I'll be back on Monday morning at 7 a.m. Maybe I could come and sit down with you on my lunch break, and we could have a chat about what I'd need to do to make that happen?"

"I'm writing you on my calendar right now."

"Thank you so much."

A little surge of excitement coursed through her as Liv made her way back toward the lobby. It was a relief to find that Sarah and her mom were no longer seated there, but she stopped at the desk just to make sure.

"The little girl and her mother," she said to the nurse behind the desk. "Are they being seen?"

"About ten minutes ago, yes."

"Great. Thank you very much."

Liv dialed her phone and folded into one of the leather chairs in the lobby.

"Yes, I have a flight from Fort Myers to Cincinnati on Tuesday. But I need to change that to tomorrow. Can you help me with that?"

❧

"I'm so sorry, Liv. I just can't leave him right now."

"I understand, I really do," Liv said, and then she moved in closer to Jared. On a whisper, she added, "But please don't make me go with Georgia. I can call a taxi."

"Don't be ridiculous," he replied. "She lives five miles from our neighborhood."

"You don't understand, Jared. She hates me."

"Hates you! She doesn't hate you."

"Are you really that dense?" she asked, wringing her hands.

"Olivia. It's a ride home. That's all."

Liv imagined a dozen different terrors in the space of those next ten seconds.

Georgia laughed maniacally as she sped the wrong way down a one-way street at more than a hundred miles per hour. Sprouting horns through her platinum blonde hair, she clenched the steering wheel and turned toward Liv with narrowed, glowing red eyes.

"Did you really think I was going to let you

take him from me? Did you? DID YOU??"

"Please, Jared. I'd much rather call a taxi."

"A taxi!" Georgia exclaimed, as she walked over to them. "Don't be silly." Turning to Jared, she smiled like the cat thanking her host for the luscious canary appetizer. "I'll see her safely home. Are you ready, Olivia?"

Liv's heart bounced against her chest, and she turned to Jared, wide-eyed and hopeful that he would read the horror there.

Jared stepped forward, put a hand on each of her shoulders, and looked down into her eyes. "I can't tell you how sorry I am about this. But I just can't leave him until Dr. Morgan arrives to consult. I'm guessing Clayton will need surgery sooner rather than later."

Liv sighed. "I understand."

"Don't be that way," he replied with a grin. "Don't understand. It's your birthday, and all of our plans—"

"Jared, as you know, I've had far worse things happen to me on my birthday than spending it alone with a flatulent dog."

He laughed out loud and pulled her into an embrace. Liv didn't care if Georgia was watching —and oh, she was watching all right! Liv slipped her arms around Jared's neck and returned the hug.

"Call me when you're through?" she murmured into his ear. "No matter when it is. Okay?"

"I promise. If you'll do something for me."

Liv stepped back and looked at him. "All right. What?"

"Put the candles on that cake and make a wish before the day ends."

"Oh, I'd rather wait."

"It has to be on your birthday, Liv. Promise."

"I promise."

"And I'll still try and make it there before the day fades completely away."

"I hope so," she said. "My flight home is tomorrow at noon."

"Ah," he groaned. "Really?"

"I had to."

"Liv, I'm so sorry."

"Ready then?" Georgia asked her, and Liv nodded.

Jared squeezed her elbow, and his hand brushed all the way down her arm and to her fingertips as Liv turned and followed Georgia toward the door. She grieved the sparks of their lost touch as their fingers parted, and she looked back only once and only long enough to return Jared's smile.

"So, did I hear Jared say this is your birthday?" Georgia asked as they pulled out to the main road.

"Yes."

"Well, happy birthday."

Liv almost burst out laughing but refrained at

the last moment. "Thank you," she managed instead.

"I guess you two had plans."

"Snorkeling."

"At least that explains what you're wearing."

Liv couldn't help herself, and she let out a chuckle. "What? You don't like it? I thought it was what all the nurses were wearing."

Georgia glanced over at her, curiosity crackling.

"Yes," Liv said, "I'm a nurse too."

"I had no idea."

"I worked in the O.R. until I had some health problems. I start back on Monday, and I'm hoping to be transferred to the pediatric clinic when I get back. At least, I hope to have that chance if there's an opening for me."

Why am I blathering my whole life story to this woman?

"You did have a way with that little girl in the waiting room."

"I love kids."

"Do you have any?"

"No. You?"

"Two daughters. They're grown and living in Charlotte."

The clackety-clack of tires against highway filled the space of the next couple of minutes while Liv tried to figure out what she was doing trapped in a car, sitting next to the one person who disliked her more than anyone else in the whole state of Florida.

"Looks like we're gonna get some rain," Georgia commented, and Liv glanced at the churning sky while Georgia clicked on the radio just as the weatherman said:

". . . could turn out to be our first tropical storm of the season. I don't see this turning into an actual hurricane, but I do feel pretty confident that we're going to see some very serious storm activity within the next twenty-four hours."

"Boy, oh, boy, oh, boy," Georgia declared as she turned down the sound.

"The storms sure do kick up quick and out of nowhere down here."

"That's the Florida motto," she replied in her thick Southern drawl. "If you don't like the weather, kindly wait an hour."

As if on cue, huge droplets of rain began to pour from the turbulent gray sky, pelting the windshield with thunderous conviction. Georgia flipped on her headlights and turned the wipers to their full speed. "Oh, my!" she exclaimed as a sudden burst of wind pushed the car until it rocked.

"Do you think we should pull over until it calms down?" Liv asked.

"We'll be at your house in just a few minutes. I think that's our best bet if we just take it slow and steady."

Liv grasped her seatbelt and squinted to keep a closer lookout on the road ahead, and then she gasped as six feet of tree branch bounced across the road in front of them. Georgia barely missed it as she swerved and navigated around it, and then she and Liv released harmonious sighs of relief.

When they finally pulled to a stop in Josie's driveway, Liv reached over and clutched Georgia by the wrist for a moment, out of instinct.

"Well, that was quite a ride, was it not?" Georgia breathed.

"Indeed!"

"I'll wait here until you get safely inside."

"Georgia, I'm thinking you should come in until the storm lets up."

"You go ahead, Olivia. I live nearby."

"Are you sure?"

Georgia nodded.

Liv hopped out of the car, grateful for the reprieve but still dreading sending someone back out into the storm, even if that someone was Georgia. She hadn't yet reached the curve of the sidewalk when a strange hissing noise drew her attention back to the driveway. Before she could even turn around, a crash sounded, and then she heard a scream.

Liv stood there with both hands over her mouth, her heart pounding and her breath sputtering.

Georgia's eyes were as wide and round as plates. A large tree had crashed down on the back of her car, and caved-in the metal down to the backseat.

"Are you okay?" Liv yelled.

"Yeah," Liv muttered as she ran toward the car and yanked at Georgia's door to open it. "This is more like it."

"What? What did you say?"

"I was just thinking that this is much more like the birthday I was expecting."

15

Prudence's donkey eyes were so wide that they ached! Despite the fact that the winds blew in great gusts, and every tree bent over beneath them, the creatures in the clearing stood shoulder to shoulder around her.

"What are they doing?" she brayed at Horatio. "What's happening?"

"You're being protected from the winds of change," her owl friend explained. "Your friends are shielding you."

"But why?"

"Because they know it needs to be done."

❧

Boofer stood before Georgia, snarling and barking like a machine gun.

Ratta-tat-tat-tat-tat.

"Boofer, please," Liv snapped. "Be quiet. I'm sorry," she told Georgia. "Just ignore her and come on in."

Georgia slipped the door shut behind her and then leaned on it as she watched the dog with caution.

"Boofer! Enough!"

Liv figured she must have struck just the right tone when Boofer's change of heart was immediate.

"She's been in the house all day. I'm going to take her out for a quick second. Just relax on the sofa, and I'll put some coffee on before we lose power."

Liv clipped the leash into place on Boofer's collar and stood at the trunk of her car near the edge of the open garage while the dog sniffed at the nearby grass and considered doing her business despite the sideways spray of rain and wind working against her.

Georgia's mangled Camry was tucked up close enough to the back of Liv's rental that there was no possibility of getting it out to take the woman home. Wasn't this just too perfect! She was trapped with Georgia Brown on her fiftieth birthday.

And the birthday curses blaze on.

I'm sure you think you're hilarious, she told the Lord in silence. But this is so not funny.

Boofer led Liv back through the garage, and she flicked the button to close the door. As she entered the house, Liv freed the dog from her leash and headed into the kitchen to start the coffee, but she found Georgia there with a pot already brewing.

"I thought I'd lend a hand," she said. "Coffee sounded pretty good."

"Great. There's no sign of things letting up out there. It's pretty severe. And even if it did let up, I can't get my car out around yours."

Georgia ran her finger around the rim of one of the two coffee cups she'd set out on the counter. Timidity was the last thing Liv expected to find in Georgia, but there it was just the same.

"You know," she began, and then she gave a quick glance upward before returning her attention to the china cup, "I am probably the last person in Florida that you'd like to be confined with for more than five minutes."

"Well . . ." Liv didn't know how to respond.

"I haven't been easy on you."

The Understatement of the Year Award goes to —

"I hope you can understand. And forgive me."

I'm sorry. What?!

"The truth is I've been hoping for something with Jared for years, and the connection just wasn't there for him."

Oh, please don't tell me any more.

"And then you came along, and the spark was hard to miss. I guess you just got my dander up."

"I didn't mean to."

What a lame thing to say.

"I know. The way you two were together today, especially when we were leaving the hospital. Well, I just don't think I've ever seen the good

209

doctor look at a woman like that in all the time I've known him."

"Thank you," Liv said in a raspy voice.

"For what?"

"For saying that."

"I just can't figure out why you're leaving tomorrow for Ohio when the love is so deep right here in Florida."

Liv stared at Georgia, a deer caught in headlights one more time.

"Well, you are in love, aren't you?"

Not a single word sprang to mind. Liv's brain was a blank, white canvas. Every paint color in the universe sat on the sidelines, brushes at the ready . . . and yet . . . nothing.

"Cake," she finally mumbled.

"Beg your pardon?"

"I have birthday cake."

"Oh. Well. All right."

Liv yanked open the door to the refrigerator and produced the white bakery box Jared had delivered that morning. Pulling back the flaps until the box lay flat beneath the cake, she discovered that two candles were taped to the inside of the box: A big, white number 5, and a matching 0, both of them with blue polka-dots.

"You're fifty!" Georgia exclaimed as Liv peeled away the tape.

"Sure am."

"Well, I hope your mama bottled those genes,

sugar. You don't look a day over forty!"

Liv couldn't decide if Georgia was sincere, or if she was still just trying to make up for the bad blood between them since the day they met.

"Well, you're full of it," Liv said with a grin. "But I'll share my cake with you anyway."

"No, honey, I'm not kiddin'," Georgia declared. "Fifty!"

Liv pressed the candles into place on top of the cake and then produced a lighter from the kitchen drawer.

"Jared made me promise I'd light them."

"And make a wish. You have to make a wish."

For a moment Liv thought about all the wishing she'd been doing, for such a very long time. She'd wished that Robert had taken better care of himself and his heart, and she'd wished that her doctor hadn't uttered the word *cancer* all those months ago. If wishes were donuts, she knew she'd easily weigh five hundred pounds.

Closing her eyes, Liv clasped her hands together.

Instead of a wish, she thought, how about a prayer? I'm just praying, Lord, that there is no more cancer in my life; that there's some joy and some love and some fulfillment instead. I'm praying that trees will stop falling on cars in front of me, and that Clayton will wake up tomorrow with your healing in his body and spirit. And I'm praying that you would please

211

take the sting out of leaving Jared behind, and that you might make the way ahead of me clear so I can't mess it up.

Liv opened her eyes again, and Georgia smiled, almost sweetly. "That was quite a wish."

"I'm very wordy."

"Blow out the candles then."

Amen, Lord. She finished her prayer, and then she blew out the 5 and the 0.

"What kind of cake is this? It smells like coffee."

Liv cut into the cake and transferred a slice to one of the plates Georgia produced. "It looks like a cream cheese filling," she said, dipping in her finger and taking a taste. "With espresso or coffee mixed in!"

"I'll have a bigger, fatter piece than that."

"Me too," Liv said with a chuckle as she added another sliver to the plate. Georgia poured coffee.

The two of them settled at the dining room table, facing the lighted patio. The storm was at full throttle, and the surface of the pool looked as if an industrial-sized fan was directed at it from one side.

"Oh!" Liv groaned as she tasted the first bite. "This is the best cake in the history of cakery."

"I do believe you're right."

"Listen," she continued, licking icing from the side of her fork, "I think you should stay the night."

"Well . . ."

"Seriously, I just think it's the better side of wisdom to just—"

Before she could complete the thought, a sudden snap cut her words in half, and a loud boom exploded in the distance. The entire house went dark.

"Your point is well taken." Georgia's voice sounded shaky from her spot in the shadows. "I think I'll stay."

❧

Jared stood next to Don Morgan, scrubbing his arms and hands. "I think that went pretty well."

"It's always such a stunner when someone in that kind of shape comes up with a blockage," Morgan commented. "The guy is active, he's fit, and yet his arteries were a mess."

"He swims laps several days a week," Jared concurred. "Goes to show how important diet is."

"The older we get, the more important it becomes."

"Well, thanks for letting me scrub in. Clayton lives on my street, and I've been his physician for years."

"I'll copy you in on my reports," Morgan said as one of the nurses untied his surgical gown.

"Be careful driving," the nurse called out as Dr. Morgan hit the door. "The weather has turned really ugly."

He nodded, waved at Jared, and then disappeared.

"Storms?" Jared asked her.

"They expect it to be classified an official tropical storm by morning," she replied as she pulled the ties on the back of his gown. "It's been pouring pretty hard—lots of power outages."

"Thanks for the warning."

Jared flicked open the last locker in the row and produced his cell phone from the shelf. Liv's number went to voice mail on the first ring.

"Liv, it's Jared. Clayton's out of surgery, and I think things went well. I just heard about the turn in the weather, and I want to make sure you made it home all right. Try my cell when you get this."

The parking lot was littered with branches and trash and even several overturned bins. After navigating his way out to the main road, Jared flipped open his cell phone and pressed the number two on speed dial.

"Rand? Hey, buddy, where are you?"

"We're at Shelby's mom and dad's on Captiva. What about you?"

"Clayton Clydesdale had a heart attack today and surgery tonight."

"He okay?"

"It looks like it. I'm headed home and just wanted to check on your whereabouts."

"Everything's cool on this end," Rand reassured him. "Are you in your car?"

"Yeah, on my way home now."

"Well, drive safe. It's a mess out there, Dad."

"Talk to you tomorrow."

A squall of sidelong rain pelted the car in gusts, and Jared could hardly see the road, even with the wipers turned up to maximum speed. He thought about dialing Liv again but figured it would be much smarter to just keep both hands on the wheel and his full attention on the road before him.

When he finally turned the corner and rounded his street, the first thing his headlights illuminated was Georgia's Toyota mashed beneath a fallen tree. Jared's heart began to pound out a wild rhythm, and he slowed for a closer look as he passed the driveway.

That girl sure wasn't kidding about birthday disasters.

As soon as his own car was parked safely in his garage, Jared jogged against the wind gusts around the side of his house and up to Josie's front door. Raindrops pelted him like sharp little needles, and the scent of burning rubber wafted past him as he made it to the front porch and pressed the doorbell.

Boofer yowled from the other side of the door and, when it opened, Liv stood before him with a burning candle in hand.

"Thank God," she exclaimed when she saw him, and she wrapped her free arm around his neck, hugging him as she drew him inside. "I was so worried."

"Is Georgia okay? I tried calling, but I think the towers are blocked by the storm."

Jared noted that another figure was bathed in yellow candlelight behind Liv, and he squinted to bring Georgia into focus.

"What in the world happened to your car?" he asked her as he strode into the living room. "I hope you two weren't in it when that happened."

"Georgia was," Liv replied. "I was heading for the front door, and she was just five seconds too long in reversing out of the driveway."

"Are you hurt?"

"No, I'm fine," she told him. "Olivia invited me in for birthday cake and coffee, and now she's invited me to stay the night."

"Did you light the candles?" he asked, grinning at Liv.

"She did. And she made a birthday wish."

"And then we ate like teenagers at a slumber party," Liv said.

"Is there any left?"

"There is. Would you like some?"

"I sure would."

"I'll get it," Georgia said, hopping to her feet. "You two sit down and relax."

"The coffee's cold by now," Liv told him. "Do you want something else to drink?"

"Just birthday cake is fine by me." He flicked the blue light on his digital watch to see that it was 11:21 p.m. "I wanted to celebrate with you on your birthday. I guess I got in right under the wire."

Jared craned his neck to make sure Georgia was out of sight, and then he slipped his arm around Liv's waist and pulled her toward him.

"Happy birthday," he said with a whisper and gave her a tender kiss.

"I'm so glad you made it."

"Me, too."

"Olivia," Georgia called, "do you want cake too?"

"Oh, my, no!"

"I didn't think so," she said, laughing. "Just thought I'd check."

"How much cake did you girls eat?" Jared teased, and Liv just shook her head furiously.

"It wasn't pretty, Jared. I think you're fortunate there's a piece left for you."

Jared and Liv shared the sofa, with Boofer wedged between them, and Georgia took the easy chair by the front window.

"Tell us about Clayton," Liv said, folding into the corner of the sofa with her legs crossed beneath her.

"The surgery went well."

"Don Morgan is one of the best," Georgia added.

"Will he recover?" Liv asked him.

"He will. He's a tough old guy."

Liv reached over the dog and quickly scooped a fingerful of icing from Jared's plate. He took a playful stab at her hand with his fork, and she poked her finger into her mouth with a grin.

"I think I'll leave you two to fight over the cake," Georgia said, and she got up from the chair and stood over them. "This has been a very long day."

"It sure has," Liv agreed.

"It's the second door on the left?"

"Yes. And I laid out an extra blanket on the chair, in case you need it."

"Thank you, sweetheart," Georgia replied, and then she leaned down and pecked Liv on the cheek.

Jared recalled Liv's pleading at the hospital not to send her home with Georgia.

She hates me, she'd declared.

"Good night."

"Night, Georgia."

Once Georgia had disappeared down the dark hall, Liv turned to Jared and smiled.

"BFFs in the making," Jared muttered.

"Who knew?" Liv replied. "And all it took was a big storm, a tree, and some really good cake."

Jared set his plate on the coffee table, and

218

then reached across Boofer and took Liv's hand in his.

"The tropical storm warning is in effect until tomorrow," he said. "I don't anticipate you flying anywhere in the morning, do you?"

"I think that's up to the airline," she said with a shrug. "If they're flying, I have to be on the plane."

"Well, then. Let's hope they won't be flying."

"Jared."

Nudging Boofer until she hopped off the couch, Jared slid toward Liv. He took both of her hands in his and gazed with a smile into her pretty green eyes.

"I can hardly stand the thought of saying good-bye to you," he admitted.

"I know. I feel the same way."

"I understand that you have a life waiting for you back there. I get that. I know how selfish it is to want you to stay, but I'm not sure how to just go back to my daily life without you being part of it anymore."

"I know."

"When Rand told me he was going to marry Shelby, I thought how young and impetuous they are. But right now, in this moment, Liv . . . impetuous doesn't seem like the worst thing we could be."

"What about the young part?" she teased. "We're old enough to know better."

Jared dropped a sigh and then fell silent. The unspoken words hanging from the tip of his tongue throbbed, aching to be released.

I love you, he wanted to declare. *I don't want you to leave. Instead, I want you to marry me and stay here and make a life with me.*

"I've loved every minute we've spent together," Liv told him, and his heart ached with the implication of her words.

But I'm going home and leaving you here alone.

"So have I," he interrupted.

"Meeting you on the plane that day was the greatest gift."

Stop now, he thought. *Enough lead-up to good-bye. Just don't say anything else.*

"I'll miss you so much," she added.

"I'll miss you too."

Jared wrapped his arm around Liv's shoulder and pulled her toward him. The last thing he wanted was for their eyes to meet at that moment and for Liv to see all the love and grief standing there.

I can't do this on my own, he thought. *Now that I've fallen for her, how do I let her go? Help me let her go gracefully, Lord.*

16

The meadow seemed so far away now. As Prudence prepared for the journey back, her heart sank lower and lower.

"It's so hard to say good-bye to all of you," she declared, her donkey eyes brimming with dewy emotion. And then her gaze met the stallion's, and the tears spilled out without warning. "I'll never forget you."

Horatio landed on Prudence's neck, and he soothed her with his outstretched wing.

"Will you ever come back?" one of her new friends asked.

Prudence lifted her lopped ear and cocked her head. "I don't see how," she said. "But I think I might believe in miracles more now than I used to."

"A good miracle is always a dandy thing to hang on to," Horatio hooted.

❧

Rain came down in sheets for most of the night, but in the light of morning it had deteriorated to a fine mist squeezed out of gloomy, gray clouds that blocked out every inch of sky.

The tow truck wouldn't get to them for several hours, and Jared, Liv, and Georgia stood inside the open garage surveying the damage beneath the broken tree.

"How will I return my rental car," Liv finally asked, "if I can't get it out of the garage?"

In another week, Rand would be going back to England with his new wife by his side. And now Jared found himself in the bizarre position of standing in a garage trying to figure out ways to help Liv leave as well.

"You can take a taxi to the airport," he offered. "I'll return the rental this afternoon, after they tow Georgia's car."

"You would do that?" she asked, turning toward him.

"Of course."

Liv twisted back again, facing outward. Jared thought the three of them must have looked like odd little birds on a wire.

"I wish I didn't have to go."

"Then why go?" Georgia asked outright, breaking the line to spin toward Liv on her left. She pressed both hands to her hips. "No, really. I don't understand. You two have obviously found something in each other that's special, am I right?"

"It's complicated," Liv told her.

"Love is not complicated," Georgia said, and then she twirled toward Jared on Liv's right.

"I haven't seen you like this with someone in a year full of Sundays, and now you're going to just let her go?"

"Liv has a job to get back to, Georgia."

"There are jobs in Florida, Ja-red."

"And friends. A house. A life."

"All of which we have here in Florida, surprisingly enough."

Jared sighed.

"All right. Fine." Georgia waved her hand at him. "I'm just sayin'." She stepped back into line with the other birds at the edge of the garage, staring out toward her battered car, scowling in silence. Three different versions of the same frozen statue.

"I guess I should go pack," Liv muttered.

"I'll check on your flight," Jared said.

And then Liv went one way, Jared went the other, and Georgia was left standing there alone.

"Talkin' to you two is like a kick in the fanny with a frozen boot," Jared heard her say.

It was all he could do to keep from laughing out loud. He kind of understood the sentiment.

"Yes. The eleven-thirty flight out to Cincinnati. Will it be on schedule?"

❧

"Do you want me to pick you up at the airport?"

"Oh, Hallie, no. I can grab a cab. I don't want you out in the cold, going all that way."

"Did you ever find it strange that the Cincinnati airport is across the river in Kentucky?" Hallie asked, and Liv chuckled.

"I have always found that strange."

"But really, I don't mind going out in the cold for you. I mean, it's cold, but it's *a dry cold*."

Laughter popped out of her, and Liv shook her head. "I've really missed you."

"You have not. But thanks for saying so."

"Tell Josie that Jared and Rand are going to watch after Boofer until she gets back on Tuesday. Oh! And Clayton had a heart attack yesterday."

"What? Is he all right?"

"He had surgery for a blockage, but Jared says he's doing really well, all things considered."

"Thank the Lord. Mama would be heartbroken if anything happened to that old coot."

"I think I would too," Liv admitted, and Hallie laughed at that.

"Really! The last I heard, you were thinking of drowning him in my mother's swimming pool."

"We've had a moment or two since then. I've kind of learned to see his better side."

"Shocking."

"You're not kidding."

"Are you sure you want to come back so soon?"

Liv squeezed her eyes shut for a moment, and then sighed.

"No. But I have to, if I want to keep my job."

"And you do?"

"I do . . . what?"

"Want to keep your job?"

"I need to, Hallie."

"Okay. Just checking," she remarked. "I'll see you tonight then. Call me when you're home, and I'll bring you some supper."

"Thanks."

"Love you."

"Love you too."

Liv tossed her cell phone to the bed, and then lifted her suitcase to rest beside it. Pushing on the top of the bag, she scissored the zipper back and forth until it closed. Boofer hopped up on the bed, and Liv dropped down beside her.

"It's been very nice to make your acquaintance," she told the dog, and Boofer reciprocated with a quick lick to Liv's hand. "You are a very nice dog, barring the Morey incident, and our initial meeting, of course. But I've appreciated your company very much."

Boofer fell over to one side and propped her head on Liv's knee. Tilting backward, she gazed at Liv, upside down.

"I know. It's so hard to say good-bye, isn't it? But it's not forever. I'll come for a visit now and then."

Liv wondered if that was true, but she knew she had to tell herself that she'd be back to keep from losing it completely.

"Oh, Lord," she prayed on a whisper, and then she clamped her eyes shut and buried her face in her hands. "I don't know why you brought me here to meet someone like Jared, only to have me leave him behind just when I'm starting to fall—" She couldn't say the words out loud, so she thought them.

—in love.

"Give me the strength to do what I have to. Help me let him go gracefully, Lord."

Boofer gave a little whimper of support, and Liv raked her fingers through the dog's fur.

"And amen from me too."

An hour later, Liv silently prayed for grace once more as the driver of the town car Jared had arranged tossed her bag into the trunk. Liv stood at the curb beneath a light mist of rain, facing Jared and Georgia to say good-bye.

"We didn't get off to a very good start," Georgia said softly as they embraced. "I'm sorry about that."

"Water under the bridge," Liv promised her.

"Y'all come back now, ya hear?" Georgia said in her best Southern twang as they parted, and Liv nodded. "I mean it. You come back."

"I will."

"I'm sorry you can't stay," Jared said, taking

her hands into his. "Rand just told me that he and Shelby are getting married tomorrow."

"Tomorrow!" Liv exclaimed.

"There's something to be said for spontaneity when it comes to love, isn't there?" Georgia rang in, but when Liv and Jared stared her down, she tossed her hands into the air. "I'm just sayin'."

Jared squeezed her hands, and Liv turned back toward him. "It's going to be a very cold summer here without you," he told her.

"But it's a dry cold," she remarked, stealing Hallie's line.

"Ha!" he laughed, and then the amusement melted from his eyes like wax down the side of a candle. "Come here."

Jared wrapped her in his arms and held her close while Liv fought back the tears that threatened to fall at any second.

Grace, she thought. *Please, give me your grace.*

"Call me when you're home safely," he whispered.

"I will."

"And maybe I can plan a long weekend up there sometime soon."

Liv gulped a pocket of air and nodded. "That would be so great."

She'd never noticed those flecks of gold in Jared's eyes before, but now she couldn't look away from them. She felt a little lost in them, in fact, like trying to swim through the inlet around Sanibel's lighthouse, with leg irons fastened securely into place.

Jared inched toward her, and then brought his hands to rest on either side of her face. He paused to guide an unruly spiral wisp of red hair back into place, and then he leaned in and kissed her with such tenderness that Liv thought it might just do her in. But the spectacle of her teeming, unpredictable emotions dissolved instead, leaving only the crushing stir of her love for Jared in their place.

"Safe trip," he said, soft and sweet.

"Take care of yourself, Jared," she replied, running one finger down the length of his square jaw. "Give my love to Rand and Shelby?"

"I will."

Georgia had moved up the driveway toward the house, shielding her helmet of teased hair from the rain. Liv caught sight of her there, one hand pressed over her mouth, watching as she bid Jared a sorrowful adieu. Liv waved at her, and Georgia tossed back a haphazard finger-wiggle. And then one last glance at Jared, and Liv dropped her eyes and climbed into the back seat of the shiny black car.

She couldn't look back, despite the inclination to do so. She just faced front with a stiff resolve as the driver added distance between her and Jared, and she felt just as gloomy and turbulent inside as the sky looked outside. And then, just like that greenish sky stretched out ahead of her, Liv's own clouds broke and down came the rain.

"Would you like tissues?" the driver asked her after a few minutes of quiet, sniffling tears.

"Yes, please."

He handed her the box over the seat, and Liv went through at least a dozen of them before they reached the airport in Fort Myers.

The winds were high, powering the assailing spears of rain, as Liv jogged toward the terminal. A strobe of lightning foretold the thunderous explosion just as she made it through the glass doors and into the building.

The terminal screen indicated that her flight was running about twenty minutes late; however, by the time she made it to the gate, the announcement was being made that Flight #2436 to Cincinnati had been canceled due to weather.

Liv stepped into the long line of passengers to inquire about an alternate flight, but no more than five minutes passed before she realized how futile it was. People were turned away in fast little spurts, and finally one of them tossed a bone to the crowd as she passed.

"They'll make an announcement in the next thirty minutes about whether we'll be able to get an alternate flight."

Liv took a seat by the massive window and

watched the clouds roll around for a while, wondering what she would tell Becky in Human Resources if she wasn't able to get home in time to report to the O.R. on Monday morning. Surely a flight would be available on Sunday, if not that day. And yet . . .

She couldn't help it. Hope that she would somehow be delayed sprouted from the very center of her. Speculation brushed large, sweeping strokes around the circumference of her mind. For instance, what might she wear to Rand's wedding? And how would she feel standing there next to Jared as Shelby and Rand skipped dipping their toes in the water in deference to just diving right into their feelings for one another.

The rain hit the window in gusts, and there was a certain rhythm to it that reminded her of something. Liv searched its melody to figure out what it was until, at last, she just smiled as she recalled the spray of salty water alongside Jared's Sun Runner as they pushed along through the Gulf. Those days out on the water with Jared were days she would never—

The jingle of Liv's cell phone cut her thoughts cleanly in two.

"Are you okay?" Hallie cried the moment she put phone to ear. "I just saw on the news that the weather down there is dreadful. Are you on the plane?"

"No. My flight was canceled. I'm waiting to hear if I can schedule the next one."

"Well, at least you're warm and dry. For the moment. How was it . . . saying good-bye to Jared?"

"Excruciating."

"Have you developed feelings for him?"

Liv bit her lip. She could hear the hopeful joy in Hallie's tone. She drummed her fingers on the arm of her chair.

"Liv?"

"Kind of."

"What does that mean?"

She groaned. "It means yes. I've developed feelings for Jared."

"More information, please."

"There's nothing else to tell," she said. "I live in Ohio; he lives in Florida. I have a job to go back to, a house I'm responsible for, and he has a whole life here."

"You know, they've come up with these fantastic new things now, Olivia. They're called *moving vans*. It's where you load up all of your belongings, and they transport them to another location. People all across the country are picking up and starting lives in other places."

"Just a couple more years, and I'm fully vested for retirement, Hallie. After that, I can go anywhere I want. But until then—"

"And what if Jared meets someone else in the meantime?"

"If it's meant to be, he won't."

"Are you kidding me?"

"Hallie, please. It's hard enough."

"But it doesn't have to be. I've known you forever. You haven't accepted a single date since Rob died, and don't think I don't know there have been invitations."

"What?"

"Ray Gillium down at the coffee bar. And the manager at the Mexican restaurant down on Fountain Square. Sam something."

Liv sniffed. "How do you know this?"

"I've got people. Anyway, now you've met someone, you've allowed yourself to fall for him, which is a bona fide miracle if you ask me, and you're sitting there waiting to fly away from him? I know you're aware of how seldom connections develop between people. Granted, I haven't seen you two together, but I do know you both. And if you're falling in love with Jared, you need to man up and make plans to bridge the gap in whatever way you can."

"Are you finished?"

"Almost. I just want to say one more thing."

"And that would be?"

"I know you think every bad thing that happens within two weeks on either side of your birthday is because of the whole curse theory, but sometimes things are thrown in your path to get you going in the right direction. Like a tropical storm that stops you from leaving the man you're falling in love with."

"So God sent a storm that would torment thousands of people on the west coast of Florida, just so I wouldn't leave Jared today?"

"Of course not," Hallie replied. "That's just the perk."

"You're a nut."

"I'm not as nutty as you are, Miss Birthday Curse Believer."

"Well, I may be rethinking that whole curse thing."

"No!"

"That's right. It's entirely possible that I am not a wretched, pitiful woman with a birthday cloud hanging over my head each and every year."

"I'm stunned."

"Imagine how I feel."

"So this year there was no crushing blow about which you'll tell the sad tale for years to come?"

"Honestly?"

"Of course."

"There were some unexpected twists and turns, like Clayton's heart attack and a tree falling on Georgia Brown's car in your mother's driveway—"

"What!?"

"—but what I'll remember from this birthday is a chocolate espresso birthday cake and a kiss at midnight from a man who makes my knees weak."

"Oh, Liv. You've got to figure out a way to make it work."

"I know. But how?"

"Any way you can find."

"I'll call you once I'm on a plane."

"Love you."

"Love you too."

Liv tucked her cell phone into her bag and sighed.

Lord, I haven't prayed as much in the last five years as I have in the two weeks since I went to church with Jared, but I'm so grateful that you've reminded me that you're still there. I've never felt about anyone in my entire life the way I feel about Jared Hunt. Please give me a sign? Tell me what to do.

"Ladies and gentlemen," the woman announced from the counter at the gate, "we want to thank you for your patience today. We do regret to inform you that Tropical Storm Millicent has been upgraded to a hurricane, expected to make landfall just north of Sarasota over the next six hours. All flights out of Fort Myers have been canceled until further notice."

Liv realized that her jaw had dropped, and her mouth was hanging open.

"Careful," her grandmother used to say on such occasions. "You'll catch flies."

Liv let the current of people move her down the long corridor, wondering whether she would be able to get a taxi when everyone else in the vicinity had the same idea.

"What are we going to do?" the woman in front of them asked her husband. "Where will we go? And, Tommy, I have to be back at work tomorrow."

"I know, baby. We'll figure something out."

Liv slowed down at the sudden whiff of brewing coffee with the thought of stopping to purchase one for the road, but she almost caused a pedestrian pileup. Skirting a collision with an elderly couple ahead of her, she stepped up the pace.

Liv jumped when someone touched her shoulder. She twirled around and looked into familiar eyes with a gasp.

"Need a ride?" Jared asked, and a smile spread across Liv's face as if someone had plugged it in and suddenly flipped a switch.

17

"You made the journey to the Enchanted Pond so that you could be refreshed," Horatio reminded her. *"But do you think you might want to stay?"*

"Stay, and leave the meadow behind?" she clarified. *"Forever?! Oh, I don't know about that."*

"Well, perhaps you'd like to take another day before we set out for home. Just to think it over."

"I don't suppose another day would hurt anything. Just to think it over."

❧

The drive back to Sanibel was treacherous in the face of storm-force winds, downpour clusters, and low visibility. Liv belted herself in and then clutched the seatbelt with both hands. Ella Fitzgerald crooned softly from the stereo, but the outside noise was so furious that, at times, Ella fell silent beneath it.

"I'll bet Boofer is scared half to death," Liv commented.

"We'll be there soon."

"Jared, have you checked on Clayton today?"

"I have. They said he's resting comfortably and requesting a better television so he can watch some special programming tonight about the next Bucs season."

Liv laughed and shook her head. "The man does love his football."

"He's a Tampa Bay Buccaneers fan, through and through," Jared replied.

"He could start a memorabilia store over at his house. Do you know he's even got Bucs plates and coffee cups?"

"The blanket on his bed is a huge Buccaneers logo."

"Oh, you're joking."

"I kid you not."

"That's classic."

Conversation took a fast and certain nosedive as two cars screeched to a stop in front of them, and then swerved around a downed tree in the road. Liv realized she was still holding her breath after Jared had navigated around it and was half a mile down the road.

"I've never seen anything like this," she said. "Have you?"

"Oh, this isn't my first hurricane season in Florida. I've pretty much seen it all. But you never really get accustomed to it. Every season brings new challenges."

"I think I'll stick to shoveling snow and layering my clothes, thank you very much."

"Ah, yes," Jared replied. "But remember, we'll get rainstorms, and power outages, but hurricane season doesn't necessarily mean hurricanes. How many winters do you have with no snow?"

"None. But ask me how many times I've had an alligator at my back door."

"That's unusual for most people here in Florida. You're just some sort of weird magnet," he chuckled.

"It's the whole birthday thing. It throws off the balance of nature."

Jared grinned, shaking his head. "After the rainy season, the rest of the year here is paradise," he reminded her. "Blue skies, 70 or 80 degrees, the Gulf breeze."

"You sound like the top salesman for Florida tourism."

"Yeah? How am I doing? Are you sold yet?"

Liv cast a quick smile in Jared's direction, and then continued to watch the road ahead of them.

"Because I could go on, you know. I could tell you about the manatees, the fresh local seafood, maybe regale you with a tale or two about being barefoot on the beach from April through October, breaking a sweat on a bike ride on Christmas Day."

"All right, all right," she said, patting him on the shoulder. "That's enough. I get it."

Liv recognized the turn into Josie's neighborhood, and she puffed out a shaky sigh of relief.

"I've got to call Hallie and Josie to let them know that I'll be staying with Boofer after all."

"Will you also call your job?" Jared asked.

"I don't think so. It's Saturday. And I might still be able to get a flight home tomorrow."

Disappointment cascaded over her even as she spoke the words, and Liv glanced over to see telltale signs of the same emotion on Jared's face.

"I was kind of hoping you'd be able to stay for the wedding tomorrow."

"Will they still have it, with the weather like this?"

"If I know my son, yes. They'll just move it indoors."

Liv noticed a few houses on the street with light shining from their front windows as Jared turned into Josie's driveway.

"It looks like we've still got power here. Do you want to stay for dinner?" she asked him. "It's just a frozen lasagna Josie left for me."

"I can be back within the hour."

When the car came to a stop, Liv reached over and squeezed Jared's arm. "Thank you for checking on my flight, and then coming to get me, Jared. I can only imagine how I'd be feeling right now if I was still stuck in the airport, wondering what to do."

"Leave your bag," he told her with a warm smile. "I'll bring it over when I come."

Liv slipped out of the car and slammed the door behind her before she took off running up the front sidewalk. The rain came down in buckets, and by the time she klunked into the house, Liv was drenched.

Boofer didn't even bark at her; she just moseyed toward her and sniffed her leg.

"Hey, girl. Didn't expect me back so soon, did you?" she asked as she sat down on the sofa and pulled her cell phone out of her bag. "Me neither," she continued as she dialed. "It's raining cats and Boofers out there, and my flight got canceled, so you're stuck with me, at least for tonight. Oh, hi. Hallie? It's Liv."

❧

The wind pounded against the walls at the back of the house, and Liv jumped as a large, unidentified item flew across the patio, past the kitchen window, and then thudded against the far wall. She peered outside as water sloshed over the side of the pool and Jared hurried around the patio securing chairs and collecting anything light enough to be carried away with another big gust.

Liv watched him for a moment more, and then she pulled on lobster claw oven mitts to remove the lasagna from the oven. She set the glass baking dish down on the stovetop and turned around to find Jared standing on the other side of the counter. He exploded with pops of laughter when he saw her there, her lobster claw hands raised in front of her.

"Only Josie," he exclaimed, shaking his head. "Who else would buy those?"

"The lasagna looks like it has spinach and mushrooms and onions," she told him, peering over the baking dish. "Maybe green peppers. I'm not sure if there's any meat. It might be vegetarian."

"It smells great, either way."

Liv handed him two plates and an assortment of flatware, which Jared organized on the counter bar while she cut two large squares of lasagna with the edge of a spatula.

"Water or tea?" Jared asked, standing at the open refrigerator door.

"Water, please."

It couldn't escape her notice how well they worked together. There was something so natural and easy about the two of them, whether they were putting together a meal or just driving down the street. Liv knew such a comfort level didn't come by often, and she was reluctant to gamble against it.

Her conversation with Hallie tripped across her mind as she rounded the counter and climbed atop the barstool next to Jared. Would their relationship remain so fresh and simple over the course of time, especially with a thousand or more miles between them? What was—

Jared interrupted the progress of her thoughts as he reached over and took her hand in his.

"How about a quick prayer?" he suggested.

Liv swallowed around the lump in her throat and nodded. Following Jared's lead, she bowed her head and closed her eyes.

"Thank you for this delicious meal," he said. "And for the company you've allowed me to keep. Now please help us find a way to keep the momentum going."

Liv opened her eyes and turned toward Jared. He was looking back at her, and the smile that curved upward was sweet and meaningful.

"Amen," she added with a whisper, and then she returned the smile. Jared squeezed her hand before releasing it.

Before much of their dinner could be enjoyed, a sudden blast of wind slammed into the side of the house. The clamor of debris accompanied a strange and strident hiss that left them in darkness.

"Not again!" Liv cried.

Jared lit several candles on the counter and grinned at her from behind their flickering yellow curtain.

"Ambiance," he declared. "Let's enjoy our dinner."

Liv wondered if he could possibly be as collected as he appeared in the face of a natural disaster that came in the form of gale-force winds and impending doom! She watched Jared as he poked another forkful of lasagna into his mouth and followed it with several gulps of iced water.

"What?" he asked when he noticed her focus on him.

Right on cue, another burst of wind sent something crashing outside, and Liv extended her hand toward the sound, palm upward.

"That," she replied. "You're not worried in the least?"

"Well, of course, I am," he told her, despite the fact that his demeanor said otherwise. Jared casually stood up and reached for her plate. "Are you finished?"

"Mmm hmm."

He gathered their plates and walked them to the sink, then he rinsed each of them before setting them down inside the large stainless steel well. He didn't even flinch when a bouncing *klunk-klunk-klunk* thumped overhead, across the entire length of the house. Liv, on the other hand, jumped to her feet, her heart pounding, her palms perspiring. Boofer pressed herself against Liv's leg, barking several times at the ceiling as if it had come alive.

"Too bad we didn't make some coffee before the lights went out."

Coffee?

"You know, Rand has a battery-operated coffee pot that he used to take on his camping trips. It's on the shelf in the garage. How about I run next door and get it?"

"No!" she exclaimed, and then she struggled to reel it back in a bit. "I don't need coffee badly enough for you to go out in this weather."

"How about a game of Scrabble?" he suggested, and it dawned on Liv at last that Jared was trying to manage her anxiety level by keeping her focused on anything but the raging storm outside. "I know Josie has a game in the front closet. She's wiped the floor with me a few times."

Before Liv could answer, an explosion of shattering glass sent Boofer into a fit of barks and snarls. Jared pressed his hands against both of Liv's shoulders, guiding her toward the barstool.

"Stay here," he said, and then he rushed down the hall toward the bedrooms.

When he didn't return right away, she took a deep breath and then headed down the hall. Jared was standing in the guest bedroom alongside a scene that was nothing if not surreal: The limb of a tree reached into the room like a bony hand, straight through the broken window. A torn, lacy green curtain waved from one of the branches like a strange wartime flag.

"I have to pull this out from the other side," Jared told her. "Then I'll go over and get something to board up this window."

"What can I do?"

"Give me time to get to the other side, and you can push from this end. First order of business is to get this tree out of the bedroom." He ran a hand down her arm as he passed, and she wondered whether it was static electricity or just the ever-present heat between the two of them that left her tingling beneath his touch.

The tree limb rocked inside the frame of the broken window. Finally, Jared called out to her, "Give it a shove."

Liv leaned her weight into the intruding branches, and her hands stung from the roughness of the bark as she pushed, but the thing didn't budge.

"I hate to ask you to come outside, but if you could pull from this end while I lift, we might have better luck," he suggested. "It seems to be stuck on the jamb of the window."

"On my way."

Liv grabbed Josie's neon yellow rain slicker from the closet in the front hall and slipped into it as she ran to the side of the house. The rain pelted her as she sloshed through the mud and, when she reached Jared, he looked a bit like a watercolor portrait left outside to face the elements. Boofer barked at them from inside the house.

"It's okay, girl," Liv promised. "Calm down. It's okay."

Jared pushed himself into the branches and managed to get a grip on two of them.

"Pull as hard as you can, on three!" he called, but his words were nearly lost behind the din of the storm. "One . . . two . . . *three!*"

Liv yanked at the tree with all her might until she finally felt it give. Jared braced both feet against the side of the house and groaned as he lent his strength to her effort. Branches snapped, wind whistled, and time seemed to stop ticking as they yanked and pulled and tugged at the encroaching tree. At last, wood cracked, and the limb broke free. Liv flew backward and slammed to the ground, the enormous arm of the battered sumac tree on top of her.

"Liv! Are you all right? Are you hurt?" Jared's tone was frantic. No more of the calm and collected storm-dweller with whom she'd shared her dinner.

"N-no," she managed, but it was hard to breathe with the limb pressed to her chest the way it was.

Jared wedged both hands under the branch and yanked it upward with a grunt, allowing Liv the freedom to wriggle out from underneath it. Once emancipated, she drew her knees upward and hugged them while she struggled to catch her breath.

Jared crawled toward her through the mud and plopped down beside her. "Are you hurt?"

She almost didn't hear him. "No."

"You sure?"

"I'm sure."

"Let's get you into the house. Then I'll go next door and get something to board up the window for the night."

Jared got to his feet and extended his hand toward her. She took it and let him pull her up.

The wind fell silent for a moment, eerily so, and then it whipped back into action, nearly stripping the jacket right off of her. But instead of moving back toward the house, Jared turned and faced Liv, taking her face into both of his hands.

A rush of adrenaline raced through her as Jared engulfed her with those chocolate brown eyes of his. The two of them just stood there beneath the ferocious downpour, anchored to one another, locked into one gaze.

"I love you, Liv."

It doesn't just happen in books. Hearts really can skip a beat!

"I love you too," she wheezed over the commotion of the storm, but she wasn't sure he heard her. So she repeated it, this time with a shout. *"I love you TOO!"*

Jared exploded with laughter, and then he

pulled her into an embrace, rocking her back and forth in his arms.

"Don't go, Liv," he said into her ear. "Don't go back to Ohio tomorrow."

She pulled back, but only far enough to look into his eyes.

"At least stay for Rand's wedding. We'll figure something out from there."

"Oh, Jared. I—"

"Shhh." He placed a finger over her lips, and she kissed it. "Just say you'll stay, just one more day."

Liv felt as if she had no control over her reply. Her job at Providence Hospital, her retirement fund, the too-big house on the hill beside Hallie's, even the pelting rain that drenched her to the core now—it all slipped away, mere dust, blown away by the raging winds around them. In that one piercing and wonderful moment, nothing mattered aside from those three exquisite words they had just exchanged.

Like the heroine in her favorite classic novel, Olivia Wallace was going to think about the consequences on another day. On this day, as she stood at the jawline of the worst storm she'd ever encountered, Liv forgot everything else and slipped her arms around Jared's neck, leaning into the warm and tender kiss he offered.

18

"What's that I hear?"

"What do you mean? I don't hear any-thing."

"That's what I mean!"

The silence was deafening to Prudence. She wasn't used to such quiet. It made her tail twitch.

∞

It was with great reluctance that Liv opened her eyes, first one and then the other. Her neck was sore, and she stretched it. Her pillow had been rolled into an awkward blob beneath her head. Boofer's face was buried in Liv's armpit, and the dog whimpered when she shifted.

"C'mon, Boof," she groaned, and she gave the dog a gentle nudge with her elbow. "Gimme a break here, huh?"

Boofer rolled away, and then released a soft, somewhat freakish squeal as she stretched and yawned.

A spear of yellow light shone through the opening in the curtains, seeming to point the way straight to the corner of the bed. Liv got up, stretched, and pulled open the drapes.

She looked up at the blue canopy hovering overhead, not a cloud in sight. What a strange dichotomy Florida was! The tail of a hurricane had walloped Sanibel Island overnight, and yet this morning—blue skies and sunshine. The only evidence of the storm was the disarray stretched out across the neighbor's lawn.

An overturned trash can rested at the foot of a tall palm tree, the grass beyond it littered with its one-time contents. Crumpled paper, a used coffee filter, and the top of a pineapple were just a few of the items Liv identified. Broken branches, several uprooted flowering plants, and a broken planter blanketed the rest of the debris.

The fragrant song of brewing coffee called to her suddenly. Liv hurried into the bathroom to brush her teeth and wash away the sleep from her eyes, but the reflection that greeted her in the mirror was enough to give pause to her efforts.

She'd been covered in mud and slime after her wrestling match with the downed tree, and she'd taken a warm candlelight shower before turning in. Drying her hair with a towel rather than an electricity-powered blow dryer had been more of an effort than she had the strength to undertake, and so she'd let her head hit the pillow before her curls were completely dry.

They're dry now! she thought.

Fuzzy spirals poked out in every direction like a confused scarecrow pointing the way. Liv frowned in disappointment as she realized the coffee (and Jared) would have to wait a few extra minutes while she pulled herself into a form that was fit for human consumption.

Thirty minutes later, she emerged with freshly diffused curls and a couple of dabs of makeup, wearing her favorite faded jeans and a pale blue, sleeveless cropped shell sweater with white enamel buttons. Her bright-white Keds were tied up with islet laces, and Boofer batted at one of them with her paw as she followed Liv to the kitchen.

"Jared?"

An empty mug waited on the counter beside the coffee pot, and she filled it before meandering over to the window above the sink. The patio was uncluttered, but a few stray leaves dotted the surface of the pool.

Jared was hard at work at the top of a stepladder in the far corner, repairing a portion of the screen that the winds had torn away from the steel frame.

Liv decided to get some breakfast started while he completed his task. She remembered a canister of cinnamon rolls she'd spotted at the back of the top shelf in the refrigerator. Fresh-baked and warm, they might make a nice addition to some scrambled eggs and sliced cantaloupe.

She'd hoped to have it all laid out on the dining table before Jared came inside, but she was still icing the rolls when he opened the glass sliders.

"What is that wonderful smell?" he exclaimed, and then leaned across the counter to have a look.

"Breakfast," she declared. "It's just about ready."

"I'll go wash up."

She didn't want to go so far as to light candles, but Liv pulled down Josie's best china and loaded the plates with all the careful precision of a sculpted masterpiece. She poured chilled orange juice into crystal wine goblets. When Jared reappeared, she was just filling two flowered porcelain cups with coffee.

"I could certainly get used to having you around," he said, standing beside the table. Liv's heart leapt.

"Back atcha." She tried to sound casual. "Thank you for fixing the screen."

As they chatted over breakfast, Liv was reminded once again how simple things were between the two of them. She tried to look back at the beginnings of her relationship with Robert so many years ago, but she couldn't remember how long it took before they found the simple groove they'd eventually slipped into. One thing she knew for sure, though, she'd never experienced with anyone the kind of heat that Jared inspired.

It was odd to be so attracted and yet so comfortable. He set butterflies to fluttering just by looking at her, sparks to blazes with his touch, and yet they could amiably converse for hours on myriad subjects.

Jared Hunt was as much an enigma to her as the Florida weather. From electrical storms to sunshine and back again.

And just then, as their eyes met across Josie Parish's mahogany table, in the hollow just above her ribs and below her heart, Liv felt the beginning rumblings of one of those electrical storms.

❧

Jared had been standing in front of his bedroom closet, tying his tie, for more than fifteen minutes. His focus wasn't on the light blue silk tie Rand had given him for Christmas, and he wasn't really even thinking about his son's nuptials, now just a little more than an hour away. Jared's thoughts were next door, on the other side of their two back-to-back swimming pools, beyond the glass sliders.

Relief had washed over him like a wave out in the Gulf when Liv called her employer and left the voice mail message.

She'd opened with, "Becky, I'm so sorry," and followed with a concise summation of her canceled flight, the hurricane, and the damage to Josie's house. But it was her closing that had Jared's gut in knots.

"I know I said I would be back to work tomorrow, but I'm just not able to do it. I'm going to try and rebook my Tuesday flight back, and I'll be in touch to let you know when I'll arrive."

Jared sat down on the corner of the bed and started over with new determination toward his necktie. When it was knotted at last, he walked over to the mirror on the back of the door and adjusted it, allowing his mind to meander back to Liv again.

She was so resolute about going back to her old life despite their obvious connection, and every one of the reasons she'd spelled out for him made perfect sense. Just one thing stood boldly out of place, and that was the love that had developed between them.

Jared was reminded of a game Rand used to love when he was little.

"Which of these pictures doesn't belong with the others?" Rand's mom would ask him, and Rand would wrinkle up his face like a prune until he figured it out.

It was hard to believe that same little boy with the furrowed brow would now be making vows to his chosen bride. Where had the time gone?

Jared slipped into his navy blue jacket and fastened the buttons down the front. He'd bought this suit for the medical conference in Cincinnati and had worn it only once. It had been hanging in the garment bag when he met Liv on the plane.

Funny how everything always seemed to circle back around to Liv these days, even his navy pinstripe suit. He'd known her such a short time, and yet she was planted, even rooted, into every aspect of his life as if she'd been there all along.

His doorbell rang just then, and Jared glanced at his watch. Five minutes early. He wasn't sure he'd ever known a woman as consistently punctual as Liv.

He opened the door to a spring bouquet on three-inch heels. She was exquisite in a straight, pale pink skirt and a silky floral blouse with fluttery ruffles framing her neck and wrists.

"You are stunning," he told her, and it thrilled him to no end that she blushed in reply.

In the car Jared queued up his favorite Michael Bublé CD and then punched through the options until he landed on the perfect song— *Everything*. The one that had reminded him of Olivia Wallace ever since the day they first met. These days, he often woke up humming it, thinking of red hair and green eyes.

Bublé continued to serenade them with an array of tunes on the drive toward Captiva, and Jared reached across the seat and grasped Liv's hand, his finger tapping out the rhythm of "their song" on her knuckle when it came up again on the menu.

Shelby's family home on Captiva was impressive. Jared navigated the curved driveway toward the large white house at the top of the hill. Stately white columns and an expansive porch lent Southern charm to the inviting architecture.

"Not a palm tree in sight once we turned off the main road," Liv noted. "It looks like it's straight out of *Gone with the Wind*."

"Welcome home," Jared teased. "To *Tah-rah*."

"I'm thinking your son is marrying into some old Southern money, Jared."

"I'm thinking so too."

Jared pulled into line behind the last car in the driveway and shifted into park.

"Are you ready for this?" Liv asked him.

"Not really."

Liv chuckled. "Well, that's honest."

"My son is getting married," he said with a sigh. "He hasn't even known her for a month, and now he's marrying her. What am I supposed to do with that? Tell him to wait? He won't listen. And he's old enough to make the decision for himself, with or without my approval. So what do I do?"

She exhaled a groan and shook her head. "I don't know. I guess you support him. You love him. And you hope and pray that he won't fall. But if he does, you're his dad and you pick him up and brush him off."

Jared's heart pinched inside his chest, and he turned toward her. "You would have made a great mother. That's excellent parental advice, Olivia."

She grinned at him and shrugged. "If that's true, it's all yours. But don't expect any more of it because that's all I got."

He laughed, squeezed her hand, and nodded in the direction of the house. "Ready?"

"When you are."

When they reached the front door, Liv slipped her arm through his, and Jared's pulse rapped against his throat. It had been such a long time since he'd felt like part of something. When Rand's mother was alive, he had another half. He was whole. He'd forgotten until the very moment he felt Liv's arm link with his, and suddenly, a missing puzzle piece snapped into place again. The thought of losing that after waiting for so long to find it—

"You must be Rand's daddy!"

The woman who opened the door was tall and thin, with an elegant smile that seemed to twinkle. Her golden hair was pulled into a loose bun at the back of her head, and expensive silver earrings dangled from her lobes to the shoulders of her lavender suit.

"Jared Hunt," he said as she shook his hand. "And this is Olivia Wallace."

"Vivian Barnes, Dr. Hunt. It's such a pleasure to meet you, and you, Miss Wallace. Please come in."

Vivian led them across the marble floor of the foyer into a great room with a wall of windows that looked out over a long, rolling green lawn. Rows of brass chairs faced a flowered arch where the bride and groom would stand. A dozen ornamental standing candelabras were placed behind the arch and ran down both sides of the room, each of them decorated with garlands of red roses and white ribbons.

"Oh, it's beautiful, Mrs. Barnes!" Liv exclaimed. "Just beautiful."

"Call me Vivian. Thank you. We didn't have much notice to pull it all together, but I don't think I've ever seen a light in our Shelby's eyes like I've seen since she met Rand. Her father and I just wanted to make sure their wedding was special."

Jared wanted to ask her how she felt about the announcement when she first heard it, or what Vivian thought about her daughter traipsing off to England in a few days. He wanted to know whether she was concerned about her daughter, the way he was concerned for his son.

"Oh, good," Vivian said, motioning to a lean man in a black suit. "Honey, come here and meet Rand's father. Jared Hunt and Olivia Wallace, this is my husband, Jasper Barnes."

The niceties bounced between them like a tennis ball before Jared finally asked them where he might find Rand.

"I was hoping to spend a few minutes with my son before the ceremony."

"Of course," Vivian replied. "Up the stairs and down the hall, the second door on the left."

Liv gave him a nod, and Jared excused himself. Once he reached the circular staircase, he took the stairs two at a time and hurried down the hall and rapped on the door.

"Oh, thank God!" Rand exclaimed when he saw his father standing in the doorway. He flicked the ends of his loose bow tie. "Help me, Dad."

Jared laughed and backed Rand into the room before shutting the door.

"Stand still," he said, and then he set about tying his son's tie. "How are you feeling? Nervous?"

"You'd think I would be, wouldn't you? But I'm really not. More excited than nervous, you know?"

"Yeah, I think I get that. No doubts then."

"Doubts about Shelby? Are you joking? She's perfect, Dad."

"It's a little hard to label perfection after two weeks, Rand." Jared tapped his son's shoulder twice and told him, "There you go. Done."

"Thank you," Rand said, and then he sat down on the bed and motioned for his father to sit beside him. "Dad, look. I know this has all happened real quick. But I feel like me and Shelby, you know, we were meant to be. She gets me. And I get her."

"Well, that's important." Jared tried not to let on how worried he really was.

"How long did you know Mom when you proposed? Something like a month?"

"Three months," Jared corrected.

"But you knew. You were sure. How is this so different? I'm sure. I can't see going back to England without her just because I haven't been sure *longer*. I don't want to be without Shelby. Can you understand that?"

Jared sighed and thought of Liv. "Better than you know."

"So just be happy for me?"

"I'll give that a go."

"Thank you."

"So are you ready to go downstairs and get married?"

"Just one thing first."

"Okay. Shoot."

"When are you going to get wise about Olivia?"

Jared wasn't sure he could stand being any wiser about Liv. But he wasn't going to share that with his twenty-something son.

"Will there be food after this thing?" he asked with a grin.

"I hope so. I could eat a cow."

"If anyone else had said that, I'd have thought they were exaggerating. Let's go get you married, son. I'm hungry."

Rand stopped him at the door with a tug to his arm. Jared turned around and, when their eyes met, he smiled. "Congratulations," he said in a whisper, and then he pulled Rand into an embrace.

"I love you, Dad."

"Of course you do. I'm a great father."

"Well, I wouldn't go that far. But you're better than mediocre."

Jared released him, and then smacked him on the back as they passed through the doorway. "It's tragic how mouthy you've become. Your mother would be so disappointed."

"Imagine if she could see how you've let yourself go. That gut alone would make her weep."

Jared shook his head and laughed as he followed Rand down the stairs. "Ingrate."

Instead of slinging something back in their usual bantering style, Rand turned toward his father and smiled.

"You're the blessing of my life, Dad."

"And you're the blessing of mine."

"Thanks for being my best man."

"Who else? You know I'm the best."

"Second best, right after me."

"Let's go get you married before Shelby realizes what a huge mistake she's making."

"Seriously," Rand said with an arched brow. "Bite your tongue."

Jared placed his hands on Rand's shoulders and looked him in the eye. "She's a lucky woman."

"I'm the lucky one."

19

The stallion stood before Prudence and whinnied. "It seems like you've only just arrived, and now you're on your way home," he said.

Home. She'd never been confused by the word before, but now Prudence was torn straight down the middle. The fragrant green grass of the meadow called to her from far away, and yet her heart told her that, if home is where the heart is, then this clearing by the Enchanted Pond had to be where she belonged.

"Another day?" Horatio suggested.

"No," she replied on a soft, mournful bray. "It's time to go."

"Are you certain?" the stallion inquired.

The truth of the matter was that Prudence wasn't sure at all. Still, she gathered her courage and said good-bye to her new friends in the clearing, and then she put one hoof in front of the other and headed . . . home.

Liv remembered Pastor Ed Phillips from Jared's church. He'd made her cry when he spoke about the return of the prodigal son. With his first few words, Liv felt fairly certain he was going to make her cry again, but for different reasons this time.

"In presenting themselves here today, Rand and Shelby perform an act of faith. After knowing one another for only a short time, both of them feel certain that a lasting and growing love, although never guaranteed, is part of their destiny. I'm not an easy one to convince of such things," he said, sharing a grin with the twenty or so guests in attendance. "But I am convinced, just the same."

Jared looked so handsome standing there beside his son, and Liv couldn't help but imagine for a moment that it was their wedding, that she was up there with him, that together they were listening as Pastor Ed assured them that a hasty marriage didn't necessarily mean a casual decision.

Liv noticed Shelby draw in a deep breath that she let out in a puff. She looked far more demure and pretty than Liv even remembered her. Her blonde hair was swept upward into a twist that was dotted with pins bearing rhinestones and small red flowers. The bodice of her white dress was sleeveless with a high neck and beading that sparkled with the reflection of the candles, and the ankle-length skirt flared only slightly with its overlay of tulle. Beaded white satin ballet slippers finished off the look, and Liv thought the bride looked very much like a regal ballerina.

"Rand and Shelby, let the foundation of your marriage be the devotion you have for each other at this moment. When trouble comes, because it always does come, commit yourselves to looking back at this day, with your friends and loved ones surrounding you, and the net of God's assurance beneath you, and stand firm. Never allow your love for each other to be blotted out by the everyday, or by the doubts of others, or by the worst-case scenarios that may play in your heads. Let your love stand strong like a house built on solid rock rather than on sand. Take comfort in what you see in one another's eyes this day, and hold it to you like a shield against anything else that would come to chip away at the foundation of what you believe in your hearts to be true: You were meant to be here, in this moment, on this day."

Georgia slipped into the row beside Liv, and she squeezed her wrist as she sat down in the chair on the aisle.

"What did I miss?" she whispered.

"They just got started."

Georgia's hand went to her heart the moment

her eyes came to rest at the front of the room. Liv wondered if Jared was the inspiration for her reaction, or Rand and Shelby. Despite the fact that they had mended their fences, Liv hadn't forgotten that Georgia's affections for Jared went far deeper than a few kind words and an appreciation for the competition.

"The bride and groom have written their own vows, which they would like to share with each other and with all of you now."

Rand looked into Shelby's eyes and gulped. They both smiled, and then he took her hand into his.

"Shell, I love you so much," he began, and then he paused and smiled as he shook his head. "I'd always heard that love was a gradual thing, that it crept in slowly when you weren't necessarily looking. But for me, it didn't come that way at all. It hit like a thunderbolt. The moment I laid eyes on you, I knew I'd found my match. And not just because you're so incredibly beautiful, but because you have a light about you, a heart like no one I've ever known before. With each passing day since that one, my love for you has grown until I can hardly contain what I feel for you. I promise to spend the rest of our lives showing you that I'm fully aware of how blessed I am to have found you. So . . ."

Rand turned toward his dad, and Jared produced the ring. His eyes sparkled as they met

Rand's, and Liv sighed. Somewhere between their conversation in the car and this moment, Jared had come to terms with his son's marriage. She could see it on his face, burning in his eyes.

". . . I give you this ring," he continued, slipping it onto Shelby's finger, "as a symbol of my vow. With all that I am, with all that I have, I honor you in the name of Jesus Christ."

Shelby's head tipped to one side as she fought back the tears. "Oh, Rand," she sniffed. "I love you so much that I feel like I could bust wide open from it. I'm so thankful that, when you looked into my eyes, you immediately felt the same as I did. I can't imagine being in love like this alone. But for some reason that I can't comprehend, that I certainly don't deserve, God chose to bless me in this way. And with our union, He's gone one further. He's allowed me to trust, without question, in something that I just don't understand. That's *SO* not me," she added, and Rand nodded.

"You're right," he said, chuckling. "It's not."

The guests erupted in laughter at that. Liv understood the sentiment. She was having trouble trusting in her own unusual emotions.

She noticed Jared give a gentle pat to Rand's shoulder, and the simple act brought tears to her eyes.

"I know," Shelby went on. "But that was the old me. This new one, the one that pledges her love and life to you today, the one that believes one-hundred percent in a future with you, this Shelby is a new creature. Today, I become your wife. I can hardly wait to see what happens next."

Shelby turned to the friend beside her, a wide-eyed brunette with a smile so big that it seemed to fold her face in half. She handed Shelby the ring.

"Please accept this ring as a symbol of my vow. With all that I am, with all that I have, I honor you in the name of Jesus Christ."

"Beautiful," the pastor commented. "Just beautiful. So now, before your friends and your family, and before the God who will nurture you and love you and protect you all the days of your life, I pronounce you husband and wife."

Rand moved in for a kiss before the pastor could suggest it, and Shelby slipped her arms around his neck with such joy that Liv's pulse raced a little.

The pastor smiled and then shrugged at the guests. "I think that's the part Randall's been waiting for. Family and friends of this happy couple, I give you Rand and Shelby Hunt."

Applause exploded in the room, and Liv hopped to her feet to join in. The tears that had welled in her eyes cascaded down her face as Jared and Rand hugged one another. She clapped her hands furiously, and Georgia put fingers to mouth and let out a shriek of a whistle.

She and Liv embraced one another as Georgia exclaimed, "What a joyous day!"

The guests tossed white confetti and red rose petals at the bride and groom as they made their way past them, and Jared followed, stopping in the aisle to give Georgia a hug. Then he reached out for Liv's hand and led her down the aisle alongside him. She couldn't imagine what Jared was feeling just then, hand-in-hand with her, sauntering down the wedding aisle, but her own heart raced with emotion.

I love this man. I love him so much.

Liv thought back to Shelby's words about feeling like she could burst with the love she had for Rand. She and Jared really did have a lot in common with the bride and groom. Except for the fact that neither of them was brave enough to take such a leap, even in the name of love.

In the dining room, a small wedding cake decorated with red roses sat in the corner on a round table. The large mahogany dining table that consumed the center of the room had been laid out with a gourmet feast of buffet items, from a four-tiered glass seafood extravaganza to a smoked salmon on cut crystal to a shining silver platter offering a scrumptious prime rib. Small matching glass bowls offered sides such as cranberry sauce, whipped sweet potatoes, steamed asparagus, and a tomato and mozzarella salad. Shelby's family had outdone themselves, and Liv marveled at it all being pulled together in such a short time.

"Please help yourselves to the buffet," Jasper announced, with his arm around the shoulder of his beaming wife. "There are tables and chairs set up through those doors, or outside on the veranda. And once the living room is cleared from the wedding, there will be music and dancing. Enjoy yourselves!"

Liv and Jared made their way around the buffet table. She lined shrimp around the outside of her plate, and placed a slice of prime rib right in the middle. One dab of this side dish, one dab of another one, and Liv's china plate was heaped with food when she and Jared made their way to a table on the veranda.

White twinkle lights glistened in the trees and around an ornate wrought iron fence, and each table had donned a dark red linen tablecloth. In the center of each sat a small glass dish that held two floating candles and one perfect white gardenia. The flowers' faint scent whispered in the air above the wedding guests who chose an outdoor setting for their meals.

"It's hard to believe it was just this morning that we were collecting the remnants after the storm."

"I was thinking that earlier," Liv replied. "Florida weather is so odd."

"Well, it's beautiful now."

"I can't believe what an amazing job Shelby's parents did putting this together," Liv told Jared in a hushed voice.

"You know what Vivian said about seeing something in Shelby that she'd never seen before?"

"Yes."

"Well, I'm not sure I've ever seen that look in Rand's eye before either. I think he's really committed to Shelby."

"Does that surprise you?"

"Maybe a little," Jared grinned. "He hasn't been the settle-down type of kid."

"Ladies' man?"

"To say the least."

"All that appears to have changed now that he's met the right girl," Liv offered, popping a large shrimp into her mouth. "I'm really happy for them both."

"You know what? I am too."

"I can tell."

Jared reached around the centerpiece and touched Liv's finger where her hand rested on the table.

"You know what I was thinking while I was standing up there with Rand?" he asked.

"No. What?"

"I was thinking how proud I am to have raised such a brave young man."

"He's remarkable, Jared. You have every right to be proud."

"I mean, when I compare Rand and Shelby to us—"

"To us?"

"Well, look at them. They met, they just knew it was something special, and, despite the misgivings about it being too soon, they had the courage to reach for it. That's very brave."

"I suppose you're right."

"I wish we were that brave."

She set down her fork and looked up at Jared. In his eyes she saw something akin to regret but also an unmistakable dash of hope.

"I think in our case," he went on, "our age and experience have acted against us. It's hard to be brave when you're so busy being sensible."

Liv laughed. *Sensible* was the perfect word for what they were—so sensible that it almost made her want to scream.

Music began to play in the distance, and Jared arched a brow.

"Old Blue Eyes," he commented, looking into the air as if watching Sinatra himself perform in the trees. "Classic. Let's dance!"

Before she could accept, he had her by the hand, leading her into the living room, which was now transformed into a beautiful ballroom with dim, gold-tinted light shining from a large chandelier. A small, six-piece orchestra sat on a platform with a male singer in front, decked out in an old-fashioned dark suit with a skinny black tie.

Jared twirled her once for dramatic flair before leading Liv toward him for a dance. They were one of only about five other couples on the dance floor, and Liv felt as if they were the only ones on planet earth, swaying to the music, she wrapped up in his arms, her head nestled into the curve of his shoulder.

And Disneyland thinks they are The Happiest Place on Earth! She had a thing or two to tell Mickey and that was for sure.

As the song drew to a close, Jared leaned back and looked into Liv's eyes. There was a sleepy, somewhat dreamy quality to his expression that sent warmth radiating from her heart, and it traveled all the way to her toes and up to the top of her head.

"Liv, I—"

"Ladies and gentlemen," the singer interrupted. "Your hosts have asked that you all join them in the dining room for the cutting of the wedding cake."

Jared sighed. "We can't miss that. Shall we?"

Liv nodded, trying to smile over the top of the disappointment that she felt certain was streaming out of her eyes. What was Jared about to say?

It wasn't until they started off the dance floor that Liv noticed Georgia was half of one of the couples alongside them out there. When their eyes met, Georgia yanked her partner by the arm toward them, grinning from ear to ear.

"Preston, this is my new friend, Olivia Wallace," she crooned. "And Jared Hunt, the father of the groom and my boss."

"Congratulations," the man said as he shook Jared's hand. "Pleased to meet you both."

"Preston is Shelby's uncle from right here in Fort Myers."

"I guess you and Jared are family now then," Liv added.

"I suppose we are. They make a nice couple."

"I think so too," Liv said with a smile. "We were just heading in for some cake. Join us?"

Preston nodded, and Liv shot a quick thumbs-up signal to Georgia from behind him. The ear-to-ear grin she returned told Liv that she may have adjusted her attention from Jared to this new and distinguished target she'd come across.

Liv guessed his age at somewhere in the late fifties. With a full head of salt and pepper hair (mostly salt), clear blue eyes, and about half a foot of height on Georgia, they made a nice-looking couple. Liv sent up a quick, silent wish that something developed between the two of them, for several reasons, but mostly because Georgia deserved to find love. And this was a realization that Liv found both surprising and somewhat comforting.

"Oh, good, Dad!" Rand exclaimed as they entered the dining room. "Come stand next to us for the pictures. Olivia, you too."

The photographer's camera clicked off a dozen times before a slice of cake made it to a plate, and then a dozen more as Rand and Shelby fed one another dainty bites. Afterward, two waiters moved in to do the actual slicing and serving of a traditional white wedding cake with butter cream icing.

"So many people have the more exotic wedding cakes these days," Liv said to Jared after her first bite. "It's so nice to get a taste of real wedding cake with no fruit filling or some gourmet fondant frosting." At just that moment, Vivian floated by them. "The cake is exquisite, Vivian."

"Oh, thank you. Jasper's niece is a pastry chef in Sarasota, and she made it for us."

"The ceremony was just beautiful too. You've done such a lovely job putting it all together."

"I appreciate your saying that. I won't kid you, I was concerned. But it all came together just as it was supposed to."

"I think you're right," Jared told her.

Vivian reached out and patted his arm. "Enjoy yourselves," she added before continuing her rounds.

When they entered the ballroom again a few minutes later, half a dozen waiters were circulating with silver trays bearing crystal glasses of sparkling cider. Jared accepted two of them and then handed one to Liv.

"Thank you all for coming," Rand said through a microphone from atop the orchestra platform. Shelby stood beside him. "I think most of you already know that Shelby and I will be leaving for England in a few days, so it means that much more to us that we had the opportunity to share this night with the people closest to us." He and Shelby raised their glasses as he added, "So here's from us to you. With deepest gratitude and love, we ask that you and your families are all blessed and healthy in the months to come as we start our life together."

Everyone raised their glasses as well, and several congratulatory wishes popped from various points around the room before they all sealed the deal with a sip.

"Olivia, how about a trip around the dance floor with me?" Rand suggested as he walked toward her.

"I'd be honored."

Jared offered an arm to Shelby, and the four of them hit the floor to an instrumental version of *Moon River*.

"I used to roll my eyes at my dad when he'd pull out his vinyl record relics and play these old songs," Rand told Liv. "But when we were talking about what kind of band we wanted tonight, Shelby and I both thought it would be cool to get someone who could sing all the classics. We heard these guys play at her parents' anniversary party last week, and we were stoked when they had the date free. I'm sure my dad is on Cloud Nine."

"Oh, he is," she said with a chuckle. "We were outside having dinner when he heard something by Frank Sinatra. He got all dewy-eyed like he'd found a long-lost friend."

Rand laughed. "I can see it now."

"It was a beautiful wedding, Rand. I'm so happy for you and Shelby."

"Thanks, Olivia. I know a lot of people think we're out of our tree, but it's right for us to be together. I don't have a doubt about that."

"Some people never find that kind of confidence in a relationship. It's awe-inspiring."

"Good," he replied. "Maybe it will inspire you and my dad to take a chance on love, ya think?"

Liv grinned, smacked Rand on the shoulder, and leaned into his embrace to continue their dance in silence. After a moment, though, she tilted her head back and laughed out loud.

As the music wound down to a close, Jared approached them with Shelby on his arm.

"What are you two laughing about?" he asked, but Rand just shook his head.

"Your son has a filtering problem," Liv told him. "Whatever he thinks in his head comes straight out his mouth."

"Don't I know it."

"It's a gift," Rand added, and then he took his bride by the hand and walked away.

"How about we get some coffee and another piece of that cake?" Jared suggested.

"Sounds like a plan."

With his hand on the small of her back, Jared led Liv toward the dining room. While she doctored the coffee, he picked up two plates of cake, and they met up at the French doors leading outside.

"It's so mild out tonight," he commented. "Why don't we sit on the veranda again?"

At the same table where they'd enjoyed their meal, Liv leaned back in her chair and glanced up at the twinkling tree branches overhead.

"I'm not so happy about a hurricane being the reason for it," she said, "but I'm so glad I got to stay and see Rand get married."

"I'm glad of that too. It wouldn't have been the same without you. In fact—"

When he cut himself off, Liv turned toward him and asked, "In fact, what?"

"Well, I was going to say—in fact—the wedding isn't the only thing that wouldn't be the same without you."

"Oh," she replied knowingly.

"Life in general wouldn't be the same. That's why I hope you'll rethink this whole idea about—"

This time, it was Jared's ringing phone that sliced through the air.

This is getting to be a little ridiculous, Liv thought.

"Sorry," he said, slipping the cell phone out of his jacket pocket. "This is Jared Hunt."

Liv sighed and took a large bite of cake.

"Josie, settle down. She's right here with me," Jared said, and Liv inched to the edge of her chair. "Start at the beginning. What's happened to Hallie?"

20

"You made the choice to leave the clearing," Horatio reminded Prudence.

"I know."

"So why are you so sad when you're only doing what you decided to do?"

"Because I've decided that I may have decided something I didn't want to decide."

❧

You have your boarding pass?"

"Yes."

"And your bag?"

"Yes."

"Okay. And I have the car keys. I'll return it after your flight leaves and take a taxi back home." They moved forward in the line toward the security gate, and Liv pushed Boofer's plastic dog carrier along with them with her foot before turning to Jared with a smile. "Thank you so much, Jared. For everything. I'm just so sorry I have to go like this, before we were able to figure out—"

"Don't be ridiculous. Hallie's hurt, and she

needs you. You go to her, and we'll talk soon."

"It's only good-bye for a little while, anyway," she reasoned. "It's not like it's forever."

"Exactly."

"It's not like I'll never see you again. I mean, there are airplanes and long weekends. People do it all the time."

"Yes, they do."

Boofer barked from inside the carrier at her feet, and Liv reached inside and tickled her chin. "Don't worry. I'll be with you the whole time."

"I would have been happy to take care of her until Josie could come back."

"We don't know when that will be," Liv reminded him. "I think it will be better for them both if I take her up there with me."

"All right," he said, and then he grabbed her hand and held it between both of his. "Have a good trip, and call me when you get there."

"I will."

"Give my love to Josie. Tell her I'm here if she needs anything at all."

"I will."

Jared gazed into her eyes for a long, pregnant moment. "I'll miss you," he told her.

"I'll miss you too."

"This has been a remarkable couple of weeks, and I've developed feelings for you that I didn't know I knew how to feel."

"Next in line," the security guard called out to her. "Let's keep it moving."

"Have you ever noticed how often our conversations are interrupted?" Jared asked her.

"I've noticed."

"Come here."

She moved toward him, and he circled her with his arms, pulling her into a lingering kiss.

"Safe trip," he whispered as he released her.

Liv picked up her bag with one hand, and Boofer's carrier with the other. Just as she turned to walk through the security post, Jared touched her on the arm.

"I love you, Liv."

Tears sprang to the surface in Liv's eyes almost the moment the words were out, and they rolled down her face in streams with no warning at all.

"I love you too," she muttered, twisting away from him. She hurried through the checkpoint and, without looking back, she rushed down the hallway and rounded the corner, Jared's declaration echoing deep within her ears.

❧

Thump—thump—thump—thump—thump.

Each time her shoe landed on linoleum, it echoed as Liv ran down the long, sterile hospital corridor. The kids were just where Josie had said they would be, and Hallie's six-year-old saw Liv first, popping to her feet and running straight at her. Liv barely had time to set Boofer down on the floor and drop her bags before Katie clunked into her arms.

"Aunt Liv, my mommy had an accident, and she broke her spare ribs."

"I know, sweetheart. I talked to Granny Josie last night. I got here as soon as I could."

"You were at Granny's house in Florida?"

"Yes."

"Is that Boofer?" she asked, wiggling out of Liv's arms and crouching down to look inside. "Hi, Boofie. Did you fly on an airplane too?"

"Hi, Aunt Liv." Ten-year-old Scotty headed toward her while Jason, his thirteen-year-old brother, didn't even glance up at her from the hand-held computer game.

"Hi, Scotty. Can you take my bag and Boofer over there with you guys while I go see your mom?"

"Sure."

Liv froze in her tracks. Turning back with a second thought, she said, "Boofer's leash is in the outside pocket of my bag. Don't take her out of the carrier until you get outside the hospital doors, okay?"

"Yeah," Scotty replied.

"And make sure you put her back inside the carrier before you bring her back in. Is that clear?"

"I think we can figure out how to walk the dog," Jason cracked without looking up.

"Are there rules about no dogs in the hospital?" Katie asked her.

"That's exactly right, and we don't want to break any rules. So you're in charge, Katie Marie. You make sure Boofer is safe until I come back, okay?"

"Okay!" Katie seemed thrilled to be in charge of something, even if it was just a mess of a dog with a tendency toward gas.

"I'll be right back."

Liv hurried down the hallway, reading off the numbers out loud as she ran by the doors.

Room 1212. At last.

Josie and Hallie's husband Jim were in chairs on either side of the hospital bed, and they both stood up when she walked into the room.

"Oh, Pumpkin, it's good to see you," Josie said as she hugged her. Jim gave her a weary smile over Josie's shoulder.

"What do the doctors say today?"

"The surgery went well," Jim replied with a whisper. "They stopped the internal bleeding from the car accident, but they want to monitor her for a couple of days."

Liv stepped up to the side of the bed and looked down at her sleeping friend. Her cheekbone was bruised, and a small bandage was angled into her hairline on the same side of her face. A patch of dried blood formed the shape of a wobbly heart on the side of her neck. Liv doused a wad of tissues with water from the pitcher next to the bed and lovingly dabbed at the blood until it was gone.

"She apparently had some head trauma," Josie said, and Liv noticed for the first time that Hallie's mother looked exhausted.

"Have they mentioned how severe? Was there any swelling to her brain?"

"Yes. The doctor said it was minimal though."

"Good. That's good."

"It is?"

"Yes. If there's—"

Suddenly, a raucous noise from the corridor barreled closer, and Liv got a rather sick feeling in the pit of her stomach when tennis shoes squeaked on the floor and a cacophony of scampering paws drew nearer.

When Josie whispered, "Boofer! My Missy Boofer!" she knew the reason why.

"I'm sorry, Aunt Liv," Katie whimpered from the doorway. "Boofer must have known Granny Josie was here."

Liv turned to find Josie cradling Boofer like a baby, rocking her back and forth and cooing over her. The dog was in canine nirvana, whining and pawing Josie's face.

"Kathryn Marie," Jim chided.

"I know, Daddy. I was in charge. And I wasn't supposed to open the door until I got outside, but Jason and Scotty wouldn't help me carry the box, and I just opened the door wide enough to click on the leash, but Boofer pushed right out of the cage. I'm sorry, Aunt Liv."

"It's okay, honey. Will you go and bring me the carrier box so I can put her back inside?"

"Okay."

Jim rubbed his temple and closed his eyes.

"Can I get you something, Jim? Coffee? Some aspirin?"

He sighed and stared at her for a long moment before he answered. "Hallie's the one who deals with everything. I don't know how she does it, Liv."

"I know the feeling. I've asked myself that question about her a hundred times."

"My own kids are giving me a headache. How crazy is that?"

"I don't think it's crazy," she said, pulling him into an embrace. "I think it's human. This is a lot to deal with."

"You can *NOT* have a dog in this hospital!"

"I know," Liv said, approaching the stern nurse who appeared in the doorway. "I'm a nurse over at Providence, so I do know the rules. I came straight from the airport, and then she got loose by accident. But there's a little girl on her way back with the dog carrier as we speak. I'll take the dog out of here as soon as she gets here with it, I promise."

Just when Liv realized that her babbling sounded

a little like Katie's explanation of Boofer's escape, the woman's hardness melted slightly, and she turned away and left without a word.

"Why don't I take the kids—and Boofer—and go to the house. I'll put some dinner together for them, make sure they're ready for school tomorrow, and you two can come home whenever you're ready."

Katie thumped in, dragging the noisy carrier behind her. "They wouldn't help me carry it," she repeated.

Josie kissed Boofer on top of the head before leaning down and nudging her into the case. Liv closed and latched the door before any more mayhem could ensue.

"Wait, how are you going to get them home?" Jim asked. "How did you get here?"

"Taxi from the airport," she said. "We'll get home the same way."

"No, look," he groaned, producing keys from his pocket. "Take the car, and Josie, you go with them. I'll get a cab home later tonight."

"Or I can come back and get you."

"I'll call you."

Liv leaned down and looked Katie right in the eye. "Go tell your brothers to get their things together. We're going home."

Katie poked her head around the corner and peered at her mother in the bed. "Did Mommy wake up yet?"

"Not yet, sweetheart," Liv told her. "She's still so tired. But sleep is very good for her right now. While she's dreaming, her body is healing itself."

Katie scuffed out into the hall, and Liv hoisted Boofer's carrier off the floor. Josie leaned down and planted a kiss on Hallie's forehead, and then she followed Liv out the door.

"Olivia," Jim called, and she turned back toward him. He looked like a somewhat deflated version of his former self, and the smile he tried to raise just didn't quite make it. "Thank you."

Liv nodded, and then she started down the hall in the direction of the dull roar of arguing children.

Spaghetti may not have been the wisest choice for a dinner menu serving three rambunctious children, but Liv hadn't thought it through beforehand, and now, as she scrubbed tomato sauce off the wall behind the kitchen table, she made a mental note for the future.

"The dishwasher is loaded," Josie announced, "a pot of tea is brewing, and the children are in their bedrooms. Let's sit down for a chat."

"I just want to put some plastic wrap over Jim's salad."

"Done. Come and sit with me."

Liv rinsed the sponge with warm water, and then washed her hands, still drying them with a paper towel when she plopped down into the padded chair across the table from Josie.

"Tell me about your trip," Josie invited as she filled two cups with hot tea. "My Halleluiah tells me you and Jared have struck up a friendship. He's such a wonderful man, isn't he?"

"Indeed."

"And Rand?"

"Oh!" she exclaimed as she stirred sweetener into the cup. "You don't know. Rand got married yesterday."

"Married?!"

"I know," Liv laughed, shaking her head. "He met a sweet girl named Shelby, the two of them just sparked, and the next thing we knew they were planning to get married before Rand left for England."

"When does he go?"

"The end of the week."

"Jared must be heartbroken. First you, and now Rand. I know what it is to feel left behind."

Liv glanced up at Josie, and she wondered about that faraway look in her tired eyes.

"Speaking of being alone, catch me up on Clayton."

"He's improving every day. I called him this morning while I waited for my flight, and he was just as feisty as ever. He asked me to send you his love, though. And Hallie."

"The old geezer has a soft spot for me," Josie

commented, shaking her head. "Truth be told, I have a bit of one for him too."

"He's a good man. Once you get past the tough metal shell."

Josie laughed at that. "He sure does have a tough metal shell, doesn't he, Pumpkin?"

Boofer moseyed into the kitchen just then, and she seemed to have a hard time deciding which of them she wanted to approach. Finally, she lay down on the tile floor, right between them.

"You and Missy Boofer appear to have become good friends," Josie noted. "I'm happy to see that."

"She has a tough metal shell too," Liv said, chuckling. "But she's all marshmallow and soft cookie crunch once you get past it."

Josie beamed.

Liv found herself yawning, and she apologized as she shook it off. "I'm just so tired," she admitted. "I think I'll go next door and take a hot bath, and then sleep in my own bed tonight."

"You do that, Pumpkin."

Liv pushed herself up to her feet and stood over Josie for a moment. "Josie, I want to thank you so much for letting me borrow your home and your friends. I feel like a brand-new person. I needed something so badly, but I just didn't know what it was. Sanibel was just the right thing."

"I can see it in your eyes. I'm happy I could play a part in you finding your way again. Just take care not to lose sight of what you've learned about yourself."

Curiosity pinched at Liv, and she cocked her head. Before she could ask Josie what she meant, the woman stood up and pulled Liv into an eager embrace.

"Would you like to ride over to the hospital with me in the morning?" Liv asked her, and Josie nodded.

"Thank you. I'd like that."

"I'll call you."

The air was brisk, and Liv hurried across the yard toward her house, her luggage in tow. She'd become accustomed to mild nights and balmy breezes. Cincinnati weather was a far cry from that, but at least there was no more snow on the ground.

The house seemed cold, both in temperature and in reception. On her way down the hall toward her bedroom, she flicked the button on the thermostat twice to make it a little warmer. She dropped her bags inside the door, and then plopped down on the edge of the bed.

Maybe I'll skip the bath and just crawl into bed.

Minutes ticked by, and she just sat there, motionless.

I think I need to get myself a dog.

When she realized that she actually missed Boofer, Liv ripped into laughter. But Boofer wasn't the only one that she missed, and that realization melted the amusement away like water on a hot sidewalk in the midday sun.

She pulled her cell phone out of her purse and dialed.

"Jared?"

"I'm so glad you called. How's Hallie?"

"She was asleep when I got to the hospital, but they have her on pain medication, so that's to be expected."

"And you?"

"Me?"

"Yes, how are you?"

"I'm tired. And cold!" she declared, and Jared laughed. "It's fifty degrees here, which at one time I would have considered lovely spring weather. But now I can't seem to get warm."

"You turned into a Floridian when you weren't looking," he commented. She had no reply to that. "How is it being home?"

"Strange. My house hasn't seemed so empty since Robert died."

Jared was silent for a long moment. Then, "I haven't died, Liv. I'm still here."

21

The grass in the meadow was long and green, and the recent rains had left it fragrant and inviting.

But inviting as it was, Prudence didn't partake. It just wasn't the way she remembered. Or maybe, because she'd tasted the lush grasses surrounding the Enchanted Pond, she just didn't like this grass anymore.

"I'll likely starve to death now," she brayed.

"You won't starve," Horatio assured her.

"I will. I don't want the meadow grass any more. I only want the faraway grasses that I can't have."

"Well, that is a dilemma. Whatever will you do now?"

"I told you. I'll probably just starve to death."

Horatio covered his beak with his wing so Prudence couldn't hear how he hooted with laughter.

"That's a terrible fate," he said. "I wonder how you can avoid it."

Preston and I are driving over to that new Chinese place for dinner. Do you want to join us?"

Jared regarded Georgia with amused curiosity. "Just to clarify. This is the same new Chinese place that you warned Rand and me away from because of—what was it? grease and MSG?"

Georgia's gaze dropped to the concrete parking lot beneath her feet, and she blushed all the way down to her shoulders.

"Likes Chinese food, does he?"

"Loves it."

"So a little grease and MSG doesn't seem so bad now, huh?"

"Do you want to join us or not?" she said, looking up and stamping her foot ever so slightly.

"Nah, you go ahead. I'm going for a bike ride and then home to make dinner for Rand and Shelby."

"I guess they'll be leaving soon."

"Another couple of days and the happy married couple will be off to London."

"Leaving the old man far behind."

"There's a lot of that going around lately," Jared remarked, pulling open the door of her rental car for her. "Have a good time, Georgia, and give my best to Preston."

"Will do, Jared. Have a good evening."

Jared closed the distance between their cars and, by the time he thought to ask how much longer it would be before her Toyota was repaired from the rumble with a fallen tree, Georgia had already pulled out of the parking lot.

He slipped into his own car and turned over the engine, but then froze slightly as the CD loaded in the stereo queued up "their song." Jared dropped his hands from the steering wheel and leaned back into the leather seat with a sigh.

Had she really only been gone for less than forty-eight hours? It seemed like a lifetime already. And as the thought occurred to him that she might never come back, a lifetime without Liv seemed far too real a possibility.

Once he arrived home, Jared changed clothes in a rush, flew into the garage, and wheeled out his bicycle. He was pedaling at full speed before he ever turned out of the driveway. Bike riding with a vengeance; it had always been his favorite way of relieving stress. But the kind of thoughts plaguing him now were far more deeply rooted and tangled up than the simple pressures of a hectic day.

He steered his way around countless other riders, never once pausing to return their greetings with a casual wave or a nod. Jared shoved pedal over pedal over pedal without restraint until his leg muscles felt scorched. It wasn't until he was already parked on the bench, downing cool water from his plastic sipper, that the memory smoldered its way to the surface.

It was on another bench, far behind him now, that he'd shared lemonade with Liv. He almost wanted to laugh out loud when he thought about her behavior that day.

"My leg. My leg! MY LEG!!" she had shouted at him. "Make it stop."

Jared remembered how he'd tried to disguise his utter amusement as he pumped her leg out and back in an effort to relieve her pain.

"Better?"

"A little."

"We'll just rest a while longer."

"Like until tomorrow?"

There was a childlike, up-front honesty about Liv that had attracted him right off. He loved that about her. She was nothing short of adorable, and as he remembered it now, he felt something inside of him go hollow.

He bowed his head and clamped shut his eyes.

How am I going to live without her, Lord? Now that I know what it is to have her at my side, I don't know if I can do it. I want her with me, every day. Please do what you do best. It was a sheer miracle that you put us on that plane together that day. I know you can do that again. Bring us back together. Somehow.

Jared remembered Rand's wedding ceremony, and he marveled again at how brave the couple had been to accept the gift they'd been given without any doubts at all. No over-thinking it, no deep analysis. Just a general assurance in their hearts that this was the path meant for them.

Why was I too dense to take the leap the way Rand did? I should have dropped to one knee and proposed to her the second I realized that she was The One.

Recognizing that Liv might have run swift and fast in the opposite direction had he done just that, Jared pondered whether everything that had happened up to that moment might actually be a part of the grand scheme of things. Perhaps things had tripped along just as they'd been meant to unfold.

Just relax. Timing is everything.

On the ride home, he wondered where such a peaceful acceptance had come from. It was so unlike him to feel denied something he wanted with all of his heart, and then to simply accept the denial as a temporary thing.

It must be you, Lord, because I don't have that kind of wisdom.

❧

Liv stood at the side of the bed, brushing Hallie's honey-blonde hair. Hallie tipped her head back and grinned at her friend, and Liv gasped.

"Don't do that. I almost brushed your face."

"Thank you for doing this, Liv."

"Well, we couldn't have you looking like a mangy dog."

"How can you talk like that about Boofer?" Hallie teased. "I thought you two were friends now."

Liv brushed Hallie's hair on each side, collecting it at the back of her head and drawing it upward into a short little ponytail. She clasped it loosely with a blue band.

"There. That's better. Do you want to brush your teeth or wash your face or anything?"

"Liv," Hallie said, taking her by the hand. "Stop being my nurse. Sit down and be my friend. Talk to me."

As Liv rounded the corner of the bed and dropped to the chair, she noticed that Hallie winced.

"Are you in pain?"

"A little."

"Should I call the—"

"Olivia."

"Sorry."

"Have you spoken to Jared since you came back?" Hallie was nothing if not outspoken.

"I have. I called him the night I got in, and we talked for a few minutes."

"And?"

"And . . . then . . . we hung up."

"Don't make me work so hard for some details. I don't have the energy. Have you talked to him since?"

"Not since, no."

"And why not?"

"Hallie."

"Come on. Give. Tell me what's going on."

"Well, there's not much to tell, really. We have deep feelings for each other. I miss him already. But it's not like we didn't know the time would come. We always knew I'd come home and go back to work and that he'd go on with his life there."

"Do you know what your problem is, Olivia?"

"I have a problem?"

"Yes, you do. It's that you are inflexible."

"Inflexible!"

"You are," Hallie said, leaning back against the raised bed. "You get one plan in your head, and then you won't deviate from it no matter what other things are tossed in your path."

"That is just not true."

"Of course it's true."

"It's not. I was heading home a couple of days ago, but all the signs pointed to me staying. Jared came to the airport, and the weather turned, and . . . and . . ."

"It was a hurricane, Liv. God had to send a hurricane to stop you in your tracks and make it impossible for you to leave because you wouldn't pay attention to the more subtle signs. *Like falling in love with someone in Florida!*"

"Don't you need some more morphine?" Liv suggested with a grin. "You look tired. It will help you sleep."

"And shut me up?"

"That too."

"You know what my mother used to say?"

Josie walked through the door at just that moment, right on cue. "Don't keep me in suspense, darlin'. What did your brilliant mother used to tell you?"

"Hi, Mama."

The two exchanged a tender hug, and Josie kissed the top of Hallie's head.

"What did I used to say?" Josie asked as she scuffed the second chair toward the bed and sat down beside Liv.

"You used to say that sometimes we're so busy following what we think are the signs that we forget to go to God and just ask for His direction."

"Oh, I still say that."

Liv chuckled.

"Laugh it up, Liv," Hallie said, shaking her finger. "But I have a feeling, if you'd just pray for a little guidance and intervention, this would all be taken care of for you."

"I keep telling her she needs more pain medication," Liv said to Josie. "Don't you think she needs a long nap?"

"I do nothing but *nap* in this bed. Right now, I'm being smart and insightful for you. Sit back and enjoy it."

"Don't you have something insightful to say to someone else? How about your mother?" Liv prodded.

"In fact, I do," Hallie replied. "Mother, would you please tell Olivia what a catch Jared Hunt really is?"

"On that note," Liv declared, "I'll let the two of you visit so I can walk down the hall and make a couple of calls."

"Jared?" Hallie asked.

Liv didn't respond. She just wiggled her fingers at them over one shoulder and strolled out of the room.

Becky sounded winded as she answered the phone in response to Liv's call.

"Becky? This is Olivia Wallace."

"Liv! Where are you? Are you all right after that terrible storm?"

"I'm safe and dry and back in Cincinnati," she admitted with some reluctance. "I got a flight out yesterday."

"Oh, good! When can we expect you back at work then?"

"Well," she hesitated. "That's a bit of a conundrum. My best friend was in a car accident. In fact, I'm over here at Good Samaritan Hospital with her right now. She cracked two ribs and has a head injury."

"Oh, my."

"And Hallie has three young children."

"I see." Becky's voice was tempered with cool anticipation. "You're not coming back to us after all, are you, Olivia?"

"Yes! I mean, I want to. I was just hoping you would reconsider the timing of it and allow me to wait until next week."

Becky didn't respond right away, and Liv imagined the worst in those seconds of silence.

"All right. Let's say Monday."

Pheeeww.

"Thank you so much, Becky."

"But I do want you to know that I've checked with Dr. Bradley, and he said they aren't going to be filling the openings at the peds clinic until late fall."

"Oh." She felt the disappointment drop within her until it thudded at the bottom of her stomach. "That's a shame."

"She's willing to consider you then," she added. "I've set up a meeting for the two of you to discuss it. Next week, Thursday, at four o'clock."

"Thanks, Becky. There's some hope then."

"Oh, there's always hope, Olivia. You would

know that better than anyone. We're so happy that you're healthy again and ready to come back to us."

Ready? That might be an overstatement.

"Thank you. I'll check in next Monday then."

Liv sat down on the edge of one of the chairs in the lobby and stared at the cell phone in her hand. When she finally dialed Jared, the call went to voice mail, and she hung up without leaving a message.

She stopped at the coffee cart and ordered two lattes and a cup of tea for Josie before heading back to Hallie's room. When she reached the doorway, though, she stopped just short of going in. She could hear Hallie whispering, and she didn't want to intrude.

"Oh, Father, she won't ask for herself," she clearly heard Hallie say. "So I'm asking you for her. Somehow, some way, Lord, if Liv and Jared are meant to be together, we just ask that you start laying the groundwork now to make it happen. They're too ignorant to do it on their own, but miracles are what you do best. So make their crooked places straight and lead them to your will for their futures."

"Oh, yes, Lord. Show them the way to their destiny," Josie added. And then they both agreed and harmonized a subdued, "Amen!"

Liv leaned against the wall outside the room for several seconds, mulling over what she'd just heard before turning the corner and joining them at Hallie's bedside.

The three of them sat in a semicircle, chatting for almost two hours over their coffees and tea. They touched on every subject under the sun, laughing like schoolgirls when Liv told them about the alligator in the swimming pool and the late afternoon bike ride with Jared that nearly crippled her for the rest of her life. Hallie and Josie gasped in unison at the tale of Morey's untimely death and Boofer's spontaneous exhumation of the body, and they roared when Liv recalled the first morning when she came across Clayton doing laps in Josie's swimming pool.

"It sounds like you had a great time," Hallie said, both arms folded across her ribs, trying not to laugh anymore and wincing when she did.

"I really did," Liv replied, dabbing at her eyes with a tissue. "I loved it down there."

"I told you so," Hallie cried. "Didn't I tell you so?"

"Well, you were right. The water out in the Gulf is just as green as an emerald, and the sky is just so perfect and blue. I think it would be impossible not to find that renewing."

"Oh, that's right," Josie exclaimed. "Hallie told me you went for a ride on Jared's boat. He's offered many times, but I've never taken him up on that yet."

"You have to, Josie. It's just exquisite out on that water. There's nothing quite like it to bring things into clear perspective."

"I'd say you need another trip out then," Hallie remarked.

Liv chose to ignore the comment.

"I thought I'd make lasagna for the children tonight," Josie told them. "Does Jim like lasagna?"

Liv's heart sank a little, and then she smiled. "Your lasagna is fantastic, Josie."

"Good. You had the one I left in the freezer for you?"

"Jared and I had it for dinner one night. We both thought it was the best we'd ever tasted."

"What a sweet thing to say, Pumpkin. Would you like to join us for supper tonight then?"

She knew it seemed silly, but Liv didn't want to have Josie's lasagna again without Jared.

"That sounds great, but I think I'll pass. I have such a lot of things to catch up on at home. But tomorrow, after the kids go to school, I thought I'd come over and help get things ready for Hallie to come home."

"Like what?" Hallie interjected. "You don't need to do that. We don't even know yet when that will be."

"I just thought of a couple of things. Like I figured I'd change the linens on your bed and maybe bring over a few pillows so you'll have some backups to prop yourself up in bed."

Hallie sighed, and her head fell to one side as tears welled in her eyes. "You're such a good friend," she said, and then she looked at Josie. "So are you, Mama. I'm so blessed."

"We're just happy to have you with us," Liv told her. "Don't ever scare us like that again."

"I'll do my best."

Just then, Liv's cell phone jingled, and she looked at the screen to find it was originating from a number in Florida. But it wasn't Jared's.

"Hello?"

"Olivia, how are you? This is Georgia Brown."

"Georgia," she said, and then pulled a face at Hallie before heading for the door. "I'm well, thank you. How are you doing?"

"I'm well too. I've just had my second date with Preston. Do you remember meeting him at Shelby and Rand's wedding?"

"Of course. Cary Grant, the later years."

Georgia cackled at that and then sighed. "Yes. We've had dinner two nights in a row now, and I have to admit to you, honey, he steams up my windows."

It was Liv's turn to laugh. "You're a hoot, Georgia."

"Listen, honey, the reason I'm calling is that I heard something this morning that I thought, well, this is just meant for Liv to hear."

"What's that?"

"Remember that conversation we had in the car the night of the first storm? When you told me you wanted to make a move to pediatrics?"

"Yes, I remember."

"Well, I was having lunch with my girlfriend, Marge, today. She works at the pediatric clinic down here, and she told me she's looking to fill two slots for nurses with emergency training. Well, you coming from the O.R. and being so wonderful with children, I had to tell her all about you. And she asked me to send you her information and maybe give her a call if you would be interested in filling one of those slots."

Liv wasn't sure which part to react to first. The fact that Georgia thought to do that, or the fact that she was making a semi-offer of employment based on something she knew Liv wanted so badly.

"Sugar? Are you still there?"

"Yes, I'm here."

"You know how those cell towers are. I thought maybe you were dropped."

"No, I'm still here. I'm just . . . well . . . stunned."

"I know, Sugar. I just have to believe this is one of those opportunities you don't let pass you by. I mean, I don't know what your plans are with Jared, and I haven't had the courage to come right out and ask him, but it could mean a reunion for the two of you, don't you think?"

"I—"

"Well, at any rate, I wanted to ask you if you have an email address so I can send you Marge's details. Then the ball is on your bat, and you can decide what to do from there."

"Yes, I have email."

"Okay, then. What's the address? I have pen in hand right now."

Liv gave her the email address, repeating it twice at Georgia's request. Her heart was racing and so were her thoughts. Hallie and Josie's prayer bounced around her brain like a roller coaster about to slip off its track.

Start laying the groundwork. Show them the way to their destiny.

Liv pushed back as hard as she could as the hope that this was part of that plan began to rise inside of her. Could this be the first section of the road that would lead her back to Jared? An old scripture played in her ears.

Hope deferred makes the heart sick.

She didn't want to start hoping too soon for something that probably wasn't going to happen.

What's the rest of that verse? she wondered. *Hope deferred makes the heart sick . . .*

"I have an old scripture verse playing over in my mind," she told Hallie and Josie when she returned to the room. "Hope deferred makes the heart sick. What's the rest?"

Josie and Hallie exchanged secretive pirate smiles.

"But when the desire comes," Josie said, "it is a tree of life."

Liv rolled the words over in her mind, and then her heart raced out of control.

When the desire comes . . .

22

"But what if I hope and hope and hope, and I never get what I'm hoping for?"

"Then all you've wasted is a bit of wishing time," Horatio offered. "But what about this? What if you hope and hope and hope, and you get what you've been hoping for? What then?"

❦

Jared couldn't help but think about the last time he'd taken someone to the airport. The citrus scent of Liv's shampoo rose in his nose and tickled him with the memory of her. It had been so hard to let her go that day, so hard to be without her every day since.

"They're going to board us in a minute, Dad."

He pushed himself up and out of the uncomfortable terminal chair and walked toward Rand, pulling him into an embrace.

"Call me when you get there."

"I'll email, Dad. It will be the middle of the night your time."

"I don't care what time it is."

"He says that now," Rand joked to Shelby.

"But when the phone rings at two a.m. he reverts into his father voice."

Shelby chuckled as she hugged Jared. "Thank you for everything," she said with a whisper as he held her. "Especially for your son."

"He's all yours now," Jared replied. "No refunds or exchanges."

"I don't think we have to worry about that."

She tucked her hair behind her ear and smiled at him as she backed away—a sweet, angelic smile that made Jared's heart thump harder. If he'd spent years searching for the perfect wife for his son, the woman who would make Rand's heart skip a beat, the one who would jump enthusiastically into a life with him with both feet, Jared wasn't sure he could have found her. Fortunately for Rand, he'd searched on his own and seemed to know just where to look to find Shelby.

"Safe trip," he called to them, and Rand gave one last wave before turning the corner, hand-in-hand with his bride.

Instead of heading straight for the car, Jared sank into a nearby chair and crossed his ankle over the opposite knee.

It seems I'm always saying good-bye to the people I love. There's something intrinsically wrong with that. Isn't it time for me to start something, rather than seeing everything end?

Liv opened the email message waiting in her inbox from Georgia@HuntFamilyMedical.com.

Olivia, here is Marge's information. She's excited to hear from you, and I'm hopeful that you'll give this opportunity a fair shake. Could be I'll see you again soon? Hope so! Sweet Georgia Brown.

She hit reply.

Georgia, thank you so much for forwarding this to me, and for putting in a good word with your friend. How's it going with Preston? Are you two in love yet?
Liv

She'd never asked Jared for an email address, but she guessed from seeing Georgia's that his would be in the same format. So she opened a new message box and addressed it to Jared@HuntFamilyMedical.com.

Hi, Jared. I hope this reaches you. I've been thinking about you so much, wondering if you'd seen Rand and Shelby off to England yet. I know it's

going to be difficult for you to say good-bye, but what a different boy who will be getting on that plane from the one who arrived. You've raised such a kind-hearted and passionate young man.

Well, I just wanted you to know that my thoughts are with you. I hope to hear from you soon.

All my love,

Liv

Liv kissed the tip of her index finger and touched it to the screen before hitting the send button.

Opening another new email screen, she pasted in the address Georgia had sent and composed another email.

Dear Marge,

Our mutual friend, Georgia Brown, sent me your email address and suggested that I contact you for more information about a position you are currently trying to fill for a pediatric nurse. I'm on the waiting list at Providence Hospital here in Cincinnati for just such a position after several years in the O.R., so I appreciate Georgia thinking of me when you mentioned your opening. I'm

not entirely certain about a move to Florida at this time, but I'm interested enough to hope that you will send me some details on the job so that I can give it consideration. I've attached an updated resume, and I look forward to hearing back from you soon. Thank you so much for your interest and attention.
Sincerely,
Olivia Wallace

It took a good deal more consideration before she clicked the send button again. But she did press it at last, and watched as the email flew away into cyberspace.

Liv deleted two weeks of spam and answered a few more entries from the inbox before she realized that new mail had arrived from Jared. She was excited to open it, biting her lip as she waited.

Liv, I'm so happy to hear from you. I don't remember giving you this address, but I'm glad that you have it. How did you come by it anyway?
Yes, I took Rand & Shelby to the airport just this afternoon, and it was a humbling experience to say good-bye yet again to someone who has brought meaning to my life. I'm feeling like the

lonely old man left behind when everyone else has moved forward with their
lives.

I was thinking on the drive back a while
ago that I'd sure love to hear from you
about Hallie, about Josie, about anything. I miss your laugh and the way
your hair smells. I miss everything about
you.

Clayton is doing well. In fact, I'll bring
him home from the hospital first thing
tomorrow. Georgia is shopping for
"healthy options" for stocking his refrigerator, and I can only imagine the reception that sort of thing will receive! Please
send everyone my love and give me a
call soon. Another thing I miss: your
voice.

Lonely old Jared Hunt, M.D.

Liv couldn't seem to wash the smile off of her
face. The joyful impact of such a short little
email from Jared bordered on the ridiculous,
she knew, and yet she felt as if she could almost
fly. Or sing. Or maybe even dance.

She wanted so much to shoot off another
email to him, telling him about the lead Georgia
had sent her way, and she wondered if perhaps
Georgia had told him already. Conflict raced
through her, and she wasn't sure whether she

was more worried about building up his hopes before she had all the facts or if the greater concern was that she would crowd him by considering a move across the length of the country to be near him. He hadn't come right out and asked her to—at least not since she'd left.

Why was she so afraid of making a grab for the brass ring? She had not one single doubt that a life with Jared would fulfill her contentment quotient for the rest of her days. So why couldn't she just let go and reach out to make it happen?

❧

Clayton refused the arm Jared offered. He seemed determined to make it up the front stairs without assistance. It took him several minutes to get through the door, but his face told Jared that he was relieved to be back home.

"Why don't you head into your room and climb into bed?" Jared suggested. "I'll sort out your medications and bring them in."

"I'm not gonna go to bed," Clayton retorted. "I'll sit right here in my easy chair so I can watch television."

"I want you taking it easy for the next two or three days, Clayton. Then I'll work with you on some stretches and merging some controlled exercise into your routine."

"Eh," he grunted, waving Jared off like a buzzing mosquito. "Ya worry too much, Doc."

"And you don't worry enough. Get comfortable, wherever you're going to be."

Clayton plunked down into his favorite chair and then yanked on the lever to lift the footrest off the ground. Jared shook his head and moved into the kitchen.

He produced a weekly pill dispenser with two rows, one for morning medications and another for the evening pills, and filled the container for the week. Just as he snapped the bottom row of lids into place, Georgia called out from the front door.

"What in Sam Hill are you doing here?" Clayton complained.

"I've come bearing nutrition," she snapped back. "Mind your manners."

Georgia stepped into the kitchen and rolled her eyes at Jared.

"He's a real charmer, isn't he?" Jared teased.

"I can hardly contain myself."

"Need some help putting that away? What do you have here?"

"I got him some fresh fruit and vegetables. I cleaned and sliced some strawberries, cantaloupe, and orange sections and put them in plastic bowls to make it easy for him to snack on. I have a bowl of tomato-cucumber salad, some asparagus, a little baked chicken with beans, and a nice gelatin salad. They're all in plasticware, labeled and ready for him to whine about."

Jared chuckled. "And you know he will."

"Yes, I'm fully prepared for that."

"For what?" Clayton barked as he appeared in the doorway. "What're you prepared for?"

"For you, you old coot."

"What's that you're loadin' into my icebox? That's not the garbage can, you know. Trash goes out back."

"Georgia put a lot of effort into making sure you have three square meals for the next week, Clayton."

"All the fresh items are cleaned and sliced and ready to eat," she told him as she stacked them inside the refrigerator. "And these up here on the top shelf are microwave ready. The heating instructions are written on the top. See here?"

"Yeah, I see it. Any cake in there?"

"No cake," she replied. "But there are some low-fat muffins over there on the counter. I baked them myself."

"Muf-fins. What in Sam Hill am I gonna do with low-fat muf-fins? 'Livia made me cake. I like cake."

"You're a piece of work, Clayton Clydesdale. I don't know why I went to so much trouble for you. Muffins are just cupcakes without the frosting. That's cake."

"Yeah? Well, I'll be the judge and let you know."

"You do that."

"Clayton," Jared interjected, "I want to see you in that chair, or in your bed. I'll bring you something to drink and go over your medications with you. Georgia will be stopping by once a day to help you get around, see if you need anything, and then I'm just a phone call away at any time."

"Eh, stop hoverin'," he said. "Just go on and leave me alone. I don't need any of ya."

He stomped out of the kitchen, and they heard the groan of the easy chair as he propelled himself into it and raised the footrest.

"Thank you for all you've done, Georgia. It's much more than he deserves."

"Ha! That's the truth."

"I'll be another ten minutes here," he said. "Would you like to have dinner after? It's on me, by way of a thank-you for putting up with this old codger."

"Really?" she asked. "After the day I've had, I would love that, Jared. Thank you."

"And if you're open to it, I'd like you to go somewhere with me afterward."

"Where?"

"Let's just save that for after dinner."

❧

Liv returned from the market with four bags of groceries. After they were put away, she unloaded the dryer for the fourth and final time that day. Her bag was unpacked, her laundry caught up, and her bed linens fresh and waiting to offer a good night's sleep.

As she folded the batch of warm towels, she considered whether to take a walk next door and check in on Jim, Josie, and the kids. Instead, she picked up her cell phone and dialed Jared.

"Liv, how are you?"

"A little restless or something today," she admitted. "I just wanted to hear your voice. Are you busy?"

"Well, I am in the middle of something. Can I call you in an hour or so?"

"Sure, I'll talk to you later."

"What? Wait!" he said, and she could hear the hum of someone else talking in the background. "Liv, are you still there?"

"Yes."

"Hold on a minute. Georgia wants to say hello."

Georgia. He's too busy with Georgia to have a five-minute conversation?

"Liv? How are you, sugar?"

"Hi, Georgia. I'm doing okay. How are you?"

"Well, I'm a little out of sorts," she replied. "Preston and I aren't seeing each other anymore."

"Oh, I'm so sorry. What happened?"

"I'll tell you all about it another time. Jared took me out for a lovely dinner, and I'm feeling better already. But right now he's hurrying me along, so I'd better go. I'll talk to you soon, all right?"

"Umm, okay. Have a nice—"

"Bye-bye, honey."

And the line closed immediately.

"Bye," she snapped, even though there was no one on the other end to hear it.

Liv's stomach began to churn and so did her imagination with a connect-the-dots progression that set her heart to pounding.

Georgia and Preston split . . . Georgia turns to Jared . . . Jared takes pity on her and takes her out for dinner . . . Now he doesn't have time to talk to me because he and Georgia are on their way somewhere else.

"What in the world?"

She'd have wagered that Georgia was going to turn out to be a friend. But now that Jared was back in her line of sight, all bets were off.

But what about Jared? Would he really strike up a relationship with Georgia? These were thoughts that just screamed out for ice cream to wash them down with.

Liv grabbed the pint of coffee-flavored Häagen Dazs she'd just put into the freezer, plucked a spoon from the drawer, and set out to do just that. Half an hour later, most of the pint was gone, but her nagging doubts about her conversation with Georgia still lingered.

23

"It's the oddest thing," Prudence confessed. "I seem to think I see the stallion a dozen times a day. Earlier, I could have sworn I spied him galloping down the hill into the meadow."

"But?" Horatio prodded.

"But it was just the shadow of an eagle flying high."

"I suppose it will be a while for both of us before we stop missing the Enchanted Pond and the new friends we made there."

"I'm not sure I'll ever stop missing them."

"I know it feels that way now," Horatio said, "but life has a tendency to move on. We'll make other friends, and so will they. Time tends to heal most wounds."

"You know what I wish? I wish we could push up the clock so our lonesome wounds would be all healed up."

꽃

Liv almost could have forgotten that she was in Ohio when her morning started out at 5:45

a.m., sounding very much like just about every morning on Sanibel Island.

She didn't have any idea how long Boofer had been barking, but by the time she limped sleepily into the kitchen, the dog was at her back door, scratching the grain right off the wood. When she opened the door, Boofer tore into the house and ran the entire length of it, from the kitchen through the dining room and down the hall into the bedroom.

"Boofer!" Liv called, and when she reached her, Boofer stood at attention in the center of her bed, panting. "What in the world is wrong with you? What are you doing over here? You belong next door now."

Boofer snarled and growled, and then the tirade resumed.

Liv approached the dog on tiptoe and then sat down on the bed beside her and stroked the top of her head and the back of her neck. In a very soft voice, she said, "Boofer, you're fine. Nothing to worry about."

The dog seemed to believe her because she circled the pillow twice and then lay down against it.

"Just like old times," Liv whispered, and then she crawled under the blanket, fluffed the other pillow, curled up next to Boofer, and closed her eyes.

Bang-bang-bang-bang-bang.

Liv popped out of bed and Boofer barked all the way down the stairs. Someone was hammering out a warning on the kitchen door. She looked at the clock and discovered that it was seven-thirty. She had slept for nearly two more hours.

"Scotty, what on earth are you doing?" she exclaimed as she opened the door to the ten-year-old.

"Boofer's missing!" he shouted, and then he scratched his head and laughed as the dog stood before him, yowling. "Oh, I guess not."

"She scratched at my door before dawn. I let her in so I could get some sleep. Go ahead and take her home, and then you get to the bus stop, young man."

"Daddy said we could stay home from school today."

"He did not."

"He did! Mom's coming home from the hospital."

"She is? When did he find that out?"

"Last night. We're gonna have a party for her. Oh, yeah. I was supposed to invite you to the party. It's at about two o'clock, and Granny Josie says you don't have to bring anything but your smile."

Liv chuckled. "Okay. Tell her I'll be there early to help you guys decorate. I'll come around noon, and we can put up signs and balloons."

"Coooo-ol," he said, bobbing his head as he thought it over. "Come on, Boofer. Granny is sure gonna give you what for."

"Tell her to give her some for me too."

Scotty snickered as he pulled the dog into his arms and headed out the back door and across the lawn.

The happy news that Hallie was being released sent a surge of excitement through Liv. She put the coffee on and made some toast with blackberry jelly. After she poured a cup, she took her breakfast with her to the desk in the corner of her bedroom.

Remembering that she still had banner paper left over from a co-worker's retirement party, Liv pulled up the banner-making application, typed in the words *welcome home mommy,* added a couple of graphics, and then loaded the paper into the printer. It took about five minutes for the entire thing to print out and feed through, so she concentrated on her toast and coffee while it did.

After she rolled the banner and fastened it with two paper clips, Liv went to her closet and stared at the contents. Even though the ground was no longer frozen over with snow and ice, she knew there would be no more sundresses, sandals, or shorts for a while. She pulled out a pair of faded black jeans that she hadn't worn in forever, and the mint green sweater she'd bought on clearance last spring and never wore because, somewhere between then and now, she'd decided the cropped sweater that laced all the way up the front with a leather cord was too "young" for a tired cancer patient with a fiftieth birthday barreling toward her.

But Liv didn't feel too old for that sweater now. Her trip to Florida and meeting Jared had revived her somehow. And to prove it, she reached into the white box at the very back of the closet floor and pulled out the other item she'd been hiding from for two years for the same reason.

After getting showered and dressed, Liv sat down on the bed and opened the large white box. She ran her hand over the long suede leg of one of the black boots tucked inside.

Nope, she decided. *These are just a little too* Pretty Woman. *What was I thinking when I bought these?!*

She used the bathroom mirror to fluff her loose spiral curls and dab on a bit of makeup. She chose a large pair of hammered metal earrings and a braided silver thumb ring to finish off the look. Standing in front of the mirror, Liv couldn't help shaking her head and chuckling. She was a different woman. And the change felt really, really good.

Even if the worst happened, and she never saw Jared again, or if he fell over to the dark side and took up with Georgia, Liv knew she would at least have this restoration. She was fifty again —not a hundred and fifty. Most important of all, she no longer saw cancer as she looked at her reflection.

All in all, two weeks on Sanibel Island had changed her, and Liv closed her eyes and thanked God for bringing her back to life.

❧

"A little more to the right. No, that's too far. Go back."

The chair wobbled slightly beneath her, and Josie and the kids screamed as Liv regained her footing.

"It's going right here!" she declared, and she poked a thumb tack into the corners of the WELCOME HOME MOMMY! banner before hopping down from the chair.

She stood back and looked at it, all three kids at her side.

"It needs something," Scotty declared.

"Balloons!" Katie shouted, and Liv nodded.

"That's it. Let's hang some balloons on each side of it."

"You blow 'em up, Scotty," Katie cried. "And Jason can tie the knots. I'll get the ribbon."

"What am I supposed to do?" Jason asked, irritated. "Just tie the knots? That's lame."

"You'll supervise too," Liv suggested. "Make sure they're hung in the right place."

Jason appeared to be all over the idea of supervising his younger siblings.

"Can we put candles on the cake, Aunt Liv?" Katie beamed. "Like if it was Mommy's birthday or something?"

"That's a great idea," Liv replied. "I'll go see if there are any candles in the drawer."

Liv walked into the kitchen to find that Josie had overheard and retrieved a box of birthday candles. She joined Josie at the kitchen table as she poked them into the top of the cake.

"What's with that smile you're sporting?" Liv asked her. "You look like you just ate the canary."

"Do I?" she replied in a sing-song voice. "I guess I'm just so happy that Halleluiah is doing so well, and coming home where she belongs."

"That's an interesting name," Liv said. "What made you name her Halleluiah?"

"Her father wanted a baby girl," Josie explained. "All through the eight and three-quarters months that I carried her, he hoped and prayed for a little girl. And when she was finally born, after the nurses counted all her fingers and toes, and they told Hosea that he'd gotten the girl he wanted, the first words out of his mouth were words of praise. And he hollered, 'Well, Halleluiah!' It seemed like the perfect name for the baby girl we'd waited so long to bring into this world."

Liv grinned. "It's a great name."

"Oh, she hated it her whole life. 'Mama, no,' she'd say. 'Don't call me that in front of my friends. Call me Hallie. I'm begging you, Mama.'"

They shared a laugh, and Liv nodded with confidence. "I can hear her saying that."

"She's a special blessing," Josie remarked, and Liv noticed that her expression had turned quite serious. "I'm so thankful that she's going to be whole and healthy again."

"You know, Hallie was a rock for me when I was sick. She cooked for me. She pushed back my hair when the chemo overwhelmed me. On the worst nights, she even sat by my bed and just read to me in that soft, sweet voice of hers. I couldn't even tell you what she was reading. Only that she created a soothing hum that carried me through."

"That must have been an awful time for you, Pumpkin."

"It was," Liv agreed, and then a smile broke over her face like the dawn of a new day. "But you know what? It's behind me now. And I'm happy and strong again. I can't really remember if I've ever felt like this."

"Must be love."

Liv's heart fluttered. "Pardon?"

"Oh," Josie said, shaking her head. "Just something my mama used to say. If something was going right, or we kids were in good spirits, she would say, 'It must be love.' "

At just that moment, Katie exploded into the kitchen, hopping from one foot to the other. "She's here! Mommy's home!" And just as quickly, she disappeared.

"Mommy's home," Liv mimicked, and she gave Josie an over-the-top excited smile. "She's home!"

Katie scuffled back into the kitchen, just long enough to shout, "Somebody's with her!"

"That's your daddy," Liv responded, but the little girl was gone again.

Josie touched Liv's arm as she passed, and Liv followed her out into the living room where they were all gathered in front of the picture window.

Jim helped Hallie out of the car while someone else stood behind the open trunk, pulling out a folded wheelchair.

"Who's that with them?" Liv asked Josie, and the woman returned an awkward shrug and then turned away.

The third person rolled the wheelchair around the car and toward Hallie. She sat down in it, grimacing and supporting her ribs with both arms.

Liv's heartbeat suddenly picked up the pace and cold perspiration percolated on her upper lip, across her forehead, and in the hollow of both palms.

"It's Dr. Jared!" Katie cried. "Dr. Jared is with them."

Once Katie was out the door, the boys followed suit. Scotty jumped the shrubs lining the sidewalk and reached Hallie first.

"Whoa, whoa, whoa!" Jim called. "Go easy. Your mom's very fragile, kids."

Jared stepped aside, allowing Jim to push Hallie up the walk toward the house. From opposite sides of the hubbub of children's voices and excited greetings, Liv and Jared homed in on one another. When he smiled, something in her stomach jumped.

"Step back, Katie. Let me get your mother into the house."

Hallie reached up and grabbed Liv's hand. "Surprise," she mouthed, and then Jim rolled her forward.

"What on earth?" Liv said, as Jared reached her and wrapped her up in his arms without a word. "What are you doing here?"

"What do you think?"

"Come on in, everyone," Josie directed. "Let's let my daughter get comfortable. What do you need, Hallie? Something cold to drink? A snack?"

"I just want to look at my family," she replied. "It's good to be home."

Jim knelt at her side, took her hands in his, and stared into her eyes. "It doesn't work without you."

Hallie tried to smile, but the tears that rose in her eyes melted it. Stroking the side of Jim's face, she told him, "I know that feeling."

"Hey, Mommy, did you see the sign?" Katie interjected.

"I did," she answered, releasing the shared moment with her husband with evident reluctance. "It's beautiful."

"Aunt Liv made it on her computer."

"Did she?" Hallie cast Liv a quick smile. "Did you kids say hello to Dr. Jared? He came all the way from Florida to see us."

Katie took Jared's hand and led him toward the kitchen. "Wanna see Mommy's cake?"

"I'd love to," Jared replied, looking back at Liv as they went along. "I do love a good cake."

"Me too!" Katie exclaimed, as if they were the only two people on earth who could truly appreciate cake.

Liv followed them and stood in the doorway as Katie led Jared toward the table and leaned in for a cautious closer look.

"This one's real good too. It's vanilla inside, with red raspberries in the middle. We had the same one for Papa's birthday, and Mommy said it was the best cake she ever had."

"How clever of you to remember that," Jared told her. "And then to get her the same one for her Welcome Home party."

"I was the one who remembered! See it? Isn't it pretty?"

"It really is," Jared replied.

His attention darted toward Liv for a quick moment, and then his focus was back on Katie, right where the little girl wanted it.

"It was my idea to put the candles on it too. Like if it was her birthday or something."

"Oooh, good one. She'll like that."

"Katie, come here, sweetheart."

The little girl tossed Jared's hand away like a used napkin and ran toward her mother's voice. Liv stepped out of the way just in time to avoid a collision.

"You're a sight for my lonesome eyes," Jared said, leaning back on the counter and regarding her like a long-lost prodigal.

"You didn't sound so lonesome," she replied. "Too busy to talk to me because you were having dinner with Georgia."

"Jealous?"

"No."

Jared beamed. "You're jealous."

"I am not."

"Come on," he said, swaggering toward her with an infuriating grin. "Admit it. You're jealous of me having a simple meal with another woman."

"Oh, please." She forced a soured expression. "You're an arrogant fool."

"Maybe so, but you're still jealous."

"Hush up."

Just as she turned away from him, Jared snatched her wrist and eased her toward him. His embrace was too much to refuse, and Liv dissolved into it with a laugh. Jared kissed the top of her head and rubbed her arms warmly.

"I'd like to tell you about that dinner, by the way."

"Oh?" She pulled back and looked at him, serious all of a sudden. "Is there something to tell?"

"Quite a bit, actually."

"Really."

Well, there it was.

"It must be staggering news to bring you all the way up here to tell me in person."

Jared cast a glance toward his shoe and, without looking at her, he softened. "Staggering is a good word for it."

Liv braced herself.

"There was a little more to it than just dinner—"

Before he could continue, Josie and Katie turned the corner.

"Olivia, if you'll bring the plates, I'm going to light the candles and we'll serve some cake."

Liv looked into Jared's eyes, hoping she could find some hint there of what might have been spilled, if only they hadn't been interrupted. But all she found was a hundred golden flecks of light, and they weren't spelling out a thing.

"Sure," she replied in resignation, turning toward the cabinet.

"What can I do?" Jared asked.

"You could get the forks," Katie suggested. "Can't have cake on plates and not have forks."

"Or napkins," Josie added as she touched the fire to each of the candle wicks. "Why don't you get those down, Katie Marie?"

"Okay, Granny."

Liv flinched with regret, her brain buzzing with possibilities about what Jared might have said.

Dinner with Georgia . . . more than just dinner . . . staggering news . . .

"Foooooooor," Josie sang as she walked into the living room, and everyone joined in right away. "She's a jolly good mommy, for she's a jolly good mommy, she's a jolly good mo-o-mmmy . . ."

Josie completed it alone. "And we're glad to have her home."

Applause erupted as Hallie blew out the candles.

"Thank you, everyone."

"It's the one with the raspberries in the middle," Katie told Hallie. "Remember we had it for Papa's birthday?"

"I do remember."

"I 'membered how you said it was the best cake you ever had. So that's the one we bought you."

"Thank you, sweetie."

"I forgot the knife to cut the cake!" Josie exclaimed.

"I'll get it," Liv said, and then she gave Jared a covert little "Follow me, for crying out loud!" roll of her hand as she passed him.

She produced a cake knife from the drawer, and then stood there waiting for Jared to make his way into the kitchen.

"Wha-at!" he asked, making no effort to disguise his amusement.

"What were you going to say before?"

"When?"

"Before."

"Before what?"

"Before, before," she replied, groaning. Why was he being so obnoxious?!

"Ohhhh," he said deliberately. "Then. Right. I think I was telling you about the night I had dinner with Georgia, wasn't I?"

"Yes. And you said there was more to it than dinner."

"Riiiight."

"Jared, why are you acting like this?" she blurted, smacking him on the arm. "If you have something to tell me, just come out and say it. If you're not interested in pursuing the relationship we started when I was in Florida, you can just be honest. You know?"

"Is that what you think?" he asked her, and his entire demeanor softened. "I'm sorry, Liv. Come here and sit down."

She let him lead her toward the table, and she felt rather numb as he guided her down into a chair. But when he sat down across from her, his smile set her at ease again. Maybe it wasn't so dire and irrevocable.

"So you and Georgia had dinner," she sighed.

"Yes. And I invited her to go somewhere with me," he explained. "Truth be told, I'd been thinking about it for a very long time. Maybe ever since I—"

"Aunt Liv!" Katie cried as she slid across the floor toward her. "We need to cut the cake."

"I'm sorry," Liv said, and she handed her the cake knife. "You be very careful with this, okay?"

"Aren't you coming?"

"In a couple of minutes. I have to talk to Dr. Jared about something first. You go ahead, and we'll be right in."

"But the cake—"

"I'll have some cake in a bit, okay, Katie?"

Josie poked her head around the corner just then, and she innocently asked, "Don't you two want cake?"

Jared smiled, and Liv sighed until she was deflated.

"Of course we do," she said. Then she looked at Jared and suggested, "Can we come back to this?"

He snickered and, with a nod, replied, "Of course."

24

Prudence rounded the corner of the glade, and she'd just set her front hoof to the path leading down into the meadow. Some fresh morning grass would surely make her feel better.

But the kind of feeling better Prudence was about to feel had nothing to do with fragrant green grass, and everything to do with the biggest and most wonderful surprise of her short donkey life.

The stallion! Her stallion. He was standing right there in front of her.

"Wh-what are you doing here?" she asked him.

"Where else would I be?" was his reply.

❧

Jared had Hallie to thank for telling him Liv's favorite restaurant and providing directions to find it.

"Take her and go," Hallie had whispered to him as her three children vied for Liv's attention to the point that he couldn't seem to finish a sentence. "Seriously. Run like the wind. Save yourselves."

Jared had rehearsed what he wanted to communicate to her for nearly the whole plane ride north. He'd even jotted down some notes to help him remember to hit the finer points. He never once thought that he should have also run through a plan to get her alone. He wasn't sure how Liv felt about being surprised, or how she would take the news that he had to deliver, and it certainly wasn't something for which they needed an audience.

The drive to the restaurant was a quiet one, and Jared pondered just pulling over to the shoulder of Sharon Road, turning off the ignition, and just blurting out what he had to say. But just about the time that consideration seemed almost worthy, he spotted a sign introducing *The Grand Finale.*

He turned into the parking lot, and Liv gasped. "This is my favorite restaurant!"

"I know. Hallie told me."

"This is where we're having dinner? I hope you made a reservation."

Jared rounded the car, opened her door, and took her hand to help her from the car. He wasn't a man given to extreme cases of nerves, but this night was an exception. He couldn't even anticipate how Liv was going to react to what he had to tell her.

The Grand Finale was a large Victorian-style house with dining areas on two floors. Antique furnishings, floral tablecloths, fine crystal, and tasteful artwork created by the restaurant's owner mingled together to create a perfect fusion of upscale comfort and ambiance that inspired instant understanding for Jared. Of course, this would be Liv's favorite restaurant. It had her name all over it.

They were seated at a small table for two near the window on the first floor. Liv's eyes sparkled with familiar appreciation for her surroundings, and she beamed at Jared.

"Isn't this place great?"

"It's beautiful."

"I've been coming here for years," she told him. "Birthdays, anniversaries, or just to reconnect. I think every milestone I've had in the last twenty years has been celebrated here."

"What's your favorite appetizer?" he asked. "Show me what's good."

"I always get the artichoke fritters," she admitted. "They're fantastic. But you would probably like the crabcakes. They come with a corn salsa and this really amazing mustard sauce."

"Let's order both."

Once the order was placed, Jared observed an awkward, let's-get-down-to-business expression that surfaced on Liv's face. There was no mistaking it. She wouldn't wait any longer for him to get to it.

"There have been a lot of interruptions today," he remarked. "It's good to finally get you alone."

"Well, now that we are," she said, "why don't you tell me what you came all this way to say to me?"

Jared couldn't help but wonder what Liv was imagining. Did she have some inkling of the truth, or was she taking a smidgen of what she thought she knew and mashing it into something else entirely?

"I'm not sure where to start."

"I do," she stated. "Start with the dinner you had with Georgia the night I called you."

"That seems like a good place," he said.

Am I sweating? Is it hot in here?

"Well, you know that Preston told Georgia he didn't think they were meant for one another."

"Yes. I was sorry to hear that."

"I had plans of my own that night, but when she told me he'd broken things off with her, and I saw how gloomy she was about it . . . well, I asked her to join me for dinner."

He paused and took a sip from the glass of cold water before him.

"After dinner, I asked her if she was interested in helping me make a decision I needed to make."

"A decision."

"So we left the restaurant and were heading

out to my car, and that's when you called."

"So you had to go somewhere to make this decision."

"Yes."

"Where?"

If only he had those notes he'd made on the plane.

"The thing is this, Liv. I love you. You know that, don't you?"

She looked away, gazing through her own reflection in the window and out into the darkness that had fallen since their arrival.

"I thought I did," she replied in a tone so soft that he had to strain to hear it.

"Well, I don't want you to doubt that, if that's what you're doing. I love you. If nothing else, believe that."

She glanced back at him and tried to smile, but it fell a little short of her eyes. "I love you too."

"I know you kept saying how your life is here in Ohio, and mine is clearly on Sanibel Island," he continued. "But when you left, I think it really hit me for the first time that you meant it."

"And so you've moved on," she surmised. "Of course, you did. That's the natural flow of things when one thing comes to an end. I mean, I know after Robert died, I—"

"What?" he interrupted. "No! I haven't moved on at all. In fact, Olivia, I'm having a really hard time even *thinking* about moving on."

The waiter arrived at the table with their appetizers. His small talk as he laid out plates and wished them a pleasant dining experience was nothing more than a hum in the background of Jared's own fast-moving thoughts.

Okay, thank you, move on, please.

"Let me know if there's anything else you need," the waiter said. "I'll be back to take your dinner order in just a few minutes."

Once he vanished Jared smiled at Liv and sighed. "Where was I?"

"Moving on," she replied as she slid the plate of artichokes toward him.

"Right. Moving on." He took a bite and brightened. "These are great."

"I love them."

Jared closed his eyes for an instant, and he rubbed his temple.

"Jared, just say it. I can take it."

He laughed. "Are you sure?"

"I survived cancer. I'm not a weak woman. Just tell me where you and Georgia went, and what decision you've come to."

"We went to Bonita Springs," he told her. "To Coconut Point."

"Isn't that—that's a hotel resort, isn't it?"

"Yes."

"You took Georgia to a hotel?"

She looked at Jared as if she were just about to ignite lift-off, and before she could blast out of her chair and run out of the restaurant, he exclaimed, "No! No. I didn't do that. I mean, yes, I took her to a hotel, but not the way you're thinking."

"Jared, you're confusing me."

Her eyes turned a stormy, deep-sea green, and Jared thought she looked like she was just about to cry.

"I know. I'm sorry. Let me just tell you this right up front: I am not, and I repeat *not*—"

"Olivia?"

Liv's focus on him was torn away like an unsuspecting flag in a hurricane, and the separation left Jared stinging.

"Becky?" Liv said.

"How crazy to run into you here," the woman said, glancing at Jared with curiosity. "My husband and I are celebrating our anniversary."

"Congratulations."

"Becky Watson," the woman said, extending her hand toward Jared.

"Oh, I'm sorry," Liv said as he shook it. "Becky, this is Dr. Jared Hunt."

"A pleasure," Jared replied once he caught his breath again.

"Becky heads up the Human Resources department at the hospital where I work," Liv explained.

"Speaking of which," the woman remarked, "we're all so excited to have you coming back to us next week. You look just phenomenal, Olivia. You really do. I'm so happy you're recovering so well."

"Thank you."

"I spoke to Dr. Bradley Bennett just this morning. He's assigned over at the pediatric clinic, and I told him about your interest in making that change."

Jared clenched his hands into one big fist beneath the table. He was pretty sure that Becky Watson sensed his impatience when she said, "I don't want to interrupt your dinner with Dr. Hunt, so maybe you can give me a call tomorrow and we can talk about it some more."

"Sure."

"Good to see you, Olivia."

"You too."

"Dr. Hunt."

"Ms. Watson."

Just as she walked away from the table, the waiter appeared, and Jared resisted the urge to let out a stress-relieving whale of a scream that would surely scare every patron in the place straight out of their chairs and through the front door.

"Can I take your dinner orders?"

"Not yet," Jared snapped, and then he caught hold of himself. "Give us a few minutes, please?"

"Certainly."

Jared sighed, trying to get himself back on track.

"So you took Georgia to a hotel resort in Bonita Springs," Liv reminded him.

"Yes. But no."

"Jared."

"I took her there, but not as guests or anything. We went there to see a buddy of mine that I knew from Chicago years ago."

"Ohhhh. Like a fix-up?"

"No. Dennis is—"

"Can I clear these for you?" a waitress asked as she reached for the appetizer plates.

"No," Jared returned, and then he pressed his lips together. "Please leave them."

"Okay."

"In fact, would you do me a favor?"

"Certainly."

"Would you tell our waiter that we are still going to have dinner, but we have to step outside for a moment? Please leave our table just as it is, and we'll be back in just a few minutes."

"All right, I'll tell him."

Jared rose from the table on sheer determination, and he took Liv's hand and urged her to follow him.

"Jared, what's going on?"

"Please. Come with me."

He knew how absurd it all was, how crazy he appeared, how out of character his behavior had become. The only thing he could hope for at that moment was that Liv knew him well enough to trust him.

And she did.

She rose from her chair, placed her napkin on the seat, and walked with him out the front door, across the parking lot, and to his rental car.

"Please. Let's get in and talk for a minute without any interruptions."

Liv didn't say a word. She just got into the car and allowed him to close the door behind her. Jared went to the other side and slid in. Once his door was shut, he sighed again, and leaned back against the headrest.

"Should I try and help?" Liv asked on a whisper. "Or just be quiet and let you get there all by yourself?"

"I'll get there. Be patient with me."

"You got it."

Silence was a thick fog inside the car. When he was finally ready to cut through it, Jared said, "Georgia told me about the opening over at the pediatric clinic. She said she'd put you and her friend together to talk about it."

"We've emailed."

"I hope you won't mind this, and I know it was a bit intrusive for me to do it, but I went over and had a talk with them myself."

"You did?" she exclaimed. "Why?"

"To see if there was something solid for you there. Something compelling enough that you might consider giving up your job here and moving down to Florida."

Liv cocked her head to the side and bit the corner of her lip. "I'm not sure I understand. What does that have to do with your friend in Bonita Springs?"

"Dennis. He's a jewelry designer, and he was in town for a big convention, and I got a look at some of his designs. Really beautiful pieces. Emerald chokers and amethyst earrings."

"You bought jewelry for Georgia?"

"No."

This was just not going as planned.

"I bought jewelry for you," he replied. "I narrowed it down to three different pieces, and I needed Georgia to help me choose."

Before she could ask another question, Jared produced the green velvet box that had been burning a hole in the pocket of his trousers since he'd left the house that morning. He opened it and held it out toward Liv.

"We both thought this one would be perfect for you. What do you think?"

Liv's eyes narrowed as she glared at the box. And then they slowly opened, wider and wider, until they were as round and shiny as quarters as she stared at the ring.

A square, one-carat diamond, surrounded on all sides by an outline of smaller diamonds, set into a perfect platinum band.

Simple, elegant, and exquisite, just like Liv.

A car pulled into the empty spot next to them, and Liv's eyes broke free to glance its way, but Jared reached over and touched her chin with two fingers and turned her head back toward him.

"No more distractions or interruptions," he said with a smile. "I have a question to ask you."

EPILOGUE

The moon hung low as Prudence and the stallion crested the top of the hill and looked down on their treasured home. They were back at the Enchanted Pond once again, and Prudence sighed in relief when she saw it.

"Are you sorry to leave the meadow behind?" the stallion asked her.

"Not at all," she replied. "That was my old life. This is my new one."

Horatio hooted at them as he flew over their heads, and Prudence laughed as he landed on the knotted branch hanging out over the pond and stretched out his wings after the long flight.

"This is where I belong," Prudence said. "I don't know why I didn't see it before."

"The old Prudence resisted change," Horatio announced from his perch. "But this—this is a brand new Pru."

❧

Liv's wedding dress was a rich champagne color, a halter swing dress from the 1950s that she and Hallie found in a vintage dress shop in Mt. Adams. The lace straps were three inches wide, and they tied at the back of the neck in a large, crisp bow. The bodice was pleated and boned for a clean, perfect fit, and the crinoline slip underneath the full skirt was pale pink so that just a hint of color peeked out from beneath the tea-length hem. Her red curls were coaxed upward and held in place with a long rhinestone clip that matched the delicate diamond choker around her neck. Her bouquet was simple: just six pink roses bound together at the stem with pink and champagne ribbon.

They were married in Hallie's church, the one with the stained glass windows, up on the hill overlooking Liv's favorite spot in the city: Winton Woods. The ceremony took place at seven thirty at night, and countless candles twinkled in agreement as they vowed to love and cherish one another for the rest of their lives. The pastor spoke a prayer over them, thanking God for this second chance for two people who thought they had experienced love and then lost it far too early, wishing them well as they said good-bye to Cincinnati and started their new lives together on Sanibel Island in Florida.

Hallie and Rand stood up for the couple, and the church was filled with well-wishers from several states. Georgia Brown sat in the second row on the groom's side, next to Dennis Pearson, the jewelry designer from Chicago. The two of them had been in constant touch since their first meeting. Clayton Clydesdale sat on the other side of Georgia, with his yellow-silver hair slicked back, and dressed in his favorite dark blue suit, the one that hadn't seen the light of day more than three times since 1998. On his lapel was a tiny stick pin bearing the team logo of the Tampa Bay Buccaneers.

At the reception, on the table beside the magnificent wedding cake, sat a smaller one bearing the words, "Happy Birthday, Olivia." That cake with the espresso cream cheese filling was a special gift to Liv from her new husband.

And so it was that Olivia Wallace's birthday curse was officially broken that day—the day that she stepped out in faith into The Great Unknown and married Jared Hunt on the moonlit night of her fifty-first birthday.

"Are you content?" he asked her from the edge of their Happily Ever After.

"Beyond content," she replied. "I'm completely brand new." With a gasp, she grinned and added, "In fact, you know what? I'm a *brand new Pru!*"

Discussion Questions

1. Each chapter is preceded by an excerpt from a children's book. What/who does Prudence the Donkey represent? Why is Prudence important to Liv's story?

2. What/who does Horatio HootOwl represent? What affect does his presence in Prudence's life have on Liv?

3. What impact did Liv's battle with cancer have on her life afterward? Is it possible for something like cancer to be a positive thing, even to be considered a gift?

4. Early on in the story, Liv refers to her ongoing "birthday curse." Do you believe in such a thing? If so, how do you explain it? And if not, how do you explain a string of negative events year after year?

5. After meeting and being attracted to Jared when they met on the plane, what was your reaction to him ending up next door? Do you believe in the role of destiny in a person's life?

6. How does Liv's relationship with Boofer evolve over time? What other relationships evolve throughout the book, and how?

7. Georgia worked with Jared for years before Liv entered his life. Was Georgia justified in her initial confrontations with Liv? What was driving her?

8. Florida is very much like another planet for Liv. What "aliens" does she meet there along the way? How is the environment different from the life she lives back in Ohio?

9. What does Jared's role as a doctor tell you about the person that he is? Or his role as a father?

10. How did you feel about the relationship between Jared and Rand?

11. Liv has a run of unfortunate circumstances (i.e., a gator in the pool, the bronzing incident, the death of Clayton's cat). Do you see any association between these instances and Liv's ongoing "birthday curse"?

12. What does Rand and Shelby's romance represent? How does it affect Liv and Jared?

13. What did you think of Liv's reaction to news of Hallie's accident?

14. Jared and Liv didn't know each other very long when they made a permanent commitment to one another. Do you think a marriage will last under those circumstances?

Center Point Publishing
600 Brooks Road ● PO Box 1
Thorndike ME 04986-0001 USA

(207) 568-3717

US & Canada:
1 800 929-9108
www.centerpointlargeprint.com